DOLPHIN JUNCTION
STORIES

Books by Mick Herron

The Oxford Series
Down Cemetery Road
The Last Voice You Hear
Why We Die
Smoke & Whispers

The Slough House Novels
Slow Horses
Dead Lions
Real Tigers
Spook Street
London Rules
Joe Country
Slough House

The Slough House Novellas
The List
The Marylebone Drop
The Catch

Other Novels
Reconstruction
Nobody Walks
This Is What Happened

DOLPHIN JUNCTION

STORIES

MICK HERRON

Published by
Soho Press, Inc.
227 W 17th Street
New York, NY 10011

Library of Congress Cataloging-in-Publication Data
Names: Herron, Mick, author.
Title: Dolphin junction : collected stories / Mick Herron.
Description: New York, NY : Soho Crime, [2021]
Identifiers: LCCN 2021018971

ISBN 978-1-64129-302-0
eISBN 978-1-64129-303-7

Subjects: LCGFT: Short stories. Classification: LCC PR6108.E77 D65 2021 |
DDC 823/.92—dc23 LC record available at https://lccn.loc.gov/2021018971

Interior design by Janine Agro

Printed in the United States of America

10 9 8 7 6 5 4 3 2 1

To Micheline Steinberg

TABLE OF CONTENTS

DOLPHIN JUNCTION
STORIES

PROOF OF LOVE

Some while ago—a few years before he died—Joe Silvermann chose a slow mid-week morning to do some heavy shifting round the office; clear away the bits of orange peel and chewed pencil ends from under the filing cabinet. So he was wearing jeans and a Sticky Fingers T-shirt, and had built up a sweat, and hadn't shaved—was everything, in fact, that the well-dressed private detective shouldn't be when four million pounds came calling.

Or forty million, you wanted to get technical. If last year's Rich List could be trusted.

"Is this a bad time?"

Joe looked down at his grimy clothing. "I've been under-cover. But I'm free right now."

He showed Russell Candy into the inner sanctum, which was more of a mess than when he'd started. Zoë was out. Joe had given up asking. When she was here, she was brain-deep in the computer, and when she wasn't she was somewhere else.

"I should have made an appointment."

"That's all right, Mr. Candy. For you, I have time."

Candy didn't look surprised Joe knew who he was—Oxford didn't have so many residents with £40 million plus that the local paper ignored them—and even less so that Joe had time for him. It would be an attitude he was used to. He was fifty or thereabouts, not much older than Joe, and his face was deeply lined, as if each million had scored its passage there. Anyone else, or anyone else with his money, might have done something about his hair, too, which had a gone-tomorrow look, and was flecked with probably dandruff, though Joe wasn't a hair expert. His suit looked expensive, or at least fresh on, and his shoes were buffed to reflective glory.

Joe plucked a jar of instant from the shelf in the corner and waggled it invitingly. "I'm out of the real stuff," he apologised, and then added, "Coffee," in case Russell Candy thought he meant heroin. "Take a seat? How can I help?"

Candy took the visitor's chair. "No coffee for me, thanks."

"Tea? Water?"

"Nothing. Thank you."

So Joe decided he didn't want coffee either, and sat behind his desk instead. "But you need a detective," he said.

"Oxford Investigations," Candy said. "You're in the book."

"We have a growing reputation."

"And you're handy. I live just up the road."

Joe nodded, as if that had been part of his plan. "I've been here awhile. How can I help you, Mr. Candy? You have a problem?"

"It's not a problem as such. More like an errand."

"An errand."

"A delivery. A collection and a delivery."

"Like a courier service."

"Pretty much. But I'll pay your usual rates, don't worry about that."

Joe said, "Oh, I'm not worried, Mr. Candy. I'm sure you can afford my rates."

"Good."

"I'm just wondering why, if you need a courier service, you hire a private detective."

"Well," said Candy. "There's the thing."

LAST TIME JOE HAD seen Russell Candy's picture in the paper he was getting married, though without the caption you'd have thought he'd been giving his daughter away. There were eight years between Joe himself and Zoë, or six once you'd rounded her up and rounded him down. You could adjust for decades in Candy's case, there'd still be a twenty-year gap. It was to do with money, of course, unless it was to do with whatever quality had allowed Candy to earn the money in the first place. But in the long run, it was to do with money. Joe wondered what it would be like, being Russell Candy rich. So rich you not only didn't have to worry about your future, but could afford to stop regretting your past.

Anyway, a good slab of Candy's wealth sat on Joe's desk now, in a padded envelope. Which made Joe a lot richer than an hour ago, even if the money wasn't his.

Odd thing, he thought, digging scissors from a drawer. If Joe had been, whatever, a geography teacher or something, it wasn't likely a passing millionaire would have trusted him with—he sliced the envelope, spilling cash onto the desk—what looked like many thousands of pounds. But being a private detective put him in a world where such things happened. To be sure, Candy had told him not to open the envelope—it wasn't like he was pretending it didn't have money in it, but that had definitely been the instruction—only how Joe worked, he had a mantra: What would Marlowe do? Would Philip Marlowe have opened the envelope? Hell, yes. So that's what Joe had done, and here it all was: bundled twenties and bundled fifties; all in used notes, obviously. Nobody wanted clean money these days. It took him half an hour to count, and the number he came up with—or at least, the number more or less halfway between the different totals he reached—was £100,000. More than he'd ever seen in one place.

Joe sticky-taped the envelope together, put it in a carrier bag, and went home to get changed.

"YOU GIVE HIM THE envelope, he gives you a package. You bring the package to me." This is what Candy had said after giving Joe the envelope.

"All this seems straightforward."

"Good."

Candy had paused, and his hand went fishing in his jacket pocket, but came out empty. It found his other hand, and they settled for a nap in his lap. Ex-smoker, Joe guessed. Dipping for his cigarettes out of habit, then remembering he didn't carry them anymore.

Joe said, "But there is a problem."

"Really?"

"You'll know that blackmailers rarely take just one bite."

"I never said—"

"Mr. Candy, please. I give him an envelope, he gives me a package? It's a blackmail scenario. I'm not being censorious. I'm just wondering, why bring a third party into it? You're not able to do this exchange yourself?"

Rather pleased with himself, he leaned back in his chair and waited.

"I want to know who he is," Candy said.

"I see," said Joe, who thought he probably did.

"You're a detective, you should be able to . . . tail him. Find out where he lives, who he is."

"I can do that. But other things—say, threats—I don't do," Joe told him. It came out like an apology. Much of what Joe said did, which was a good reason for not doing threats. "Violence either," he added, perhaps unnecessarily.

"You won't need to. Once I know who's behind this, I can make sure it doesn't happen again. But there'll be no violence, Mr. Silvermann. I'm a businessman, not a gangster."

"This is good to know," Joe said.

WHEN HE WASN'T UNDERCOVER, or shifting furniture, Joe dressed conservatively: shirt and tie, usually; fawn chinos; a tweedy-type jacket he'd long been trying to upgrade from without success. A few years ago, when he and Zoë were still holidaying together, he'd snagged a bargain at an Italian street market: a leather jacket black and shiny as night, with a strap around the collar that buckled separately. Zoë had paid eleven times as much for something similar in a high-end shop. His had fallen apart the following spring, and she was still wearing hers. But despite all that Joe had liked Italy, once he'd worked out that zebra crossings were designated accident spots, not safe places to cross.

So he was wearing shirt and tie, fawn chinos and tweedy jacket when he got back to the office and found Zoë in residence: bent over a monitor, as usual. The information superhighway—wasn't that what people were saying? Joe had no complaints about the new technology, but was well aware of his own place in it: by the side of the road, his thumb in the air.

"Hey, Zoë," he said to his—technically—wife.

"I'm busy, Joe."

"With credit checks," he said helpfully.

"And reference checks."

"And reference checks."

"Which pay the bills."

"You don't get bored? Staring at the screen all day, not to mention what it's doing to your eyes?"

She didn't reply.

"Because it's not a secret, you can damage your health sitting at the computer all day long. Your posture suffers."

"You have a problem with my posture, Joe?"

"I'm only saying."

"You think I slouch? I don't stand straight enough?"

"You stand fine, Zoë. You always have. I'm just worried you don't get enough fresh air."

"So now I'm pale and wasted, right? You don't like my pasty complexion?"

"Can I get you a cup of coffee, Zoë?"

"We're out of coffee."

"I think there's some instant."

"What do you want, Joe? I'm busy."

"We've got a job."

"'We'?"

"A piece of proper detective work."

He was looking over her shoulder as he said this—at the screen on which it was so easy to go back and delete what had just been keyed—and thought: Push straight on, or beat a retreat? Push straight on.

Zoë said, "Prop—"

But Joe was way ahead of her: "Not *proper*, no, stupid word. 'Traditional' is what I meant to say. Yes, traditional. You know, out on the mean streets, dealing with actual flesh and blood and real live criminals. The kind of thing we always wanted to do, remember?"

"I remember the kind of thing you always wanted to do, Joe. Trouble is, it had nothing in common with real life." She pushed her chair from the desk, and Joe had to step aside smartish not to be run over. She looked up at him. "If you want this to be a success, you could do a little less wittering about mean streets, and a lot more studying what I do. Before you wind up on the wrong end of a credit check yourself."

"Blackmail," he said.

"It's not blackmail, it's common sense."

"No, blackmail. That's the job."

"Doing it or stopping it?"

Joe had to think about that. "Well, paying it, technically. Then making sure it doesn't happen again."

She pursed her lips.

"It'll be a lot more fun than credit checks," he unwisely added.

"Which provide eighty percent of our income."

"Yes but—"

"And of which I do one hundred percent."

"It's not a competition, Zoë."

"If it was, I'd win."

She pushed herself back to her keyboard and began stabbing it viciously; possibly randomly. The screen underwent various transformations. It was like looking through fifteen windows at once.

Joe waited until the clock in the monitor's corner clicked onto the next minute, then said, "Zoë? I can't do it by myself."

He liked to think of this as his trump card.

Her fingers had stopped rattling, and she was using the mouse instead: clicking here, clicking there. But Joe was pretty sure she was slowing down.

It was just a matter of time.

The clock in the corner turned over.

Zoë said, "I bloody hope he's paying well."

IT WAS DARK IN South Parks. A lot of private detectives were former policemen, or had wanted to be policemen but had failed to make the grade, but Joe wasn't among them: being a policeman would have meant working nights, and Joe didn't do so well in the dark. Which was one of the reasons he'd told Zoë he couldn't manage this on his own; another being, he wasn't sure he could manage this on his own. Tailing someone—an entry-level PI skill, if the books could be believed—was a lot harder than it looked. You couldn't count on the bad guy being unobservant. On the other hand, if you could, a lot of novels would be short stories.

He was hunkered down on a bench: that was the word. The jacket had given way to an overcoat, and Joe had his arms wrapped round him; less as a shield from the cold than to keep Candy's padded envelope secure—it was too big to fit his pocket. "Too much money to fit my pockets." It sounded like the opposite to a blues song. The bench was at the top of the long slope running down to St. Clement's, and there were trees behind him, and a brick toilet off to his left, and further in that direction the gate that was locked by now, so anyone turning up to collect the envelope would have to scramble over the railings, unless he was already hiding among the trees. Joe had considered doing that himself—the railings were high, and looked apt to cause horrible injury—but in the end was less worried about impaling himself than being found lurking by one of the groundsmen. "I'm a private detective," he'd have had to explain. "I'm a sex pervert," they'd have interpreted. From the bench, looking down towards the city, the streets were a blur of traffic and misty movement. A dog barked, too far off to be a worry.

"I meet him on the bench at midnight. I give him the envelope. He gives me the package."

This was what he'd said to Russell Candy.

"And then you find out where he goes. His car registration. An address. Something to know him by."

"This is personal, Mr. Candy."

"What do you mean?"

Joe had said: "It's not business. You're a rich man, forgive me. There's nothing wrong with being rich. Sometimes it means making enemies, but that's not what's happening here, is it?"

"You sound very sure of that."

Joe shrugged. "You're a rich man," he repeated. "For business-type problems, you'll have people. But you come to me."

Even Zoë would have admitted, this was Joe at his best. It helped that he looked like Judd Hirsch, who'd been in that old show *Taxi*. Not a dead ringer, but the same kind face. People often wanted to confide in him. He made friends the way other people make appointments. And sitting in that half-tidied office—the filing cabinet plonked mid-floor like a half-arsed installation—Russell Candy, he could tell, was having what Zoë once called a Joe moment, which in this particular case meant forgetting that he was rich and that Joe was for hire. They were just two men sharing a trouble.

So Candy had told Joe about his wife's brief movie career.

JOE SAID, "THE THING is, Mr. Candy, this is not like buying a manuscript. It's like buying a book. Somebody else can still buy it too. There are bookshops all over." Deciding he'd taken the analogy as far as was useful, he added, "Video shops, too."

"It's eight years old. Seven, anyway. She used a false name, and wore a sparkly wig. It's not like anyone would recognise her. Not without being told." Candy paused. "What I'm buying is his silence. That's what he's selling."

Joe said, "But an actual movie, a film, if it's out there in distribution—"

Candy said, "There weren't many copies made. Between three and four hundred. A lot'll have gone abroad, Europe, the Far East, and besides, how many eight-year-old videos do you have? Most'll have worn out years ago. And this market . . . there's a lot of turnover."

It would have cost him too much to say it, Joe thought. This market: porn. "He provided a lot of information, your blackmailer."

"You think I'm about to give him *this*"—this being the envelope—"without good reason? I wasn't born yesterday."

He said, "Mr. Candy. Forgive me, I don't wish to step on toes. But is your wife aware of what you're doing?"

"No."

"So you haven't, ah, verified—"

"I knew about the film, Mr. Silvermann. She told me before we were married."

"Oh."

"She didn't have to. I could have walked away, called the wedding off. You know how much bravery that must have taken?"

Joe said, "I couldn't begin to guess, Mr. Candy," and meant every word.

Candy leaned forward. "She was nineteen. And hurting for money. I can remember what that felt like."

"The money part, me too," Joe agreed. "Nineteen's a bit of a stretch."

"You've got to allow for gender differences," Candy said. "Girls growing up faster, I mean. Plus the fact that everybody gets older faster now anyway. So Faye's nineteen was probably more like your or my twenty-five. Anyway, that's not really the point. She wasn't a bad girl, is what I'm saying. It wasn't like this was a step on a road she was taking. It was an offer made at a time she really needed . . ."

"An offer?" Joe suggested.

"She saw it as an opportunity. You know, like it was going to get her into movies, make her a star. I don't blame her. And I'm not just saying that because I love her. I haven't always been rich. I know the things being poor can make you do."

Joe nodded wisely. "Half the world's woes," he said. "Did I say half? Ninety percent. Caused by not having what we need when we need it." Candy was still leaning forward, his hands splayed flat on Joe's desk. Joe reached out and patted one of them. "You're right, though, Mr. Candy. It was bravery itself, her confession."

"Oh, tell me about it. Tell me. I treasure the moment. It's how I know she loves me." He eyed Joe as if Joe were his favourite bartender. "I'm worth a lot, Mr. Silvermann."

"Please. Joe."

"I'm worth a lot, Joe. A hell of a lot. But take that away, I'm a catch? I've never been much in the looks department. Since meeting Faye I've been making an effort, but what you see is how far I've got. She tells me how to dress, and I still look like an accident in a charity shop. But you know and I know, I could have married years ago. It's just, I never met a woman I wanted I could believe wanted me and not my money."

Because he paused, and because Joe was still there, Joe said, "I understand, Mr. Candy."

"If Faye was just after my money, she'd never have told me about this."

"I understand."

Candy said, "He sent me a photocopy. Of the video cover. It's her. Sparkly wig, but it's her. He saw our wedding photo in the local paper. Says he recognised the blushing bride. She— Faye—she has a tattoo. Small, very tasteful." He tapped his left shoulder with his right hand. "It's there. It's there."

And then he'd started to cry.

SO NOW IT WAS nearly midnight, and here was Joe on a bench. Soon this blackmailer would turn up, and Joe would take the video and give him the envelope in return, making the nineteen-year-old Faye Candy's sole movie one of the priciest properties he'd ever heard of. Not that she'd been Faye Candy at the time, of course. And anyway, had used a false name. Well, you would, wouldn't you? If he, Joe Silvermann, ever made a dirty movie, he was pretty sure he'd do it cloaked in anonymity, even if he wasn't cloaked in anything else.

"He gives me the video, I give him the envelope," he murmured. Not that he was in danger of forgetting the procedure; he was just spooked by the dark, and the nearness of trees.

And then would come the tricky bit, which was finding out where the blackmailer went. A car registration. An address. *Something to know him by.*

He'd thought he was alert; ready for the slightest clue. A twig snapping, or a rustling of paper. But when someone arrived out of nowhere, and sat down hard next to him, Joe yelped.

"You Candy's man?"

That's what Joe thought he said. And in the split second that followed, he had a near-perfect vision of the fiasco about to be born: one in which Joe, mistaken for a local candyman, ended up holding a few grubby fivers, while this dopehead wandered off with what he expected was a bag of crack, but was in fact a beautiful fortune. The next moment thankfully blew that nightmare away.

"From Russell Candy, yeah?"

Joe said, "And you're the blackmailer."

As mentioned, it was dark. The faraway lights didn't do much to reveal the newcomer, beyond that he was male, about Joe's height—though slenderer—and fuzzily chinned, as if a beard were considering its options. Joe couldn't really tell what he was wearing. Jeans, probably. A jacket of some sort. His voice quavered, so he was possibly nervous. If there was an accent, Joe couldn't place it.

"Did you bring the money?"

"That's why I'm here," Joe said, without reaching for it.

"Don't spin this out, man. We just make the exchange, and go our ways."

"You could be anyone."

"Didn't I just say Russell Candy? You think that's some sort of cosmic coincidence?"

Joe said, "Do you want to show me the merchandise?" He wasn't sure why he'd said that. Merchandise. "The film, I mean?" he amended.

The man—he was a young man, Joe realised; had the fluidity of movement of younger men—rustled about in the folds of his jacket. Then he was handing Joe a videotape-shaped object, wrapped in a plastic carrier bag.

Joe put his hand to it, but the man didn't release his grip. "The money," he said.

"How do I know it's the right film?"

"You got a machine handy?"

Joe didn't have an answer for that, so did what he usually did at such moments: said nothing, and waited.

After a moment, the young man pulled the bag back, and rustled some more. Then a torch snapped on, one of those pencil-sized lights, and Joe—once temporary blindness passed—was looking at a video box: *Bedroom Stories* ran the title, over a picture of a glitter-wigged girl trying to look mean; topless, but with her arms folded over her breasts. What might have been a dead moth decorated one shoulder. Trudii Foxx, it read below the title: two *i*s, two *x*s. A false identity, like Russell Candy said. Though Faye Candy wasn't, when you came down to it, that bad a blue-movie name itself.

"Seen enough?"

The young man turned the torch off as he spoke.

Joe said, "What guarantee do we have this is the end of it?"

"My word."

"Excuse me, but you're a blackmailer. Maybe your word is not so bankable. How do we know, a month down the line, you won't be back for more?"

"Because I won't have the movie, will I?"

Joe opened his mouth, then closed it again: it's not the movie, it's the knowledge it exists. *What we're buying is your silence.* But it was not his plan to outline any wiggles that this blackmailer hadn't discovered himself. So he said instead, "And how do we know you haven't made copies?"

"Do I look like a . . . technician?"

"I'm not sure what you're asking me."

"How would I copy a video? It's not like taping off the telly. You'd need a special machine to record a videotape."

"I think maybe you can do it with two video machines."

"Really?"

"I think so. With some kind of cable." Joe wasn't a technician either, but he was pretty sure this could be done. "You connect the two machines with the cable, then put a blank tape in one, and play the film in the other, and bish-bosh. Just like recording it off, as you say, the telly."

Both men considered this for a while. Then the blackmailer said, "Would you have to actually be playing the film? While you recorded it?"

"That, I'm not sure about."

"Okay."

Joe tightened his grip on the parcel.

The blackmailer said, "So, anyway. The price."

"I have it here."

"I figured. You going to hand it over?"

Joe had to ask. "Are you proud of yourself?"

"I need the money, man."

"We all need money. We get jobs, we save up."

"Look. I saw a picture in the paper, this rich bloke getting married. I recognised her from a dirty film. It was an opportunity, and I don't get so many of those. All right?"

He remembered Candy saying something like that. *She saw it as an opportunity.* There was maybe a moral here, or some kind of mirror-imaging, that might repay thought later, but for the moment all he could do was fish the envelope out from beneath his coat, and hand it over.

"Thanks, man."

"You don't have to thank me," Joe began, but he was alone by the second syllable.

That far-off dog barked again. After a while Joe got to his feet, and went off to tackle the railings once more.

THERE WERE GUIDEBOOKS AVAILABLE—etiquette for beginners, that sort of thing—but Joe doubted any of them covered this set-up: your knock answered by the star of the porn film you were clutching in your spare hand. Faye Candy was sporting a lot more clothes than on the video's cover, and had shed the sparkly wig, but was, no question, the same girl. Eight years older, but you'd not have guessed it. If her husband's face wore the marks of four decades spent shinning up the money tree, Faye's was clear and fresh, as if her greatest struggle to date had been finishing *Heidi*. Looked, in fact, like butter wouldn't melt, Joe thought, before pushing away an unsolicited memory of *Last Tango in Paris*.

This morning, Mrs. Candy was wearing black leggings that stopped three inches above her ankle and what looked like a man's shirt: doubtless her husband's. It was collarless and stripy. Blue on white. Unwigged, her dark hair dropped to shoulder length, and her skin, though white, looked prone to blooming pink at a moment's notice.

"I'm, er—"

"You're Joe?"

"Yes. Of course I am."

"Russell's expecting you. He's in his study."

The line should have thrilled him more—he'd never called on anyone who had a study. But he felt awkward in her presence, and suspected that the tape in his carrier bag glowed like phosphorus. When she led him down the hall, she moved with what Joe could only call grace, to which various adjectives jostled to attach themselves, *lithe* winning by a head. He felt like a heffalump, tromping in her wake. She was tall for a woman, and slim of build, though that shirt (he hadn't been able to help noticing) didn't do all it might to conceal her charms. "Slim of build" didn't cover the whole picture.

. . . He hadn't watched the video. Would Philip Marlowe have watched the video? The answer, true, got more flexible if you counted Elliott Gould's shopsoiled version in the Altman movie, but there were rules, so Joe hadn't watched the video. He'd left it on the table in the sitting room. Taking it into the bedroom would have been a tarnished act.

Come the morning he'd found Zoë in the kitchen, drinking coffee.

"I didn't hear you coming in."

"Joe, you wouldn't hear a brass band coming in."

It was true, he'd slept heavily. Actually, always did.

"So, last night—"

"Did I follow him?"

"Did you?"

"Did I get an address? A name?"

"You got his name?"

"Am I a detective?"

"What is this, the first to answer a question loses?"

"You're asking me?" Zoë said.

He'd had to laugh. When it came to finding ways of getting under his skin, Zoë had yet to run out of inspiration, but she could always make him laugh. Or whenever, he amended, she felt like it, she could make him laugh. He was usually glad they were married, and often wondered if they'd one day make it work.

"So . . ."

"You lose."

"And for losing, what do I get?"

She'd reached into a pocket and handed him a folded piece of paper: a name, address, phone number, car registration.

"This, this is genius."

"I followed him, Joe. It was no huge deal."

It hadn't even involved scaling those railings. She'd been waiting outside, in her car, all that time.

"And then you hunted him down on your internet."

"It's not entirely my internet," she said. "Joe? Did you really give him all that money?"

"You think I kept it?"

"He didn't stop to check. It could have been cut-up newspaper. You'd still have the video."

"He insisted," Joe said. "Candy, I mean. He insisted."

"I know he's rich. But that's plain dumb."

"I think he saw it as a proof of love. To match his wife's."

"Like I say," Zoë said. "Plain dumb."

And now Joe was standing outside Russell Candy's study, the unwatched videotape tucked under his arm.

Faye didn't come in with him; she just opened the door, said, "Darling? Your man for you," then smiled at Joe, waving him in and closing the door behind him. Stuff to do, Joe supposed; whatever stuff needed doing when you were married to forty million pounds. Perhaps it needed counting.

Russell Candy said, "Mr. Silvermann. I didn't hear the door."

"Your lady wife let me in. And it's Joe, remember?"

"You didn't—?"

Joe made a zipper motion, finger and thumb to his lips.

"Then, Joe. Come in. Sit down."

The room was what Joe'd have guessed a study to be: largely book-lined, with a lot of possibly walnut panelling. But it was the photos you noticed. These were all of Candy's wife: in her wedding dress, at a party, on the deck of a yacht. Only one showed her and Candy together: a studio shot; the groom looking hot and blistered under the lights; Faye radiant, as in all the others. As Joe looked, he realised Candy was staring at him. Or staring, rather, at the package under his arm.

Joe handed it to him as he settled into a chair.

"This is—?"

"Yes."

"And did you—?"

"No."

Candy closed his eyes for a moment. When he opened them, he was still holding the package. Gingerly, as if it contained a bomb, he removed the videotape from the bag, closing his eyes again briefly as he registered its cover, then slid open a drawer and hid it from view. All this, Joe watched with compassion. None of it could have been easy.

After a moment or two, Candy said, "Thank you, Joe."

"It was my job. There's no need for thank-yous."

"You followed him?"

"I have his address," Joe said. "His name. A few other details."

"Who is he?"

"Mr. Candy, are you sure—"

"Like you say. Your job."

"McKenzie. He is a Mr. Neil McKenzie." Joe offered a piece of paper across the desk. "You know the name at all?"

Candy thought about it. Decided he didn't. Shook his head.

"No reason you should," Joe assured him. "He only knows you through your picture in the paper. And he recognised your wife, of course. But he made no copies of the film."

"He told you that?"

"I believed him. He didn't seem—he was not what you'd call a technician."

"And you're a good judge of character?"

Joe shrugged modestly. "In my line of work, it's a bonus."

"So I won't be hearing from him again?"

"I wish I could make promises. But a blackmailer, he's more a jackal than a lion. And you've given him one good feed already."

"But now I know where he lives." Russell Candy's hand wrapped itself round Joe's slip of paper.

A good judge of character would recognise this as a Moment.

Joe said, "Mr. Candy. Russell. You don't mind?"

"It's fine."

"Russell. You will forgive me for asking. We are not friends exactly, of course not. You're paying for my services." It struck Joe that this wasn't the right line, and he changed tack. "But I feel responsibility. I gave you these details, McKenzie's particulars, so that if he tries his blackmail tricks once more, you can go to the police. This is not just the right thing, Mr. Candy. Russell. It is the only thing."

"He's a vile little—"

"He is vile, yes. Maybe not so little, but that's neither here nor there. And I'm not pretending he doesn't deserve punishment, but what I am saying, Russell, is that it would be a matter of grave regret. To take vengeance into your own hands, I mean."

"Trust me. I wouldn't regret it."

"Trust me, Russell. You possibly might."

"Is this part of your service?" An edge entered Candy's tone: He was a rich rich man, and Joe was offering him advice? "Am I paying extra for this part?"

But Joe was already showing his palms in surrender. "Please, I didn't mean to offend. It happens, sometimes, that I get carried away. My wife—"

"You're married?"

"She's called Zoë. She likes to remind me of a case, this was a few years ago, that I got arrested while looking for a missing dog. It's a long story and I won't worry you with it now, but what I'm saying is that sometimes I go further than I should. Such as giving you unnecessary warnings just now. It's over-involvement, Russell, that's all. I don't wish to see you in awkward situations."

Candy looked like he felt he was already in one. "I appreciate that, Mr. Silvermann. Joe. Appreciate it in all senses. And I don't plan to do anything—unto*ward*, anything untoward, with the information you've given me. It's security, that's all." He fetched his cheque book from a drawer: not the one he'd deposited the videotape in. "If the bastard returns, I'll be prepared. And yes, you're right, it'll be a matter for the police." He scribbled a cheque; didn't even appear to notice the sum he was scrawling. "And I don't have to ask you—"

"Discretion, of course, it's my middle name. Though not for banking purposes," he added. "Thank you," he said, taking the cheque.

He didn't see Faye Candy as Russell showed him out. Or anyone else: the multimillionaire did his own opening and waving away—there were those, no doubt, who'd regard this lack of staff as cheap, but Joe wasn't among them. He saw it, rather, as adding substance to the man's homelife. Just him and lovely Faye, to protect whose reputation he'd secretly shelled out a hundred grand. Not to mention the substantial payment he'd made Joe himself. He'd called Faye's confession a proof of love, and his own behaviour showed this true of himself also: there was love in this house, Joe thought, as its door closed behind him. It would be a terrible shame if Mr. Candy endangered it by acting foolishly.

SURVEILLANCE SOUNDED LIKE A French word, though whether that meant the French invented snooping probably depended on who you asked. Either way, Joe was in no position to throw stones. For the past two hours, while the evening died, he'd been sitting in his car surveilling a closed post office; closed in the sense that it wasn't open, and closed also in the sense that it had shut down some while ago, and had boards over its windows. There'd been little to see, though an hour back— long enough that he could think on it nostalgically as a crazy, fun-packed moment—a woman had passed with a Chihuahua shivering on a lead. Joe liked to think he could empathise, but there were limits. That anyone could walk into a dogshop, point at a Chihuahua and say "I want that one" baffled him.

Darkness had painted the sky its favourite colour before anything happened to interest Joe.

IT WAS A CAR. The make escaped him: cars didn't do much for Joe, which he conceded was a drawback in his chosen career, but he had the excuse right now that it was dark, and the car arrived lightless, and the streetlamps round this part of town—he was as far east as he could get and still claim to be in Oxford— weren't as maintained as they might be. But car schmar: its details didn't matter. It cruised to a slow halt and its driver killed the engine. He got out, came round to the pavement, looked down at his hand, then back up at the deserted post office. Something about this scene, the slope of his shoulders broadcast, was wrong.

Joe nodded to himself twice, not without hope. He too emerged from his car. The sound of its door drew the other man's attention.

"You."

"It's me, yes."

"Your information—"

"Was not what it might have been. Russell, I'm sorry. There was no intention to deceive."

Russell Candy held out the piece of paper Joe had given him that morning. "Neil McKenzie? 24 Linden Road?"

"There was some intention to deceive," Joe amended. "But for the best of possible reasons."

"This place looks like it's been closed for years."

"And to whose benefit?" Joe asked. "A post office, it's a lodestone of the community. A lodestone."

"That's not really the point, is it, Silvermann?"

"Please, the surname. It's an unfriendly approach." Joe, standing close to Candy now, pointed at the empty building. "This, yes, was a ruse. But forgive me, your coat's lopsided." He moved surprisingly quickly; his hand dipping into Candy's pocket before the man could stop him. What it came out with was small, black, leather, heavy, and had a strap at one end.

"Oh, Russell," Joe said, more in sadness than reproach.

"That's not—"

Joe slipped the strap round his right hand; slapped the sap into his left. The noise echoed fleshly round the dark. "Not which? Not a toy? It certainly feels like it's made for harm." He magicked it inside his coat. "Russell, I owe an apology, yes. There is no Neil McKenzie. Or there is, rather, but that's not what he's called." He nodded at the post office. "And that's not where he lives. I mean, you've noticed this already."

"You let him get away."

"No. I traced him." He gave a small shrug. "There was help. Internet-wise, you know?"

It remained dark, but Joe could tell there were internal struggles occurring: anger and relief. Russell Candy was a battleground. Joe was glad the leather sap was no longer within his reach.

"But you've decided not to tell me who he is."

"For the good of all concerned."

"For his good, sure." This with growing heat. "Not mine. What I want more than anything right now is—"

"More than love? More than marriage?"

"I have those already."

"But to keep them, that's the trick." Joe tapped a hand against his breast; the pocket into which he'd slipped the sap. "You think violence in one area does not seep into another? It's dark here, Russell, and certainly, maybe, you could wreak vengeance then slip off unaccosted." He thought about this, then said: "If McKenzie was here, I mean. And called McKenzie. But what I'm saying is, nobody walks unharmed from a beating. Not the victim. Not its perpetrator."

"You think I paid a hundred thousand for a lecture? I wanted his *name*."

"You paid a hundred thousand for a videotape, Russell. You paid me for a name. Generously, yes, but not a fortune."

"But—"

"You could hurt him, Russell, yes, hurt him badly. With your imposing physical presence. Plus your weapon. But he has knowledge, remember? About your lovely wife's past? And that's the one thing you can't take from him. Unless you planned more than a simple beating."

Candy began to speak, then changed his mind.

"And in that case, Russell, believe me, there would be no winners. There would be a dead blackmailer, yes, but also a

sick worm burrowing into you, and it would burrow and burrow until there was nothing left inside, Russell—nothing at
all, no love, no satisfactions. You think your marriage would
survive? And that, like I say, is if you walk away unaccosted.
If you don't . . ." Joe shrugged. He was still close to Candy: all
this information as confidential as it was urgent. And while he
shrugged Candy shrank a little, as if Joe's as-yet-unspoken conclusions were already hitting home. "If you don't, it comes to
nothing. Everything you wanted concealed will be out in the
light. Everything your wife confessed—her proof of love—just
a cheap noise in the tabloids."

Russell Candy shivered.

"Listen." Joe briefly rested his hand on the man's shoulder.
"Russell, listen. You want the truth? Go. This man, this blackmailer—yes, he's vicious, but who knows? Maybe he has needs,
maybe this is the only escape he has. Okay, you don't care about
his problems. But like I told you, he made no copies of the film.
He'll take your money and disappear. His problems, well, now he
has the resources to confront them. So, Russell, go home to your
lovely wife and put this behind you. It's over. The violence, your
ugly weapon—Russell, trust me, you want no part of any of that.
All the things you want, you already have."

He came to a halt, aware that to go further would be to
risk repeating himself. For a few moments—which felt much
longer—the two men stood on the dark silent street; one
of them reaching out tentatively, his hand just falling short of
plucking the other's sleeve.

At last Candy said, "I can't stand the idea of him getting
away with it."

"It's my belief that nobody gets away with anything," Joe said, letting his hand drop back to his side. "Besides, I think what you mean is, you can't stand the idea of him knowing what he does."

"Yes. That too."

"But that fades to nothing, Russell, when you think of all he doesn't know. That your wife, your Faye, loves you enough to have risked everything—that she told you of this unfortunate film exactly when the information could have put your life together at risk. She trusted you. What is one little secret, lost to a stranger, compared to that?"

"If she hadn't told me, I'd never have believed the bastard," Candy said.

"Of course you wouldn't."

Candy shivered again, as if aware how nearly disaster had kissed him. "He'd have had to show me the damn movie."

Joe wanted to know, but didn't dare ask. Candy told him anyway.

"I destroyed it," he said flatly. "Burned it. Unwatched. I wish I could burn every copy."

"No one else will ever know. The coincidence, already, was huge. What were the chances, an eight-year-old film made for a . . . specialist audience, and this young man being local, and recognising the wedding picture in the paper?" Joe shook his head, wearied by how unnecessary it had all been. "But he's gone. It's over. And if it isn't—if he ever makes contact again—you let me know. And I will take care of it."

For the first time, Candy looked Joe directly in the eye. "You're sure? It's over?"

"I'm sure," Joe said firmly. Just the saying of it cemented it as fact. He was sure.

"Thank you, Joe."

"No need, no need." Here was another Joe moment, only this time it was Joe himself in the grip of it. The successful conclusion of a case: it demanded the grand gesture. Fishing inside his coat, he produced the envelope containing Candy's cheque. "Here—I insist. You were right, perfectly right. You wanted his name, you paid me for his name. Which I did not provide. I did not earn my fee."

"You did your job," Candy said.

"But not what you asked. You wanted his name, his particulars. I thought it best you not have them. That was my decision. Not something you paid for."

"Joe—"

"Please—it would be a portrait of Madison. You follow the reference?"

Candy's bafflement glowed in the dark.

"*The Long Goodbye.* It's not important. But trust me, I cannot take your money." To prove it, Joe tore the envelope in half. Then quartered it. It would have been satisfying to cast the pieces into the night, but hardly sociable. He stuffed them into his pocket instead, then extended a hand. "Russell. Trust me. All this, you can put it behind you. Your life is what happens from now. Go home to your Faye."

Candy took Joe's hand in both his own. "Thank you."

"Please. I'm just glad things worked out."

They walked to their separate cars in the dark. Candy's started first time, and disappeared smoothly into the night.

Joe's gave him trouble, and it was twenty minutes before he could leave.

THERE WAS A SLOW-BURN conversion in process by which the city centre was being made more cosmopolitan, a metamorphosis most obvious in its cafés. The square behind the bus station boasted plenty, all with outside tables at which customers could read newspapers or chat with friends; an increasing number doing the latter via mobile phones. This was a passing fad, Joe had often mentioned in Zoë's hearing. Why cart round items of domestic equipment when we could be paying attention to people and nature and the happy accidents that make life worth living? Most people were best ignored, as far as Zoë was concerned, and nature wasn't at its best in an urban environment. As for happy accidents, she hadn't the faintest clue what Joe was on about.

The woman at this particular café had evidently not long finished a conversation: her chunky mobile sat beside a large cappuccino, which she raised to her lips as Zoë approached. Zoë put her espresso on the table. "Mind if I join you?"

"Oh—no, that's okay."

Though there were other, unoccupied tables nearby.

Zoë said, "I like your tattoo. A butterfly, yes?"

The woman looked at her.

"On your right shoulder? Or is it your left? I always get muddled when it's someone facing me."

"Is this a joke?"

"Oh, right. You're wearing a sweater." Zoë took a sip of her espresso. "But if I could see your shoulder, it'd be a butterfly, wouldn't it?"

Faye Candy put her cup down. "Do we know each other?"

"Not in the flesh. But I admire your work."

"I don't know what you're talking about."

"Fourteen seconds. Pretty good. I was expecting that line when I mentioned the tattoo."

"I think you should leave."

Zoë said, "Let me ask you something. Girl meets boy. They fall in love. Girl then meets man. Man falls in love with girl. Man very rich. What's girl do?"

"You're annoying me. I'm going to call for help."

"Honey, I'm telling a story. An audience is the first thing I want. So anyway, of course you marry him. He's rich, for God's sake. You give up, what, two years? Three? Then one smart lawyer later, you're on easy street for life."

"You're a lunatic."

"I watched the film."

Faye Candy opened her mouth. Closed it again.

"Joe left it out. It was a point of principle with him not to watch it." Zoë lit a cigarette. "It wasn't with me."

"Who are you?"

"Name's Zoë Boehm. And you want to know something? She does look a bit like you, the woman in the film. Even with the glittery wig and all that makeup. Not so much a stranger might notice, but a definite resemblance if you're looking for it. And then there's the tattoo, of course. The clincher. But then, that's why you had yours done, isn't it?"

"You," Faye Candy said slowly. "Interfering. Bitch."

"Thanks. Let me tell you what I think happened. You marry the millionaire, of course. Who turns down a once-in-a-lifetime chance like that? And you promise your boyfriend it won't be forever, that you'll be coming back to him, only richer. Did he believe you?"

"It's true!"

"Maybe so. But he wanted a down payment, didn't he? Something to tide him over. And this is what the pair of you came up with. He didn't go looking for the film, did he? I mean, he'd already seen it, noted the resemblance. That's what gave him the idea."

"We'd watched it together," Faye said. "Nothing wrong with that."

"Sure."

"He's a college porter. You know how much that's worth, being a college porter?"

"I'm guessing not a lot."

"But he's got talent. He's a writer. He writes all sorts— poems, stories."

"Blackmail notes. Was it his idea you got the tattoo? To put the resemblance beyond doubt?"

"I'm admitting nothing."

"And then you faked the cover, of course. Must have been fun. Bit of a gamble, because the woman on the box clearly isn't the woman in the film, but—and here's the beauty of it— it doesn't matter, does it? The rich man doesn't need to see the film. All that matters is he knows that it exists. Because Russell Candy's hardly going to think you confessed to making a blue movie if you didn't. Who in her right mind would do that, and put her wedding to a rich man at risk?"

She tapped ash into her empty coffee cup.

"It took pluck, I'll give you that. He could have walked away. But he didn't, so you're home free. Candy knows the blackmail's for real, because you've told him about the movie. No way is he going to shout for the cops, when all that'll do is make your dirty secret public. No, the confession was a touch of genius. Poor sap probably thinks it proves you love him."

Faye Candy said, "I'll be with him. One day."

It was clear she was talking about her beloved blackmailer.

Zoë ground her cigarette out. "The cheque Joe tore up was for a grand. You can make the replacement out to me. That's Zoë B-o-e-h-m. Don't worry, he'll get his share."

"Will you tell him?"

"Joe? I would if I thought he'd learn from it. But he's set in his ways."

"I meant Russell."

Zoë said, "I've got your boyfriend's name and address. Try another bite at the cherry and I'll blow you both out of the water. Otherwise, how you live your life's up to you. But you might want to get clear on the details in future."

"Meaning what?"

"You got the wrong arm. The woman in the film? Her tattoo's on her left shoulder. Yours is on your right."

She waited while Faye Candy wrote the cheque, then folded it and stowed it away inside her leather jacket. When she left, a chill breeze was just making itself felt, and cups were rattling in saucers around the square. But Zoë didn't look back, and was in the bank before the rain arrived.

REMOTE CONTROL

It starts on a train. Maurice's fault. Maurice is about my age, but since his divorce, he's let himself go: his suits overdue a dry-clean; his shirts frayed at the cuff. Some days, he could stand a little closer to the shower. To hear him tell it, though, he's better off.

"Finally I get a little peace," he says. "That woman could talk for England. They should record her phone calls for training purposes."

But for all the spin, it's not just his cuffs that are frayed lately. Small things rattle Maurice's cage. Some days we don't get a seat—it's a busy service—and once he'd have grinned, and deployed those origami skills commuters develop for reading newspapers upright in a crowd. Now he seethes instead, staring grimly out of the window as if, instead of fields and dormitory towns, we're flashing through a post-nuclear landscape. His hair needs attention. He still has good teeth, though.

"Jesus," he tells me. "They should make it a crime."

"Make what a crime, Maurice?"

"Coming into the capital without due purpose," he says. "Some of these dumbbells, they're going shopping, can you believe it? They get on a train, eight-ten in the morning, they're going shopping on Regent Street. So us poor working stiffs have to stand. Hell of a way to prepare for the day ahead."

"Most of them have jobs, Maurice."

"The ones that don't should be stuffed in the luggage racks."

I have a job. I work in corporate finance, and earn nicely without causing outrage. And Maurice has a job. His company operates CCTV systems. I sometimes wonder if it's the vaguely Hollywood flavour of this that has tinted his speech with Americanisms. And, too, he sees a lot of bad behaviour. Maurice doesn't monitor screens himself, but what he calls the showstopper stuff gets spliced onto tapes and shown at parties. His outfit has a security contract which puts cameras along the South Bank, all the way to the Isle of Dogs. He's seen people screwing against the wall in broad daylight, and not just professionally either. Muggings, of course; rapes, fistfights, stabbings. Politicians arm in arm with local gangsters. Last year he seemed happy in his work, but as the days grind by, the wells we draw from sink deeper. Maurice has a new boss, and this is a travesty of justice. Maurice should have been the new boss—not this punk, which is how Maurice refers to him. "This punk," he says. "This goddamn kid." This goddamn kid is ten years younger, two stone lighter and fifteen grand a year richer than Maurice is right now. Maurice feels he's been gazumped. "That was my job," he says. "Goddamn punk came out of nowhere."

Remain detached, I want to tell him. *Stay in control.* Or you will rupture one day; burst one of those complicated valves that keep the heart pumping. *Once you let the rage inside, it's hard to get it out.* Trust me. I know about this.

Maurice hasn't mentioned the boss in a while. New angers blossom daily.

"Fuckin' personalised numberplates," he says this morning. "Don't you hate them?"

"They have their uses," I say. "Easy to remember."

"Yeah, well, I'm not forgetting this one in a hurry."

And he goes into a spiel about being cut up by a red sports car at the weekend. Maurice was entirely in the right. These twits in their flash motors: decapitation would be too quick.

"She was driving," he says. "But it's him I remember. Shaved bald, and when did that get to be cool? I remember in the good old days, your chrome-domes had the grace to be ashamed."

He wore an earring too, and Maurice has much to say on this subject.

"I figure he had his hand up her skirt, and that's how come she was in a rush. Looked old enough to be his big sister."

The train pulls into platform 8, and the long forever begins of its gradual halt; the release of its doors.

"Whoosh," he says, and I think he's imitating the doors, but he isn't. "WHOO5H. The *S* was a five."

On the concourse, we make our usual farewells.

"Don't let the bastards grind you down," he warns me.

"Remember," I tell him. "They can kill you. But they're not allowed to eat you."

But I say it distractedly, because my mind is elsewhere.

IF YOU WANT TO know where it gets you—letting the rage inside—keep your eyes open as you slog around the city. You'll see people behaving like all kinds of weather at once: fizzing and spitting; boiling and baked; grey and grim. Just by walking where somebody else wants to be, you're making mortal enemies for life. Somebody asked me "What the fuck?" last week because I slowed to inspect a shop window, and I've no doubt he thought it a reasonable question. Trench warfare has its critics, but city life is no picnic either. A *Daily Mail* columnist once spent a morning on the pavement outside Bond Street station, and not a soul stopped to check he wasn't dead. Though to be fair, they might have recognised him. One less *Mail* columnist would brighten anyone's day.

Remain detached. Stay in control. Or you will rupture; burst a complicated valve.

Trust me, because I know about this. I killed a man once. It was mostly an accident. It happened years ago, when I was a student, over a girl: a girl I hadn't even spoken to, but told a friend about, and next thing I knew they were going steady. It seemed to me that he would never have looked her way if I'd not pointed her out. You dream your dreams aloud, and they come true for someone else. I waited for him after the pubs shut one night, on the towpath he used as a shortcut. He was drunk, and might well have ended up in the canal even if I'd not been there—which, as far as the world was concerned, was the case. The following day it seemed like a strange dream. Now I recall it as a warning: *remain detached; stay in control.* There are angry places in each of us, and we visit them at our peril. I can't even remember that girl's name.

The things that are precious remain worth fighting for. But I've learned to let go of the space around me. I don't ask strangers "What the fuck?" because I already know what the fuck.

I've only ever told one person about the man I killed.

I DON'T SEE MAURICE on the evening train, because he usually goes to the pub. Instead, I stare out of the window as the world goes whooshing by. I have bought flowers for Emma, which is something I do: it's not a birthday thing, or an anniversary thing, or even a Friday-night thing. It is a recurring statement of intent: *I will always bring you flowers*. Tonight they are roses, and to my fellow passengers possibly look like an apology. But I have nothing to be sorry for, and intend to keep it that way.

Emma hums as she arranges the roses in a vase.

"How was your day?" she asks.

"It was fine. Yours?"

"Same old same old," she says, and this is our private joke. Emma does not work—I earn enough for both of us—and her same old is someone else's leisure.

I potter around the sitting room as she prepares the supper. I drink a glass of white, and pick things up, and put them down—ornaments, books, a candlestick; a pale silk scarf left draped across a chair—and remember where each came from, and which were my gifts to her. It is not only flowers I bring her: I buy gifts. That scarf; this candlestick. I made her a present long ago of my deepest secret: of the man I killed on a lonely stretch of canal, unobserved by God or anyone. She wept—we both did—but she understood what my telling her meant: that I was placing all I was, and ever hoped to be, in her hands. Ever since, I've known we'll never drift apart.

I bought her those books, those CDs, and the pictures on our walls.

And last year, for her birthday, as a special treat, I bought her a smart red sports car.

With a personalised numberplate.

REMAIN IN CONTROL. STAY detached.

Maurice says, "Why so interested? I told you all this yesterday, you're like, Yeah yeah, are we nearly there yet?"

We have seats this morning. There's never any telling which days are going to be crowded; which are going to be like somebody declared a bank holiday, and never told you. Maurice sits opposite me, and I can see he's missed a spot shaving; one of those difficult places under the chin which mirrors don't always notice, but wives do.

"It's just bad behaviour," I tell him.

"Well, it wasn't the only kind of bad behaviour on their mind. I can promise you that."

He reminds me that it happened in the Cotswolds, then goes off on a tangent, telling me why he was there himself. I spend the interlude recalling that Emma had gone shopping on Saturday afternoon.

"Couple of miles along the road, I see the car parked by a wood. Like they're nature lovers, right? Guy with a shaved head, a fuckin' *earring*, the only wildlife he's interested in is a bit of outdoors horizontal jogging."

Maurice can be loud sometimes. His words riffle through the carriage like a cat in long grass.

That day, I call Emma twice from work. She answers both times. I say I just wanted to hear her voice.

"That's sweet."

And in the evening, I dig out our most recent phone bill. There's no earthly reason a landline should betray her, but even so, there are numbers I don't recognise. But Google tells me they're innocent. Mail-order firms; the local library. A plumber. For a while I entertain visions of Emma wrapped in highly coordinated intercourse with an overalled handyman, plungers and piping arrayed all around. But then I recall a leaky tap in the upstairs bathroom. Of course she called a plumber. Who else is going to fix a leaky tap?

"You're very quiet," she says over supper. "Is everything all right?"

She's a beautiful woman, Emma; more beautiful to me than anyone else, it's true. But beautiful. It always surprises me that she doesn't take a good photo. I buy her gifts; when you get down to it, I feed and clothe her. But none of this makes her my possession. She is my wife, and that places her deeply inside my space, but she's not my possession. In my absence, who knows where she walks?

"I'm fine," I tell her. "Everything is fine."

"WE'RE STRICTLY AUDIO-VISUAL, OUR end," Maurice says. "And v. much above board. Public stuff, like the South Bank getout, plus offices and home security systems and all that. What you're talking about's bugging. You can buy phonetaps over the counter, or over the internet, same difference. But it's legally touchy. You put up signs saying THIS AREA'S UNDER REMOTE SURVEILLANCE, everyone knows where they stand. Nobody puts up a sign saying THIS PHONE'S TAPPED. And if you did, you could put up another one saying OUT OF ORDER, you'd get more traffic on it."

THE DEVICE, WHICH ARRIVES at my office from friendlyear.com, is no bigger than a watch battery, and transmits to a recorder the size of a memory stick. *Feel more secure,* the packaging invites, though its actual purpose is to confirm one's insecurities. The instructions read like they've been translated from the Portuguese by someone who speaks only French, but owns two dictionaries.

It weighs my pocket down as I leave, and I wonder if the dogs at the station will bark me out—the police dogs that wait on the concourse, trained to sniff for bombs, guns and fear.

On the train, Maurice says, "You're looking pressured. Markets heading for a fall?"

It is such a surprise that Maurice notices anything beyond his own concerns that I'm not sure how to answer. "Same old same old," I say at last.

He looks out on a darkening view of warehouse yards and traffic jams. "Tell me about it. We've got a citywide systems check on—every camera, every lens, every angle. Guess which muggins gets to coordinate that little lot?"

"Don't the cameras get checked all the time?"

"Individually, yes. This is a systems audit." He leans forward. "Means we have to close whole chunks of it down. You want to pull some riverside mischief and not get caught, this week's good."

"I presume you're not advertising that."

"Jesus, don't joke." He brushes imaginary crumbs from his lapel. The real ketchup stain on his tie is unimpressed. "Big Brother never sleeps. That's our story, anyway."

At home, I place the bug on the standard lamp. The recorder goes in a drawer. It's noise-activated, which means that when nothing's happening, it goes to sleep. Along with hours of sound, it can capture aeons of unremembered silence.

"What are your plans for the rest of the week?" I ask Emma over supper; a strangely formal construction.

"I thought I might go up to London one morning. Do some shopping. But don't worry, I'll avoid the commuter crush."

"That's good," I say. "Maurice doesn't like non-combatants stealing our seats."

She smiles at this. She knows Maurice.

All night it rains, and I lie awake wondering if the pattering on the windows will trigger the bug. Already I can picture myself listening to it: hours of secondhand rain; a memory of overnight weather.

EMMA HUMS AS SHE moves from room to room; she hums as she changes the roses' water. And talks to herself too, snatches of dialogue—single words, mostly—meant to act as memos-to-self: *milk*, she will say, for obvious reasons, or *oven*, less obviously. She takes a call on her mobile, and walks out of range while gossiping with a book-club friend. I hear all this hours later, in the bathroom, the recorder's earpiece clamped to my head.

She interrupts my surveillance by calling upstairs.

I go down to eat, and admire her food. I applaud the industry with which she passes her days. I notice that the oven sparkles; its ceramic buffed and polished. My attentions amuse her.

"Sometimes you act like a brand-new husband," she tells me.

"Would you like a brand-new husband?" I ask.

"I'm quite content with the old one," she says. "But it's nice to be appreciated."

Later, I return to the bathroom, and continue listening to the day's messages.

More humming.

Lightbulbs.

The friendly clatter of a woman preparing to go out, followed an unknowable amount of time later by the sound of the same woman returning home.

She takes a call on her mobile.

Yes . . . Tomorrow, that's right. Well, thank you for confirming. What time's check-in? Any time after eleven? That's fine.

Damn, she tells herself some time later. *I forgot to buy the bread.*

I hear myself arriving back from work, and removing the recorder from its drawer.

And then all I hear is silence, taking place in real time.

IN THE MORNING, BEFORE she's up, I take her mobile from her coat pocket, and jot a number down from the call register. When I ring it from my own phone, a hotel reception-ist answers. I find I can't speak.

Emma emerges, in her dressing gown. "I'm going to London today too," she says. "But I'll go in on the ten o'clock."

"Shall we come back together?" My voice is rusty, as if it belongs to somebody older.

"Oh, I'll be home before rush hour." She kisses me on the cheek. "I'll leave the rough stuff to you men."

On the train, Maurice complains about the continuing rain. He also complains about fare increases, the government's pensions policy, and the number of reality shows on TV.

"Don't those guys know their T. S. Eliot?" *Those guys* are the guys we all hate: the ones responsible for whatever disgusts us at that moment. "Humankind cannot bear too much reality. Did they think he was kidding, or what?"

"I don't think modernist poetry factors much in TV scheduling, Maurice."

"Well, I don't think basic intelligence factors much in TV scheduling. They got fuckin' cheerleaders doing the weather, for God's sake." He pauses. "Actually, that bit's not all bad."

On the concourse he says, "Let's be careful out there."

"Do it to them before they do it to you," I tell him.

BUT I DON'T HEAD for the Tube. Instead I make for the daylight, or what little there is of it—it's wet and grey as I walk to Hyde Park Corner, where I buy a cup of coffee in a franchise opposite the Victoria Hotel, and use my mobile phone to call in sick. There's a newspaper on my table, and I pretend to read while I watch the comings and goings.

At ten to eleven a shaven-headed man with an earring pauses at its steps, checks his watch, then goes in.

At ten past, my wife arrives in a taxi. She smiles as she tips the driver.

STAY DETACHED. REMAIN IN control. Let go of the space around you.

But everything inside that space is yours.

I spend so long in that café, it starts to feel like my kitchen. I drink so much coffee, I start to feel like hell.

In the newspaper I'm not reading is a grainy picture from CCTV footage. It shows two kids in hoodies stomping a homeless man to death.

Three hours later, Emma leaves the Victoria. Through a circle I've rubbed in the steamed-up window I watch as she sets off for the station, and she looks the same to me as she always does. There's no scarlet letter branded on her forehead. She might have been taking a business meeting in the hotel's conference room. Out of view she walks, her good grey coat and umbrella keeping her dry. Once she's gone, I return my attention to the hotel entrance. It swims a little, but I blink away newfound knowledge. When the shaven-headed man emerges five minutes later, my vision is clear again, my purpose undimmed. I pay the bill and follow him round the corner. I'm half an escalator behind him as he dips into the underground.

THE TUBE MAP HAS been played with many times; its stations replaced with constellations, philosophers, authors, famous drunks. It is an attempt, I think, to find poetry in the ordinary. He changes trains, then, at the Great Bear, and I loiter yards from him as he waits on the platform. Every so often he checks his watch. Perhaps he's heading back to work—playtime over; alibi used up. I wonder what excuse he phoned in before heading for the Victoria: A dental appointment? A checkup? He is wearing a suit beneath his raincoat, and his earring flashes when it catches the light. I imagine him in the passenger seat of my wife's red car, his hand up her skirt; or in a hotel bedroom, that suit folded onto a hanger before their fun begins. Then the Tube arrives in a silvery whoosh, and we board the same carriage, and sit ten seats apart.

Dylan Thomas; WB Yeats; Ezra Pound . . . The carriage fills, but no one sits next to me. Perhaps I'm giving off the wrong signals. Perhaps no one wants to check if I'm dead. I feel dead, it's almost true, as we reach our destination, and emerge into the same grey grubby weather of twenty minutes ago. He walks across Hungerford Bridge, collar pulled up to protect his shaven skull. I follow some way behind. My hair is plastered to my head, and rainwater pours down my neck. Everyone I pass has the same expression stamped onto their features: a look that says *stay out of my space*. On the South Bank he veers left, and heads towards Tate Modern. Before reaching it he turns from the river, and without ever looking behind him—as if he enjoys a clear conscience—leads me to an office block, into which he disappears.

Forever, I wait in an alley opposite. Ages of unrecorded time, whose silence spools into nothingness.

When he emerges, it's long past office hours. Perhaps he's compensating for his morning's absence, or perhaps his office role is important enough to spill into the evening shift. He seems tired when he appears at last, talking into his mobile phone; shaking his head and waving his free hand around in a pointless underlining of his words. This conversation lasts way up the South Bank, where he stops at a pub beyond the Globe.

From a corner table I watch as he drinks his way through three large scotches.

Outside, it's full-on dark. The rain is back with a vengeance, and has cleared the evening streets. I nurse a single pint until he rises to leave, then follow him along the unwatched river, heedless of the switched-off cameras we pass. He is somewhat drunk, I expect. I'm mildly wobbly myself, after beer on an empty stomach.

What happens next—the sudden acceleration, the blow to the head, the heave into the water—seems both familiar and surprisingly straightforward. For a minute afterwards I stand there, hardly able to believe that such a large problem can vanish so instantly. In the morning, I expect, it will feel like another strange dream.

And then I catch the last train home, to find Emma waiting, anxious.

"You're so late!"

"I went for a drink. Sorry."

"You could have called."

"I know. I'm sorry."

"Are you sure you're all right?"

"I'm fine," I say. "How was your day?"

"Same old same old," she tells me.

THE PAPERS MAKE GREAT play of the irony: the murder of the London head of a global security outfit captured on his firm's CCTV. There are shots of me trailing him halfway up the river. Even I recognise myself in the blown-up footage. But at the trial I don't mention Maurice's subterfuge about the system being shut down because—as both he and Emma point out—last thing I need is another drowned body surfacing. Even a twenty-year-old murder would muddy the waters. One life sentence is enough.

They send me a photo from the wedding. This takes place the week after our divorce comes through. Maurice looks fit and spruce, but then he has no further need to play down-at-heel, and the extra £15k for stepping into the boss's shoes can't hurt. He's maintained his predecessor's habit of holding brunch meetings at the Victoria, I gather. Its conference room is ideal. I sometimes think about Emma killing three hours in the café there, and wonder if she drank as much coffee as I did while waiting for suspicion to harden.

In the photo, she looks beautiful.

LOST LUGGAGE

Her name was Jane Carpenter, she worked at an estate agent's, and she'd been taken at 7:26 that morning as she cut across the playing field behind the secondary school to reach her bus stop on the other side. She was twenty-three. She had wavy brown hair with fresh blonde highlights. Maybe she would, but probably she wouldn't, go to Malta with her sister this summer; she had hopes her boyfriend Brendan would suggest they go somewhere together instead. These and other details still fizzed through her unconscious, but mostly what she was now was a machine for not dying: an unwilled continuation of heart, lung and nervous system that pumped away, undeterred by the narcotics in her system, the ropes binding her ankles and wrists, the gag, the blindfold, the car boot's lock.

Her name was Jane Carpenter, but she was currently luggage. And if nobody found her soon, she'd be lost.

THE CAR WAS PARKED mid-morning at a motorway service station. The restaurant there was brightly lit, and its furnishings fixed in place, so the symmetry didn't spoil. Laminated menus offered pictures of the food on offer, and the sound system regurgitated an inoffensive medley to match. A man in jeans and scuffed black leather jacket left the counter, carrying a tray with the mixed grill option and a large mug of tea. He hadn't shaved in a while, nor shampooed, by the look of it. He took a seat near the corner, facing out towards the car park. There weren't many people in the restaurant, and he wasn't sitting near any of them.

"What about him?"

"Whom?"

She liked it that he said "whom."

The couple talking were Peter Mason and Jennifer Holmes, and they'd been an item for somewhere approaching eight months. In that time they'd done most of the usual getting-to-know-you dances, and made one or two of the usual surprising discoveries about shared interests and passions. They'd spent a few weekends together, and enjoyed what they'd learned, but this was the first time they'd come away as a couple—they were heading for a cottage Pete had got hold of, up in the Peak District; somewhere pretty isolated—and their mood was a little scatty. A bit off-the-leash. On the way here they'd talked about their respective weeks at work, then moved on to mildly salacious hints about what the weekend might hold, before reverting—not to get too ahead of themselves—to inconsequential stuff: movies, music, childhood friends. Now they'd stopped for coffee, which had turned into coffee and sandwiches, and Pete had been talking about people-watching; a hobby-horse of his. It was amazing, he maintained, what you could tell about someone just by observation. Provided you looked in the right way, and picked up on the available clues.

"With a name like yours, this shouldn't be any big surprise."

"Jennifer?"

"Ha ha. Holmes, pumpkin. As in Sherlock."

"The great detective."

"Who could deconstruct a character soon as look at him. No villain was safe. No secret undiscovered."

"Didn't he have expert knowledge, though? Couldn't he always tell, I don't know, that you had your hair cut by a one-armed barber who plied his trade on the Strand every second Tuesday? That kind of *cheating* knowledge no real person could have?"

"Well, yeah. But the theory is absolute. Observation brings knowledge."

"You reckon."

"I reckon."

"What about him?"

"Whom?"

Jennifer nodded towards the man who'd just sat down on the far side of the restaurant. Sitting side by side the way they were, both were facing him, though he was facing the window. "Him."

Jeans and scuffed black leather jacket with a faded tee underneath. Probably with logo or slogan, though it was impossible to see from here. He must have been early forties, with shaggy dark hair and a sallow complexion.

". . . Well?"

It was meant as a challenge, he could tell.

They couldn't be overheard. There was no harm in this. The man was a stranger.

Peter said, "Okay. He's used to these places. Motorway service stations."

"Everyone is. We've all been places like this."

"But they're a way of life with him."

"Evidence."

"He's not looking round. He's focused on his food, see? The surroundings mean nothing to him."

It was true: he was.

"Maybe he's hungry."

"Maybe he is."

"And it's not like the surroundings are worth paying attention to."

"I wouldn't say that. They're not tasteful or pleasant, true, but that doesn't mean they're without interest. I notice you took in what the menu had to offer. And you checked out the coasters and everything. The posters on the walls."

"Is that shallow?"

"No. I did too. I've been places like this before, but I've never been to this particular place. There's always something new. But I'm guessing there's a saturation point, and our man's reached it. Because he didn't look around when he came in. He barely glanced at the menu. It's like everything is so familiar to him, it's not worth paying attention to."

"Good," she said. "More," she said.

Peter thought. "Okay. When he was fetching his food, he didn't have to puzzle out the system. He already knew what was going on, that you fetch your food that side and pay this side. And where the drinks are, and everything. He didn't have to go back and fetch a teacup once he'd got to the hot water urn. He knew to pick up the cup first."

"I didn't see any of that."

"Well, I did. Trust me. And another thing. See where he's sitting?"

"What about it?"

"Perfect place. He can eat and still keep an eye on his vehicle. That's the kind of precaution you take when we're talking about livelihood."

"Ah. He travels for a living."

"I think what we've got so far is bringing us to that conclusion, yes."

"Salesman?"

"He's not really kempt enough for a salesman, is he?"

"Kempt," she thought. That was up there with "whom."

"So I don't know. Maybe a courier of some sort."

Jennifer turned and looked out into the car park. There were no delivery vans out there. One estate car had writing down the side panels—something about double-glazing—but they'd decided he wasn't a salesman.

Peter was ahead of her. "There's all kinds of couriers these days. You don't have to wear a uniform and drive a brown truck. Maybe he delivers cars."

"Cars?"

"You hire a car to take you to the airport, but for one reason or another you don't need it for the return journey. Maybe you're flying back somewhere else, because you got a deal on the flight or you're going to visit your mother or something." He shrugged. "Somebody has to fetch the car, take it back to its starting point."

"You know so much."

What he liked about this was the absence of any trace of sarcasm.

"It's all just speculation," he said modestly.

"Well, of course it is. But what speculation. Tell me more."

He said, "Well . . . Looks to me like he's on the skids."

"I'll go along with that."

"But he used to be prosperous. This motorway service station life, this is something that's happened to him. It's not the way he started out."

"Evidence," she said again.

He was ready for this. "Take his jacket. It's nice, but old. You buy a jacket like that because you want to look good, you want to look cool."

"Leather jackets get cooler, the more worn they are."

"Point. But you have to wash your hair for the full effect. Nobody interested in their appearance is going to leave their hair unwashed for so long that you can tell from this distance it's dirty."

"So what do we deduce from that, Sherlock?"

Peter said, "Like I said, he's on the skids. He used to be a man who wears a jacket like that, and now he's a man who's still clinging to the jacket, but can't do the rest of it anymore . . . Watch his hand as he raises his fork to his mouth . . . There!"

"He's not wearing a wedding ring."

"Clever girl. But what else?"

"You're going to tell me there's a white band of flesh there. That he used to wear a ring but doesn't now."

Pete was shaking his head in admiration before she'd finished. "Damn, but you're good at this."

"Sure. Except I don't believe it. I can't see any such thing from here, and you can't either, can you?"

"Well, no. But what are the chances a guy who used to wear a jacket like that never had the chance to marry? And he's certainly not wearing a ring now."

"Perhaps he's gay."

"Perhaps he is. But in the absence of evidence one way or the other, let's go with the odds."

"His marriage went down the pan."

"About the same time his old job disappeared."

"And you can tell that from . . . ?"

"That's the way it so often happens, isn't it?" For a moment they shared a look brimming with confidence that this wouldn't happen to them. "One day you've got it all nailed down, but when one thing gives, everything else follows."

"The domino effect."

"They wouldn't have given it a name if it didn't happen."

"Whoever 'they' are."

"Oh, they're a smart bunch. Your turn. What do you think his old job was?"

Jennifer watched the man for a moment or two. He didn't look their way. He glanced at the car park once, just for a second, but other than that he concentrated on his food.

She said, "I think he wore a uniform."

He said, "Evidence?" and enjoyed saying it.

"He has that air of invisibility. I mean, when you wear a uniform, you get noticed, right? Except you don't, not really. People see the uniform, but they don't see the person wearing it. So if you ask somebody to describe, say, a policeman, they'll say, well, he was a policeman. He was wearing a police uniform."

"Uh-huh."

"And the way he's sitting there now, you can tell, I don't know . . . that he doesn't expect to be noticed. And that he's used to that. It gives him a kind of freedom."

"Freedom," Peter said. "That's interesting."

"Not the open-road freedom he gets from his courier job." She flashed him a smile with this. "A different kind of freedom. The kind that lets you get away with stuff."

"Stuff."

"You know. A life spent tootling up and down motorways, there's lots of temptations out there. The kind of person who's used to being invisible could get up to mischief."

"He could pick up hitch-hikers, for instance," Peter said.

"He could pick them up," Jennifer agreed. "And then . . . whatever."

"Jesus," Peter said. "I think we've just caught ourselves a serial killer."

They both laughed.

Their sandwiches were finished. They still had some way to go, and neither of them had to say it out loud for both to know they should be on the move. But as they stood, Peter said, "You know, I think I'll go have a word with him."

"You can't!"

"'Course I can. It's no big deal. I'll just verify one fact."

"Which fact? How?"

"I'll tell him we had a bet. That he used to wear a uniform. What harm can it do?"

"He might get angry."

"I've never met an angry man yet," Peter said, "that I wasn't able to run away from. You go out to the car. I'll join you in a second."

SHE STOOD BY THE car, waiting. Peter came out two minutes later, holding his mobile to his ear, but whatever he was doing with it he finished before he reached her. "Just checking my messages," he said, putting it in his pocket.

"And?"

"Nothing important."

"No, silly. The man. What did you find out?"

"Well . . ." He was drawing this out. Then he smiled. "You were right, clever girl. He used to drive a bus."

"A uniform. But completely invisible."

"Well," he said, "I don't suppose that actually makes him a serial killer."

She looked back through the restaurant window. The man was still sitting there, but he was watching them now; the look on his face completely unreadable from this distance. Or maybe it would have been unreadable even close up. He had the air of being one of those people it wasn't possible to know much about, no matter how good you were at observation. She shivered a little, then got in the car.

"Cold?"

"No, I'm okay."

"Good."

"A little excited, to tell you the truth."

Turning the ignition, Peter smiled at her. "Good," he said again. Then they drove off.

Their names were Peter Mason and Jennifer Holmes, and in the eight months they'd been together, they'd made one or two surprising discoveries about shared interests and passions. And now they were heading for a cottage Pete had got hold of, up in the Peak District; somewhere pretty isolated, for a private little party. Just the two of them, plus their luggage.

Everything they needed was in the boot.

MIRROR IMAGES

He didn't keep count, but he must have dispatched upwards of thirty people. Few had given him sleepless nights. Death was part and parcel of what he did, and if some of his initial methods had been a little off the wall (he had once strangled a bus conductor with the sloughed skin of a boa constrictor), he had calmed down since, and now generally shot, stabbed or bludgeoned his victims to death without undue fuss.

But last night, three in the morning, he'd sat bolt upright in bed thinking: Harry.

Couldn't even remember Harry's surname at first, it had been so long ago. Harry Cudlipp. He'd been a nobody, Harry Cudlipp, but he'd seen something he shouldn't have seen, and reckoned to profit by it, and thus his uneventful life reached its eventful close. All, as stated, long ago.

So why is Harry at the foot of the bed, three in the morning?

Not literally, of course. Not literally. If Nigel Reeve-Holkham believed in ghosts, he'd not have gone in for this particular line.

He'd got up and closed the wardrobe door, hiding its mirror from sight, then returned to his pillows, but sleep held off, only taking him back in its sly embrace moments before the alarm clock screeched the morning into life. He'd risen heavy-lidded, with unresponsive limbs. Black coffee left him just as exhausted but with a tic at his eyebrow. And when he'd shaved, there'd been that nudge from his subconscious again; an awareness of Harry. You couldn't put it stronger than that. It wasn't as if Harry Cudlipp appeared in his bathroom cabinet mirror—not even in that classic double-take shock, when you open the cabinet, then shut it again and *yeek*, there he is, beside you—but as Nigel put razor to cheek, tracing those bumps on his reflection's right jaw that were a perfect match for those on his own left, back Harry arrived; swimming into mind as if he were a long-term resident of Nigel Reeve-Holkham's mental aquarium, instead of a passing guest some sixteen years gone.

Sixteen years gone, Harry had been on a boathouse balcony, looking across the river to the meadow. Quite probably he'd been remembering that thing he'd seen that he shouldn't have seen, and musing on the profit he might turn. A certain smile had played across his lips. Then Harry Cudlipp—who had not been at the boathouse as a rower, student, or college chap eager to watch his alma mater's crew put through their paces; he'd been there because that was his job, cleaning out the boathouse of a morning—had stubbed his cigarette in the hanging basket to his left, yawned, stretched, and *crack!*, a shot had rung out.

Stubbing one's cigarette out in a hanging basket is impolite but not, perhaps, a capital offence. Still: *crack!* A shot had rung out.

And Harry Cudlipp had been effectively remaindered.

Nigel Reeve-Holkham sighed, and continued shaving.

He nicked his chin in the process, and bloodied a clean towel.

AFTER THAT, IT WAS all about Harry. Not that Harry dogged his steps (this wasn't a literal haunting. Nigel Reeve-Holkham was coming to caress that scrap of comfort), but he'd spring to mind a dozen times a day, mostly when Nigel caught his own unexpected reflection—shop windows, mirrored pillars in stores; the distorting surfaces of passing cars. Why was that? Nigel Reeve-Holkham in no way resembled Harry Cudlipp. Harry Cudlipp had been gaunt, with cheeks that sucked in as if he had a lemon drop under his tongue. His hair had been thinning too, catching up with the rest of him; Harry's hair had been no more than a few stray wisps, Brylcreemed into place. He'd smoked constantly. And his clothes had been rubbish: a mishmash of garments over which he pulled a stained apron every morning as he set about tasks which remained, in Nigel Reeve-Holkham's mind, vague and undefined, but which had doubtless involved the application of industrial-strength cleaning fluids and mops and buckets and other details.

Nigel himself was abstemious; immaculate. His cleaning fluids came in polite plastic bottles with spray-nozzles. They rarely intruded on his consciousness.

But all this Harry stuff: it was getting him down. He was starting to wonder who else was going to turn up out of the long-dead blue—that bus conductor? The one who didn't like snakes? Or maybe the woman thrown from the roof of that chi-chi hotel in Paris. She'd landed spread-eagled near a fountain, whose reach had been just enough to rinse her life's-blood from the flagstones, and drag it in a pinkening swirl to the gutters of the rue Pigalle. But there was nobody. Only Harry. No one else made a peep.

A couple of afternoons after that first visitation, Nigel took his newspapers to the recycling bins near the local park. There were a lot of them; his haul included Oxford's daily *Mail* and weekly *Times* as well as the decent nationals, not that either had given him joy. And as he was hoisting them through the letter-box mouth of the bin, he saw Harry again. There were swings and roundabouts over the park's far side—the infants' play-area was fenced off, to keep monsters at bay—and that was where Harry stood, leaning against that very fence; smoking, and wearing rubbish clothes. He was staring in Nigel's direction.

And then Nigel blinked, and he was gone. There was a man over there, that was all; a man who not only wasn't Harry, he wasn't even smoking. Nigel shook his head. It was early, but already he knew today would be a wasted day. He'd spend most of it gnawing on this new non-encounter; a reminder of something that had been put to rest years ago, but apparently wouldn't lie down.

He was beginning to think that in killing Harry Cudlipp, he'd made a terrible mistake.

JOE SILVERMANN HAD A lot of sayings, and one of them was, there was no such thing as an ordinary case. "People, they come in all sizes. Their problems, likewise." This was largely theoretical, because he didn't work much. And the problems that didn't come in different sizes—the problems that were always the same: the credit checks, the reference evaluations, the child support defaulters—were dealt with by his wife and partner, Zoë Boehm, on the grounds that they paid the rent and didn't need screwing up.

Her words.

Where she was right now, he didn't know. As for Joe, he was in the office of a couple of upstairs rooms on North Parade, which was a confusing mile or so south of South Parade. And he had a client with him. His client was a small man, sinisterly well-dressed: he had long fingers and small teeth, and a tic at his left eyebrow. And he'd just told Joe he was being haunted.

"Haunted?"

"Not literally."

Joe nodded sagely. He didn't believe in ghosts—Zoë would have given him a hard time if he had—but didn't mind talking to people who did. He just had to be careful not to absorb any supernatural beliefs by mistake. Like any virtue, empathy had its downside.

"It's more of an . . . awareness."

"Ah."

"You see?"

Joe nodded politely. He was hoping matters would become more specific. Otherwise—well, this wouldn't be the first interview with a prospective client where he'd never worked out what he was being hired for.

"But some things trigger that awareness more than others."

"And they would be . . . ?"

"Well—when I'm shaving. I'm reminded of him when I'm shaving."

"You see him when you look in the mirror."

"I'm reminded of him when I look in the mirror."

Joe raised a finger to make his point. "There's a difference."

There followed a slight pause during which both men became aware of a bluebottle on the window, fizzing like an electric charge.

"I know," said Nigel Reeve-Holkham at last. "That's why I made the distinction."

"As you say," said Joe. Positive responses, he'd read, were a good thing, so he'd memorized a couple. "But I'm wondering how you think I can help." Less positive, but it had to be asked.

"You're a detective."

"I am," Joe said.

"You solve problems."

"Mmm."

"Well—this is a problem."

"But you don't think it's one perhaps better addressed by . . ." A slight nervousness had him split the word in two. He was as good as calling the client a nutter. "Psycho analyst?"

"I have an analyst. We've discussed the matter."

"And he, ah—?"

"She thinks it's guilt."

Analyst, thought Joe. He/she. Schoolboy error.

"But you disagree," he said.

"Well, obviously."

"And what do you think it's down to?"

Nigel Reeve-Holkham said, "I think I made a mistake in killing him. And I need to know what it was, so I don't make the same mistake again."

"Pardon me one small moment," Joe said. He rose, walked round his desk, and raised the sash window six inches; enough that a brained creature would take the hint. But the bluebottle rose with the glass, and continued to rage against its invisible enemy. Still: a step forward had been made. An opportunity offered. There was a chance that within the next little while the bluebottle would find freedom.

Joe returned to his chair.

"Sorry about that," he said. "Where were we?"

FOR A WHILE AFTER his new client left, Joe sat listening to the bluebottle buzz. Eventually he decided that opening the window had only irritated the creature, and tested this theory by closing it. The bluebottle subsided. Problem solved. The fact that the bluebottle remained on Joe's side of the glass was a matter to be dealt with later.

This new client, though. This new client presented a problem unlike any Joe had come across before.

His normal reaction to a new problem was to seek Zoë's input, ideally without her noticing that he was unsure what to do next. The word "ideally" was unavoidable here, as Zoë not noticing never actually occurred in practice. But somehow Joe felt that this situation wasn't one Zoë would find sympathetic. Zoë's qualities, all of which he theoretically prized, included a low tolerance for the supernatural, and when Zoë's tolerance was low, matters swiftly became critical. By and large, it was Joe they were critical of. This looked like being a solo job.

Which left Joe's fallback position: What would Marlowe

do? To which the answer was obvious. Marlowe would get out on the mean streets.

Even if those streets weren't actually streets.

NOW THIS—THIS WAS SOMETHING you did not see every day.

Had Joe's thoughts been broadcast alongside footage of the scenery he was gliding through, many would agree with him. Here were trees bending low over the water, as if stooping to drink; and beyond the bushes lining the riverbanks, meadows stretched into a friendly distance. Cows could be spotted, grazing and suchlike, and Joe had seen a small animal scrabble into a muddy hole in the bank. And not long since, a heron had flown overhead. Joe was almost certain it had been a heron. For some seconds before its appearance he'd been aware of its flapping, deep and hungry as a monster's heartbeat, and just for a moment he'd suspected there was something he'd never been told about Oxford; that it involved the occasional unexpected hazard, such as a giant bat. But then the heron had flown round a bend in the river and passed no more than two yards over his head, its stick-legs trailing in its wake like a kite frame. Its wing-breeze had ruffled his hair. That, too, didn't happen every day.

But what he actually meant by *this*, the this you didn't see much, wasn't the trees or the water or the cows or even the heron; it was *this*: Joe Silvermann, in a punt. Poling upriver. With water rolling up his arms. And how did that happen, anyway, water rolling up his arms? It must be a punting thing; some freakish bending of the laws of physics. Because every time Joe lifted the pole clear of the water (which almost made him fall over, because this was not a steady surface: it was like balancing on three planks of wood, which he had nobody's word for but the young woman hiring out punts at the Cherwell Boathouse were riverworthy anyway. "It's sinking," Joe had pointed out, to which she'd replied, "It's got a bit of water in the bottom, that's all." "That's how sinking starts," Joe had said. But she'd sworn this was normal), he felt his elbows getting wet, even though they were raised at this point. Five minutes in he'd had to stop to remove his jacket, and the punt pole had rolled into the river, and it taken another ten minutes' paddling to retrieve it, all of which had taken place within clear view of that same young woman, who was either finding all this very amusing, or was remembering something funny that had happened to her once.

And now his jacket was folded and carefully placed on the bench in the middle of the punt; his sleeves were rolled up; the riverbank was gliding past in a reasonably steady, panic-free manner; and Joe had to admit there was a certain elegance to this mode of travel. From a distance, he probably looked in control of things. Which was just as well, because if his mental map was working, he must be approaching the place he'd been looking for.

What Nigel Reeve-Holkham had told him was that the boathouse where Harry Cudlipp had worked had stood just beyond the bridge across which the main road rumbled. "On the left. As you're heading upriver."

"But it's not there anymore," Joe had said. Just to be clear on this point.

"No."

This was a thing about boathouses in Oxford. They had a tendency to burn down.

"And this happened . . . ?"

"The same year."

"And you think there's a connection between, ah . . ."

Nigel Reeve-Holkham had stared at him as if he'd sprung a leak. "How on earth could there be?"

"No. Good point."

The bluebottle had rattled the glass again.

Joe had said, "You'll excuse me, I can be slow." Then mentally kicked himself: not a great admission to make to a client. "But my being there? This place that burned down, sixteen years ago? How precisely might this help? There'll be evidence?"

Any remaining evidence, he'd been told, was of the circumstantial kind. The boathouse might not be there any longer, but the river hadn't changed. And it was from the river that the bullet that had killed Harry Cudlipp had been fired.

"From a punt, to be precise," Nigel Reeve-Holkham had said.

"I see." A longtime resident of Oxford, Joe had never been nearer a punt than looking down on one while crossing Magdalen Bridge. "And that was—that was a straightforward business? Was it?"

"I thought so at the time. But now I'm worried that it wasn't. That something in fact went wrong, without my realising it."

"And you think that's why Harry Cudlipp is haunting you now?"

"Yes."

Joe had nodded.

"But not literally."

Joe had kept nodding.

"Do you think you can help?"

Well, no. No, he didn't. How could he help? This was out-side sense. But there was no doubting Mr. Reeve-Holkham needed somebody's aid, and if his analyst couldn't supply it, Joe felt duty bound to step in. People, he hadn't forgotten, came in all sizes. Their problems likewise. The sign on his door didn't specify that some of those problems, Joe didn't want to know about. The sign in question had actually fallen off the door some weeks ago, but that didn't alter the facts. The bluebottle had buzzed again. Joe had taken a deep breath. "Yes," he'd said. "Yes. I can help."

And so here he was. This was the place Nigel Reeve-Holkham had meant. It was where the old boathouse had stood.

He raised the pole from the water, and the punt came to a gentle halt. Or that was the plan, but in fact the punt contin-ued to glide upriver. For a moment Joe simply stood, confused by the way things weren't turning out as he'd intended. And then the familiarity of this circumstance asserted itself, and he groped for a contingency plan. Sooner or later, the punt would run out of steam. It was, after all, headed upriver. There were only so many laws of physics one punt could break. So think-ing, he lowered the pole into the water again, to act as a drag, and steered into the bank.

Okay. That worked too.

A few minutes of uncoordinated flapping about later, Joe had the punt more or less stationary; its pole jammed into the riverbed, acting as a kind of anchor. A tree spread low overhead, its branches gnarled and stumpy. Joe sat in its shade, in the punt, facing the far bank. Somehow, before he'd set off on it, this had seemed a sensible venture. Now he was here, the theory—that punting upriver to look at something that wasn't there anymore would cast light on events buried way in the past—held less water than the punt. He'd been reminded of how much this was when he'd sat, and put his feet into that puddle.

Not far away, the pleasant whizz of cars was a reminder that mechanised life carried on. Across the river, long grass bent in the breeze. Nothing else happened. There were no other boats on the water, and nobody walking the fields either side. Cows didn't count. Marlowe, Joe guessed, would have savoured the moment. Marlowe would have lain back in his bone-dry punt, pulled a hat over his eyes, and smoked himself to sleep. Joe didn't smoke, didn't wear a hat, and having a nap wouldn't help. He checked once more that there was no one around, and raised an imaginary rifle to his eyes. Sighted down its imaginary scope. Over there—on the long-gone balcony—Harry Cudlipp stood smoking like Marlowe; gazing across at a landscape which must have been much the same as it was now. He'd been remembering something he'd seen which he wasn't supposed to have seen, and a certain smile had played across his lips, because Harry Cudlipp had been sure that his knowledge was going to make him rich. Instead, it made him dead. He had stubbed the cigarette out in the hanging basket to his left, yawned, and stretched. Joe squeezed an imaginary trigger. Bang. A shot had rung out. And Harry Cudlipp died.

Sixteen years ago, this had been. He'd been dead all that time. Why would he stand up now?

Joe toyed again with his imaginary rifle. Maybe it was as simple as this: that hitting a stationary target from a floating boat was a lot trickier than pretending made it seem. With the thought, he shifted position, and the punt shied like a pony. That would be enough to take the edge off a sharpshooter's talent, wouldn't it? He counted out loud, and made it a full sixteen seconds before the punt settled down. And then he raised the imaginary rifle again. Bang. That would rock the boat even more. And would the rocking start a nanosecond before the bullet left the barrel—enough to throw it off—or would the bullet be long gone before its departure made waves? "Bang," he whispered. What sort of distance was involved? Where precisely had the boathouse stood? How high was its balcony?

And then he put down his imaginary rifle, and shook his very real head. Joe Joe Joe, he told himself. This is not the answer. The answer is not, Harry Cudlipp didn't really die. We know Harry Cudlipp died. The question is, what went wrong?

He turned and surveyed the nearer side of the river; the side where his punt was moored. The bank rose steeply for a yard or so, and he had to stand to see the view. When he did, it hadn't changed: same fields, same long grass. Same buzz of cars in the distance. Light flashed from windscreens where the road dipped. He sat down; gazed back at where the boathouse once stood. There is more than one kind of ghost, he decided. Not that ghosts exist, he noted, in case Zoë ever acquired a transcript of his thoughts, but still: there's more than just one kind of thing we might describe as a ghost. Places, too, can have spirits. Maybe this place still missed its boathouse.

A shiver ran down his spine then; a shiver the punt felt too. It wobbled once more on the water.

Joe stood, unfixed the pole from the riverbed, and pushed off from the bank.

Heading back was easier than heading out. Partly, this was because he was now going with the flow, but mostly it was down to increased competence. Any form of transport in which the human was in control—that is, any which didn't involve animals—and a learning curve was there for the taking: any competent person—hard to avoid the word "male" here, but Joe managed it—could pick up the basics of something like punting within a very short space of time. One little trip upriver was all it took. Heading to the boathouse that was no longer there, he'd been an amateur. Poling back to the one he'd hired the punt from: you couldn't say expert. But experienced, yes. An experienced puntsman. This time, he knew what he was doing.

ZOË SAID, "SO YOU fell in."

"There was some kind of surge."

"A tsunami."

"You can mock. But there's a special wave, there's a word for it—what do they call it? The Cherwell Bore? I think that's what I encountered."

"They'll probably cover it on *Newsnight*. What were you doing on a punt anyway?"

"Nothing," said Joe bravely.

The fifteen-minute walk back from the boathouse had taken thirty. He'd not have thought the human form, with just the usual number of clothes on its back, could absorb so much water; water he'd shed like a colander all the way. *Hey, mister? You're melting.* Joe, not normally one to shun an opening gambit, had tried to pretend he hadn't heard. But it was difficult maintaining a lofty dignity with your underwear growing tighter at every step.

At least Zoë wasn't around, he remembered thinking as he'd reached the office at last. At least he had that to be thankful for, he congratulated himself as he dripped up the stairs. But of course there she'd been, at her computer, watching as he opened the door.

"Nothing?" she repeated.

"Just punting."

"Punting's almost a sport."

"So?"

"An athletic activity."

"So?"

"So when they wanted you for the Rose & Crown darts team, Joe, you turned up with a doctor's note. You don't do sports. What the hell were you doing on a punt?"

"Oh," Joe said, as if remembering. "I was on a case."

"Why does that not surprise me?"

"You're an astute and—"

"Don't."

"Just telling it like it is." The best they'd managed for a towel on the premises was hand-sized and not especially clean, but Zoë had found an old Sticky Fingers T-shirt, which Joe now wore. His trousers were draped over the windowsill in the faint hope this might dry them out a little. Bare-legged, he was perched on a wooden stool. He'd felt more ridiculous, but not since turning ten. "But it's an interesting business, Zoë. When I tell you about it, you'll be . . . interested."

"The only interesting thing so far is the way you're avoiding telling me anything."

"Our new client. He has a situation."

"Leaving 'our' aside for the moment, and without bothering just yet to tell me about the client, what's 'situation' mean?"

"He's, ah . . . haunted."

"Haunted?"

"But not literally."

"Well, I'm glad not literally, Joe. Literally would mean he's mad and you're bonkers. Who's he not being haunted by, then? Literally?"

"One of his murder victims."

Zoë opened her mouth, then closed it again. Looked as if she regretted being here. Then said, "Joe? We really need to talk."

"'A SHOT RANG OUT'?" Zoë asked.

"He's a writer."

"You think? 'A certain smile played across his lips'?"

"He's not on the syllabus," Joe conceded.

"I doubt he could spell 'syllabus.' And as for the sex scene . . ."

Joe's non-committal look was the big giveaway.

"You haven't actually read this, have you?"

"He provided the essential details."

N.R. Holkham's *Death at the Boathouse* sat on Zoë's knees,

a shadowy figure in a punt gracing its front cover. It had taken her roughly half an hour to get through the 250-page paperback—Joe suspected she hadn't read every word—and as soon as she'd reached the end, she'd flipped back to the crucial passage where Harry Cudlipp had his drop-dead moment. "Hell, Joe. He finds out you haven't bothered to read it, he'll probably come round and commit murder in real life."

Joe said, "I've been busy. Is it any good?"

"Those were the best bits. A shot rang out. A certain smile played across his lips." Zoë slapped the book on the desk. "And this is it? He wants you to investigate a murder that happened in one of his own books? It didn't occur to you to suggest that he might be better off having his head examined?"

"Well, I—"

"But oh no, that's not your way, is it? The brilliant detective Joe Silvermann. No problem too small, no client too flaky. He is paying for this, isn't he?"

"Of course," said Joe, with some dignity.

"Well, that's a start. So what's your plan?"

"My plan," Joe said carefully. Then he nodded. "It's, ah— not fully formulated yet."

"But it involves ridding Mr. Reeve-Holkham of his troublesome ghost."

"That would be the ideal outcome."

She shook her head. "Are you aware how crazy this is? Your client writes a book sixteen years ago. Some character—and I'm being generous here, because Holkham's a better typist than he is a writer—some 'character' gets shot dead three chapters in. A murder that's solved by chapter twelve. And now Holkham's waking up nights thinking he's made some dreadful mistake? Damn it all, Joe, if he's sorry he killed the guy, why not just bring him back to life? Write another book. Put Harry in it."

"That would be cheating."

"He could set it earlier in time."

"Unworthy gimmick," Joe sniffed. "Besides, you're missing the point. Mr. Reeve-Holkham doesn't care about Harry Cudlipp. He's just worried that when he described Harry's murder, he made a mistake of some sort. That what he wrote couldn't actually happen. And that bothers him because he takes great pride in his research. Apart from anything else, when you make mistakes, readers send letters pointing it out. Or pencil snide comments in library copies."

"Readers actually do that?"

"Apparently."

"What a bunch of losers. And has he had many letters?"

"He didn't mention receiving any, no."

"I guess that makes him a bigger loser. What's that buzzing noise? Is that you?"

"Not me, Zoë. I don't buzz."

She picked up last week's *Oxford Times*, which was topmost of the pile of newspapers waiting to go for recycling, and rolled it into a tube. Then she swatted the bluebottle, and flicked its mangled corpse into the wastepaper basket.

"One problem solved," she said. "When did this trauma start?"

"A week or so ago," Joe said.

"And this non-ghost, this not-quite-literal haunting, it mostly happens when Holkham's looking into mirrors."

"Reflections set it off. Is what he tells me."

Zoë shook her head. "People lose cats every day of the week. But do they come to you for help? No, you have to end up with the lunatic fringe. No client too flaky." She was repeating herself. Never a good sign. "Did your trip upriver help?"

"It's always useful to view a crime scene," Joe said.

"I'll take it that's a no."

"It was a thought, that's all."

"I'd not dignify it quite that much. When are you seeing your client again?"

Your, Joe noted. Not *our*. *Your*. "Tomorrow morning."

"Well," Zoë said. "Good luck with that."

She stood, still holding the rolled-up newspaper.

"You might want to mop the stairs dry before then."

And off she went.

THE TIC AT NIGEL Reeve-Holkham's eyebrow had got no better. Joe found it difficult not to address his opening remarks to it. "Please," he said. "Please—take the weight off. Have a seat."

"Thank you, Jack."

"It's Joe."

"I beg your pardon."

"An easy mistake to make."

Both men sat, and it was a toss-up which looked worse for wear. Joe himself had been awake much of the night. Partly this was due to worrying that he might have contracted something unpleasant in the Cherwell. Rats swam in it, and even the less obviously disgusting river-dwellers such as ducks did not lead hygienic lives. There was a medical dictionary somewhere, and

Joe would have had an anxious browse through it over breakfast if he'd felt like breakfast, and if Zoë hadn't hidden the book because reading it affected his blood pressure. But the other worry, of course, was the client.

"If I believed in ghosts," Nigel Reeve-Holkham had said, "I'd not have gone in for this particular line. I'd have written horror stories."

And that was the problem in a nutshell. How did you get rid of a ghost when the haunted didn't believe in them? The attitude rendered traditional cures useless. Exorcism demanded the cooperation of all involved. Even the ghost.

"I take it the problem's no better," he said.

Though the tic had already answered that one.

The client said, "I cut myself shaving again." He tilted his chin so Joe could see a nasty-looking nick, from an old-fashioned cut-throat razor. Something larger than a duck walked across Joe's grave. "It's not that he looms up behind me or anything. He's not a physical presence. Nor even a spiritual one. He's just . . . there. The memory of him is there. And I don't understand why."

"I went to the boathouse yesterday. To where it used to be, I mean," Joe said.

"And what did you think?"

"Well, it occurred to me that it wasn't such an easy thing to do, to shoot a man from a punt. Maybe this is the mistake, in a nutshell. That you chose a murder method that was not so simply done. That wasn't entirely . . ."

He trailed away, the effort of avoiding the word "credible" getting too much for him.

"The killer," Reeve-Holkham said, "had SAS training."

"Of course," said Joe. "I hadn't forgotten that."

This was true. He hadn't forgotten because he'd never known it.

"One of the world's finest marksmen."

"So a shot from a punt . . ."

"Would have been child's play," Reeve-Holkham confirmed. "And besides. If that were the trouble, why would it wait sixteen years to disturb my sleep? I publish a book a year. I've lost count of the number of murder victims, and not one has come back to haunt me except Harry. Not one. No, the solution lies in the more recent past."

The pair fell silent. The problem with this problem, Joe thought, was that it fell outside the realm of clues and answers. Nigel Reeve-Holkham was a writer. His troubles would be best addressed by medication.

Downstairs, the door opened. He recognised Zoë's footsteps.

"I perhaps should warn you," he said, "that my partner—"

But it was too late. Zoë had arrived.

"You'd be the writer," she said.

"Well," Reeve-Holkham demurred modestly. "I'm *a* writer, certainly. Only my agent thinks I'm *the*—"

"That's what I meant."

Zoë was wearing jeans, a red top, her black leather jacket. She was reaching into her jacket pocket now; pulling out a folded-up page from a newspaper. "Do you read the local press, Mr. Reeve-Holkham?"

"Nigel. Please."

"Do you read the local press, Nigel?"

"Not usually."

"How about last week? Did you see the *Oxford Times*?"

"Well, yes. Yes I did, as a matter of fact."

"New book out?"

"I thought it might be carrying a review," he admitted.
"But it didn't."

"It's hard to get your books noticed these days, if you're
not a celebrity," he said. "But I'd have thought the local press
would at least—"

"That must be a drag. So you didn't actually read the paper?
After finding out there wasn't a review of your latest in it?"

"Well, I probably leafed through it. But I didn't read every
word, no."

Joe, listening to this exchange, began to nod. He had no
idea what Zoë was about, but didn't want to feel left out.

Zoë unfolded the page, which came, Joe saw, from last
week's *Oxford Times*. The *Times* had a supplement: arts and
culture, local events, and if N.R. Holkham's latest had been
awarded a review, this was where it would have appeared. He'd
have thumbed through it to the books section, then put it
aside, disgruntled. Zoë spread the page on the desk. It hadn't
been torn cleanly, and a triangular inch was missing from one
edge, but there was no mistaking what the article was about.
The upper half of the page was a photo of a boathouse.

"There are plans to build another one on the same site,"
Zoë said. "Hence the article."

Nigel Reeve-Holkham picked the page up and studied it carefully. He wasn't reading the article, just looking at the picture.

Joe was nodding more vigorously now. This, he knew, was

a clue. He had been mildly off-target a short while ago when he'd toyed with the idea that this was not such a case; on the other hand, he'd been bang-on yesterday, visiting the scene of the crime. That was exactly the approach to be taken; the business-as-normal approach. Nigel Reeve-Holkham's problem, he now realised, fell precisely within the domain of the detective. Its exact location, Zoë was about to reveal.

But the client didn't need further explication. Already he was shaking his head. "I'm an idiot," he said. "Something as simple as that? I'm an idiot. I'm surprised I didn't get letters."

He sat back in his chair, allowing Joe a clearer look at the photograph.

Which revealed little. There wasn't a lot of variation when it came to boathouses. They all tend to have big doors at ground level, behind which lurks a garagey space full of long canoes and racks of oars, and a balcony upstairs. The glass doors on this particular balcony, Joe supposed, would lead to a bar, but the photo didn't penetrate that far.

What could be seen quite clearly was the hanging basket to the left of the door. The basket Harry Cudlipp had stubbed his cigarette in, as he stepped outside.

Nothing that amounted to a clue, as far as Joe was concerned.

Something in his face must have betrayed this, because Nigel Reeve-Holkham said, "You don't see?"

Joe said, "So, this SAS-trained marksman—"

"He's pulling your leg, Nigel," Zoë said. "Joe read your book as carefully as I did. We all know this photo makes it look like you got things wrong."

Nigel Reeve-Holkham said miserably, "Harry steps through

the balcony doors, and stubs his cigarette out in the hanging basket. On his left."

"On his left," Zoë repeated.

"Then he's shot dead."

"It burned down before you wrote the book, didn't it?"

"That's what gave me the idea to use it as a setting," Reeve-Holkham said. "I put the fire in the final chapter. I'd never even been inside, but I'd punted past a time or two. I could have sworn I had a perfect mental image of it. But I must have got it twisted. The hanging basket wasn't on Harry's left. It was on his right."

"That's it?" said Joe. "That's the mistake?"

Nigel Reeve-Holkham stared at him. "Isn't that enough? I research my books thoroughly. Down to the finest detail. I'm not the kind of writer who makes elementary mistakes, Jack."

"Joe."

"That's what I meant." He picked the page up, studied it closely, then put it down again. "I must have seen this last week. I didn't pay it any attention. But it took root in my subconscious."

Zoë said, "And that's why reflections keep reminding you of Harry. It's the left/right switch. When you look in the mirror, your reflection's right is your left. A dormant part of your brain's picking up on this, and nagging you with it. You just didn't know why, that's all."

"Or didn't know you knew," Joe said brightly.

It felt like the right moment to make a contribution. It was, after all, his case.

"Well," Reeve-Holkham said after a while. "At least that

explains why Harry Cudlipp's been on my mind. So thank you for that. But it doesn't really help, does it?"

But Joe had seen films with psychiatrist heroes. "I think you'll find," he said, "that now you know *why* you've been bothered, it'll stop bothering you."

"No," Reeve-Holkham said. "Now I know for sure I made a mistake, I think I'll find it'll bother me even more."

"Except you didn't make a mistake," Zoë said.

Joe wished he'd said that.

Reeve-Holkham's finger jabbed the photograph. "Nice thought. But here's the picture. And there's the book. It's black and white. The hanging basket is on the left of the door. I made a mistake. I misdescribed the scene."

"No, you got it right," Zoë said. She took the page and held it in front of her so the two men could see the picture. "It's the photo that's wrong. It's been flipped."

As far as Joe could see, the hanging basket hadn't changed position. But enlightenment was beginning to spread across the client's face.

"Flipped," he said.

"Flipped?" Joe said.

"Left and right have been transposed," Zoë said. "It's a common enough practice in newspapers. Sometimes for artistic reasons. And quite often by mistake. With this one, I don't suppose anyone noticed, or cared. But it's been flipped. It shows everything in reverse. The hanging basket isn't to the left of the door at all. It's to the right."

"So," Joe said, light dawning, "it would have been to Harry's left as he stepped outside."

"Exactly as you described in your book," Zoë said.

And at that moment, the tic in Nigel Reeve-Holkham's eyebrow ceased.

A LITTLE LATER, JOE sat musing over the photograph.

"It's lucky you happened to notice this," he said to Zoë.

Zoë was in the reception room, bent over her computer, but the door was open.

"Luck had nothing to do with it," she said. "It was obvious something recent triggered this 'haunting.' And odds on it was local, because the book was set in Oxford. So the recent edition of the local paper's the first place to look for clues, wouldn't you say?"

"It was the very next thing on my list," Joe agreed. "Except you'd walked away with it." He fingered the triangular inch that was missing from one edge of the photo. "There's a bit torn off here."

"I was in a hurry."

"Not like you to be careless."

"I tend to be busier than you, Joe. Doing the work that keeps us afloat."

This would have been grossly unfair were it not manifestly true.

He examined the rip more closely. It had been quite neatly torn, in fact. Almost deliberately.

"How easy is it to tell if a photo's been flipped?" he asked.

She didn't answer.

"Zoë?"

"I'm busy."

"But how easy is it to tell?"

He waited.

"Depends," she said at last.

"On what?"

"Well," she said. "If there's any writing in the photo. That would be a giveaway."

"You mean, if there'd been a sign in this missing bit for instance, that read, say, Mind the Step—that would have come out backwards, would it?"

"Precisely."

"If the photo had been flipped."

"Are you trying to make a point, Joe?"

"No," he said. "Not really."

He slipped the page into his desk drawer. It wouldn't be hard, he supposed, to track down another copy of last week's *Times*; take a look at the intact photo. But really, what use would that be? Problems came in different sizes. Solutions, likewise.

At the window, another bluebottle began to buzz.

"Don't worry, Zoë," Joe said, getting up. "I'll take care of this."

DOLPHIN JUNCTION

i

"Don't try to find me," the note began. It was written on the back of a postcard. "Believe me, it's best this way. Things aren't working, David, and they haven't been for a long time. I'm sorry, but we both know it's true. I love you. But it's over. Shell."

On the kitchen wall, the clock still ticked, and outside the window, one of the slats in the fence still hung loose, and the fence remained discoloured where ivy had been peeled from it during the garden makeover two weeks previously. The marks where it had clung still resembled railway lines as seen on a map. If you could take a snapshot of that moment, nothing would have changed. But she was gone.

"AND THIS CARD WAS on the kitchen table."

I had already explained this. I explained it again. He laboriously made a note; perhaps a duplicate of the one he'd made the first time.

"And there's no sign of a break-in, no disturbance, no—"

"I've told you that too. There's no sign of anything. She's just disappeared. Everything else is the same as always."

"Well. You say disappeared. But she's fairly clearly left of her own accord, wouldn't you say?"

"No. I wouldn't say that at all."

"Be that as it may, sir, that's what the situation suggests. Now, if there were no note I'd be suggesting you call her friends, check with colleagues, maybe even try the hospitals just in case. But where there's a note explaining that she's gone of her own free will, all I can advise is that you wait and see."

"Wait and see? That's what you're telling me? I should wait and *see*?"

"I've no doubt your wife will be in touch shortly, sir. These things always look different in the plain light of day."

"Is there someone else I can talk to? A detective? Somebody?"

"They'd tell you exactly what I'm telling you, sir. That ninety-nine point nine percent of these cases are exactly what they appear to be. And if your wife decides to leave you, there's not a lot the police can do about it."

"But what if she's the point one percent? What happens then?"

"The chances of that are a billion to one, sir. Now, what I suggest you do is go home and get some rest. Maybe call into the pub. Shame not to take advantage, eh?"

He was on the other side of a counter, in no position to deliver a nudge in the ribs. But that's what his expression suggested. Old lady drops out of the picture? Have yourself a little time out.

"You haven't listened to a word, have you? My wife has been abducted. Is that so difficult to understand?"

He bristled. "She left a note, sir. That seems clear enough to me. Wrote and signed it."

"But that's exactly the problem," I explained for the fourth time. "My wife's name isn't Shell. My wife—Michelle—she'd never sign herself Shell. She hated the name. She hated it."

IN THE END I left the station empty-handed. If I wanted to speak to a detective, I'd have to make an appointment. And it would be best to leave this for forty-eight hours, the desk sergeant said. That seemed to be the window through which missing persons peered. Forty-eight hours. Not that my wife could be classed a missing person. She had left of her own accord, and nothing could convince him otherwise.

There'd be a phone call, he said. Possibly a letter. He managed to refrain from asserting that he'd put good money on it, but it was a close-run thing.

His suggestion that I spend the evening in the pub I ignored, just as he'd ignored the evidence of the false signature. Back home, I wandered room to room, looking for signs of disturbance that might have escaped me earlier—anything I could carry back to the station to cast in his smug stupid face. But there was nothing. In fact, everything I found, he'd doubtless cite as proof of his view of events.

The suitcase, for example. The black suitcase was in the hall where I'd left it on getting home. I'd been away at a conference. But the other suitcase, the red one, was missing from its berth in the stair-cupboard, and in the wardrobe and the chests of drawers were unaccustomed gaps. I have never been the world's most observant husband. Some of my wife's dresses I have confidently claimed never to have seen before, only to be told that that's what she'd been wearing when I proposed, or that I'd bought it for her last Christmas. But even I recognised a space when I saw one, and these gaps spoke of recent disinterment. Someone had been through Michelle's private places, harvesting articles I couldn't picture but knew were there no longer. There were underlinings everywhere. The bathroom cabinet contained absences, and there was no novel on the floor on Michelle's side of the bed. Some of her jewellery was gone. The locket, though, was where it ought to be. She had far from taken everything—that would have entailed removal lorries and lawyerly negotiation—but it seemed as if a particular version of events were establishing itself.

But I didn't believe Michelle had been responsible for any of this. There are things we simply know; non-demonstrable things; events or facts at a tangent from the available evidence. Not everything is susceptible to interrogation. This wasn't about appearances. It was about knowledge. Experience.

Let me tell you something about Michelle: she knows words. She makes puns the way other people pass remarks upon the weather. I remember once we were talking about retirement fantasies: where we'd go, what we'd do, places we'd see. Before long I was conjuring technicolour futures, painting the most elaborate visions in the air, and she chided me for going over the top. I still remember the excuse I offered. "Once you start daydreaming," I told her, "it's hard to stop."

"That's the thing about castles in Spain," she said. "They're very Moorish."

Moorish. Moreish. You see? She was always playing with words. She accorded them due deference. She recognised their weight.

And she'd no more sign herself Shell than she'd misplace an apostrophe.

When I eventually went to bed, I lay the whole night on my side of the mattress, as if rolling onto Michelle's side would be to take up room she'd soon need; space which, if unavailable on her return, would cause her to disappear again.

ii

The mattress is no more than three inches thick, laid flat on the concrete floor. There is a chemical toilet in the opposite corner. The only light spills in from a barred window nine feet or so above her head. This window is about the size of eight bricks laid side by side, and contains no glass: air must come through it, sound drift out. But here on floor level she feels no draught, and outside there is no one to hear any noise she might make.

But he will find her.

She is confident he will find her.

Eventually.

iii

Much of the next day, much of the day after, I spent on the telephone, speaking to an increasingly wide circle of friends, which at its outer reaches included people I'd never met. Colleagues of Michelle's; old university accomplices; even schoolmates—the responses I culled varied from sympathy to amusement, but in each I heard that chasm that lies between horror and delight; the German feeling you get when bad things happen to other people.

At its narrower reach, the circle included family. Michelle had one parent living, her mother, currently residing in a care home. I'm not sure why I say "currently." There's little chance of her future involving alternative accommodation. But she's beyond the reach of polite conversation, let alone urgency, and it was Michelle's sister—her only sibling—whom I spoke to instead.

"And she hasn't been in touch?"

"No, David."

"But you'd tell me if she had?"

Her pause told its own story.

"Elizabeth?"

"I would reassure you that nothing bad had happened to her," she said. "As I'm sure it hasn't."

"Can I speak to her?"

"She's not here, David."

"No, it certainly sounds like it. Just put her on, Elizabeth."

She hung up at that point. I called back. Her husband answered. We exchanged words.

Shortly after that, I began drinking in earnest.

THURSDAY EVENING WAS THE forty-eight-hour mark. I was not at my best. I was, though, back at the police station, talking to a detective.

"So your wife hasn't been in touch, Mr. Wallace?"

I bit back various answers. No sarcasm; no fury. Just answer the question. Answer the question.

"Not a word. Not since this."

At some point I had found a polythene envelope in a desk drawer; one of those plastic flippancies for keeping documents pristine. Michelle's card tucked inside, it lay on the table between us. Facedown, which is to say, message-side up.

"And there's been no word from anyone else?"

"I've called everyone I can think of," I said.

This wasn't quite true.

"You have my sympathy, Mr. Wallace. I know how difficult this must be."

She—the detective—was young, blonde, jacketless, with a crisp white shirt, and hair bunched into the shortest of tails. She wore no makeup. I have no idea whether this is a service regulation. And I couldn't remember her name, though she'd introduced herself at the start of our conversation. Interview, I should probably call it. I'm good with names, but this woman's had swum out of my head as soon as it was spoken. Then again, I had distractions. My wife was missing.

"Can we talk about background details?"

"Whatever will help."

"What about your finances? Do you and your wife keep a joint account?"

"We have a joint savings account, yes."

"And has that been touched at all?"

"We keep our current accounts separate." It was important to spell out the details. One might prove crucial. "I pay a standing order into her account on the fifteenth, and she deals with the bills from that. Most of them. The mortgage and council tax are mine. She pays the phone and the gas and electricity." I came to a halt. For some reason, I couldn't remember which of us paid for the water.

"And your savings account, Mr. Wallace," she reminded me, quite gently. "Has that been touched at all?"

I said, "Well, yes. Yes, it probably has."

"Emptied?" she asked.

"No," I told her. "Quite the opposite. Well, not the opposite. That would be doubling it, wouldn't it?" Rambling, I knew. I took a breath. "Half of our savings have been withdrawn," I told her.

"Half?"

"Precisely half," I said. "To the penny."

She made a note on the pad in front of her.

"But don't you see?" I told her. "If they'd taken it all, that would have alerted me, alerted *you*, to the fact that there's funny business going on."

"They?" she asked.

"Whoever's taken her," I said. "She hasn't just left. She can't have."

"People do leave, Mr. Wallace. I'm sorry, but they do. What is it your wife does? She works, is that right?"

"She's a librarian."

"Whereabouts? Here in town?"

"Just down the road, yes."

"And you've spoken to her colleagues? Have they . . . shed any light on your wife's departure?"

"Disappearance."

She nodded: not agreeing. But allowing my alternative term the way you might allow a child to have his way on an unimportant matter, on which he was nevertheless mistaken.

I said: "She put in her notice."

"I see."

You had to hand it to her. There was no inflection on this.

"And when did she do that, do you know?"

"A few days ago," I said. Suddenly I felt very tired. "On Monday."

"While you were away."

"That's right."

"Didn't she have notice to serve? Under the terms of her contract?"

"Yes. But she told them that she had personal reasons for needing to leave right away. But . . ." I could hear my voice trailing away. There was another *but*; there'd always be a *but*,

but I couldn't for the life of me work out what this particular one might be.

"Mr. Wallace."

I nodded, tiredly.

"I'm not sure we can take this matter further." She corrected herself. "We the police, I mean. It doesn't seem like a matter for us. I'm very sorry."

"What about the handwriting?" I asked.

She looked down at exhibit one, which just now seemed all that remained of my wife.

"It's a postcard," I explained. I was half sure I'd told her this already, but so many facts were drifting loose from their moorings that it was important to nail some down. "It didn't come through the post. It's just a card we both liked. It's been on our fridge a long time. Years, even. Stuck there with a magnet."

In a few moments more, I might have begun to describe the magnet it was stuck with.

"And you recognise it?"

"The card?"

"The handwriting, Mr. Wallace."

"Well, it looks like hers. But then it would, wouldn't it? If someone was trying to make it look like Michelle's?"

"I'm not sure that impersonating handwriting is as easy as all that. If it looks like your wife's, well . . ." She glanced down at whatever note she'd been making, and didn't finish.

"But the name! I keep telling you, Michelle wouldn't call herself Shell. It's—" I had to stop at this point. *It's the last thing she would do* was what I didn't say.

"Mr. Wallace. Sometimes, when people want a new life for themselves, they find a new name to go with it. Do you see? By calling herself Shell, she's making a break with the past."

"That's an interesting point—I've forgotten your name. Whatever. It's an interesting point. But not as important as handwriting analysis. Maybe, once that's been done, we can discuss your psychological insight."

She sighed. "Handwriting analysis is an expensive business, sir. We're not in the habit of diverting police resources to non-criminal matters."

"But this is a criminal matter. That's precisely what I'm trying to get across. My wife has been abducted."

I might have saved my breath.

"When your wife's worked out her new place in the world, I'm sure she'll be in touch. Meanwhile, do you have a friend you can stay with? Someone to talk things over with?"

"You won't have the card analysed," I informed her. We both already knew this. That's why I didn't make it a question.

"There's nothing to stop you having it done privately," she said.

"And if I'm right? *When* I'm right? Will you listen to me then?"

"If you can provide credible evidence that the note's a forgery, then we'd certainly want to hear about it," she said.

It was as if we'd sat next to each other at a dinner party, and I'd described a trip I was planning.

Well, if you have a good time, I'd certainly like to hear about it.

The kind of thing you say when you're certain you'll never meet again.

iv

I've read books where they say things like *I took an indefinite leave of absence*. Do you have a job like that? Does anyone you know have a job like that? By Friday, my phone was ringing off the hook. Was I sick? Had I forgotten the appropriate channels for alerting HR to health issues? I spat, fumed, and mentally consigned HR to hell, but once I'd raged my hour I bit the bullet and saw my GP, who listened sympathetically while my story squirmed out, then signed me off work for the month. I returned home and delivered the news to the fools in HR. Then I fished out Yellow Pages and looked for handwriting experts.

Here's another. Have you ever tried looking for a handwriting expert in Yellow Pages?

Nothing under *handwriting*. *Calligraphy* offers sign-writers and commercial artists. And—

And that's all I came up with.

I sat next to the phone for a while, useless directory in my hands. What other guise might a handwriting expert adopt? I couldn't imagine. I failed to deduce.

In the end, I looked up detective agencies instead.

YOU'RE PROBABLY THINKING THAT was the thing to do. That once the professional arrived on the scene I'd fade into the background where I belonged, while some hard-bitten but soft-centred ex-cop with an alcohol problem and an interestingly named cat reravelled my life for £250 a day plus expenses. But it was just another trip to Dolphin Junction. I gave my story twice, once over the phone and once in person to an acne-scratched twentysomething who couldn't get his digital recorder to work and forgot—thank God—to take the postcard when he left. I didn't hear from him again. He probably lost my address. And if he couldn't find me, missing persons were definitely out of his league.

Anyway. I went back to the police.

V

This time, it was a man. A thin, dark-featured man whose tie featured small dancing elephants, a detail which stuck with me a long time afterwards. He was a detective sergeant, so at least I was being shuffled upwards, rather than down. His name was Martin Dampner, and I wasn't a stranger to him.

"We've met before, Mr. Wallace. You probably don't remember."

"I do," I told him. "I think I do. When Jane was killed."

It would have had to be then. When else had I been in a police station?

"That's right. I sat in on the interview. Don't think I said anything. I was a DC then. A detective constable."

"It was a long time ago," I said.

He digested that, perhaps examining it for hidden barbs. But I hadn't meant anything special. It had been twelve years ago. If that was a long time to rise from DC to DS, that was his problem.

He said, "It was a bad business."

"So is this."

"Of course," he said.

We were in an office which might have been his or just one he was using for our conversation. I've no idea whether detective sergeants get their own office. My impression was that life was open-plan at that rank.

"How are you?" he now asked.

This stumped me.

"What do you mean?"

He settled into the chair his side of the desk. "How are you feeling? Are you eating properly? Drinking too much? Getting to work okay?"

I said, "My GP signed me off."

"Sensible. Good move."

"Can we talk about my missing wife?"

"We can. We can." He put his hands behind his neck and stared at me for what felt a long while. I was starting to quite seriously wonder if he were mad. Then he said, "I've looked at the notes DC Peterson made. She seems convinced your wife left of her own accord."

"Well, it's nice to know she's formed an opinion. That didn't take much effort on her part, did it?"

"You're underestimating my colleague. She followed some matters up after speaking to you. Did you know that?"

I didn't. And had more important subjects to raise: "Did she explain about the name? The name the note was signed with?"

"Shell, yes?"

"That's right."

"For Michelle."

"My wife never called herself that. Never would. She hated it."

"I got that much. But if you don't mind my saying so, Mr. Wallace, that's a pretty flimsy base on which to assume—what is it you're assuming? Abduction?"

"Abduction. Kidnapping. Whatever you call it when someone is taken against their will and the police won't do *a bloody thing about it!*"

I was shaking suddenly. How did that happen? For days I'd been calm and reasonably controlled, and now this supercilious cop was undoing all that work. Did he have any idea what I was going through? These days of *not knowing*; these endless nights of staring at the ceiling? And then, just when it felt the dark would never end, light pulling its second-storey job; bringing definition to the furniture, and returning all the spooky shapes to their everyday functional presences. With this came not fresh hope. Just an awareness that things weren't over yet.

Days of this. More than a week now. How much longer?

"Let's calm down," he suggested.

"Why," I asked, pulling myself together, "did you agree to see me? If you've made up your mind nothing's wrong?"

"We serve the public," he said.

I didn't have an answer to that.

"My colleague, DC Peterson. She did some follow-up after you spoke." Martin Dampner pushed his chair back, to allow himself room to uncross his legs, then cross them the other way. "She went to the library where Mrs. Wallace worked. Spoke to the librarian."

"And?"

Though I knew what was coming.

"When your wife handed her resignation in, she was perfectly in control. She handed her letter over, discussed its ramifications. Refused to be swayed. There was no coercion. Nobody waiting outside. No whispered messages for help."

"And I'm sure you've drawn all the conclusions you need from that."

He steamrollered on. "She also went, DC Peterson, to your building society. Where she didn't just ask questions. She saw tape."

I closed my eyes.

"They record everything on CCTV. You probably know that already. DC Peterson watched footage of Mrs. Wallace withdrawing money, having a brief chat with the cashier—who has no memory of their conversation, other than that it probably involved the weather or holidays—and leaving. On her own. Uncoerced."

It was like pursuing an argument with a filing cabinet. I stood.

"Mr. Wallace, I am sorry. But you need to hear this."

"Which is why you agreed to see me. Right?"

"Also, I was wondering if you'd had a handwriting test done."

I stared.

"Have you?"

"No. No, I haven't."

"And does that mean you're now convinced it is her writing? Or so convinced it isn't that mere proof isn't likely to sway you?"

"It means, Sergeant, that I haven't yet found anyone that'll do the job for me." I didn't want to tell him about the spotty private eye. I already knew that was a road heading nowhere.

"And I don't suppose you're about to tell me you've had a change of heart? And will do it yourselves?"

He was shaking his head before I'd finished. "Mr. Wallace. Believe me, I'm sorry for what you're going through. I've been there myself, and there aren't many I'd wish it on. But the facts as we understand them leave little room for doubt. Your wife quit her job, withdrew half your savings, and left a note saying she was leaving. All of which suggests that wherever Mrs. Wallace is, she's there of her own accord."

"My wife's name is not Shell," I said.

He handed me a piece of paper with a phone number on it. "They're pretty good. They won't rip you off. Take another sample of Mrs. Wallace's writing with you. Well, you'd probably worked that out for yourself."

I should have thanked him, I suppose. But what I really felt like was a specimen; as if his whole purpose in seeing me had been to study what my life looked like. So I just shovelled the paper into a pocket.

"You've aged well," he said. "If you don't mind my saying."

"I'm surprised you've not made inspector yet," was the best I could manage in reply.

BACK HOME, I SAT at the kitchen table and rang the number Martin Dampner had given me. The woman who answered explained what I could expect from her firm's services: a definitive statement as to whether the handwriting matched a sample I knew was the subject's. There was no chance of error. She might have been talking of DNA. She might have been talking of a lot of things, actually, because I stopped listening for a bit. When I tuned back in, she was telling me that they could also produce a psychometric evaluation of the subject. I wasn't thinking of offering the subject a job, I almost said, but didn't. If they couldn't work that out from the postcard, they weren't much use to anyone.

There was a notepad on the windowledge, as ever. I scribbled down the address she gave me. And then, before anything could prevent my doing so, I transferred my scribble to an envelope, found a stamp, and went out and popped my wife's last words in the post.

vi

She does not have much spatial awareness—few women do, many men say—but sees no reason to doubt the information she has been given: that this room measures twenty-four feet by eighteen, with a ceiling some twenty feet high. It is a cellar, or part of a cellar. The handkerchief of light way over her head is the only part of the room set above ground level. Built into a hillside, see? *he'd told her.* Yes. She saw.

Apart from herself and the mattress and a thick rough blanket, and the chemical toilet in the corner, this room holds three articles: a plastic beaker three inches deep; a plastic fork five inches long; and a stainless steel tin-opener.

And then there is the second room, and all that it contains.

Had I been asked, during the days following, what I imagined had happened to Michelle, I would have been unable to give an answer. It wasn't that there was any great dearth of fates to choose from. Open any newspaper. Turn to any channel. But it was as if my imagination—so reliably lurid in other matters—had discreetly changed the locks on this particular chamber, deeming it better, or safer, if I not only did not know what had occurred, but was barred from inventing a version of my own. I can see Michelle in our kitchen last week—of course I can. Just as I can see no trace of her here today, or in any other of her domestic haunts. But what happened to merge the former state into the latter remains white noise. Who stood by while she wrote that note and packed a case? What thrill of inspiration moved her to sign herself Shell? And in quitting her job, in withdrawing half our savings, what threat kept her obedient; made her perform these tasks unassisted?

And underneath all this a treacherous riptide that tugged with subtly increasing force. What if all this was as it seemed? What if she'd left of her own free will?

Things aren't working, David, and they haven't been for a long time. I'm sorry, but we both know it's true.

That's what her note had said. But that's true of any marriage. All have their highs and lows, and some years fray just as others swell.

These past few years you could describe as frayed. We'd had fraught times before—the seven-year itch, of course. A phrase doesn't get to be cliché just by being a classic movie title. If ever the wheels were to come off, that would have been the time. But we survived, and it bonded us more securely. I truly believe that. And if these past few years had been less than joyful, that was just another dip in a long journey—we've been married nineteen years, for goodness' sake. You could look on this period as one of adjustment; a changing of gear as the view ahead narrows to one of quieter, calmer waters; of a long road dipping into a valley, with fewer turnings available on either side.

But maybe Michelle had other views. Maybe she thought this her last chance to get out.

Once, years ago, a train we were on came to a halt somewhere between Slough and Reading, for one of those unexplained reasons that are the motivating force behind the English railway network. Nearby was a scatter of gravel, a telephone pole, a wire fence, and a battleship-grey junction box. Beyond this, a desultory field offered itself for inspection. On the near side of the fence, a wooden sign declared this Dolphin Junction.

"Dolphin Junction," Michelle said. "If you heard the name, you'd summon up a picture easily enough, wouldn't you? But it wouldn't look like this."

Afterwards, it became part of our private language. *A trip to Dolphin Junction* meant something had turned out disappointing, or less than expected. It meant things had not been as advertised. That anytime soon would be a good moment to turn back, or peel away.

And maybe that was it, when all was said and done. Maybe Michelle, during one of these dips in our journey, caught a glimpse of uninspiring fields ahead, and realised we were headed for Dolphin Junction. Would it have taken more than that? I didn't know anymore. I didn't know what had happened. All I knew, deep in the gut, was that all wasn't, in fact, said and done.

Because she had signed her name Shell. Michelle had done that? She'd have been as likely to roll herself in feathers and go dancing down the street.

She just wouldn't.

A FEW DAYS LATER the card came back. Until I heard the thump on the doormat I hadn't been aware of how keenly I'd been awaiting it, but in that instant everything else vanished like yesterday's weather. And then, as I went to collect it, a second thing happened. The doorbell rang.

She's back, was my first thought. Swiftly followed by my second, which was—what, she's lost her *keys*?

Padded envelope in hand, I opened the door.

Standing there was Dennis Farlowe.

There are languages, I know, that thrive on compound construction; that from the building blocks of everyday vocabulary cobble together one-time-only adjectives, or bespoke nouns for special circumstances. Legolanguages, Michelle would say. Perhaps one of them includes a word that captures my relationship with Dennis Farlowe: a former close friend who long ago accused me of the rape and murder of his wife; who could manage only the most tortured of apologies on being found wrong; who subsequently moved abroad for a decade, remarried, divorced; and who ultimately returned here a year or so ago, upon which we achieved a tenuous rapprochement, like that of a long-separated couple who remember the good times, without being desperate to relive them.

"David," he said.

"Dennis."

"I'm sorry about—" He grimaced and made a hand gesture. Male semaphore. For those moments when speech proves embarrassing.

We went into the kitchen. It's odd how swiftly an absence can make itself felt in a room. Even had Dennis not already heard the news, it wouldn't have cost him more than a moment's intuition to discern a problem.

"Good of you to come," I said.

Which it probably was, I thought—or he probably thought it was. Truth was, he was the last man I wanted to see. Apart from anything else, the envelope was burning my fingers.

But he had his own agenda. "You should have called."

"Yes. Well. I would have done." Leaving open the circumstances this action would have required, I put the kettle on instead. "Coffee?"

"Tea, if you've got it."

"I think we run to tea."

That pronoun slipped out.

It was history, obviously, that had prevented me from phoning Dennis Farlowe; had kept him the missing degree in the circle I'd rung round. Some of this history was the old kind, and some of it newer. I poured him a cup of tea. Wondering as I did so how many gallons of the stuff—and of coffee, beer, wine, spirits; even water—we'd drunk in each other's company. Not an unmeasurable amount, I suppose. Few things, in truth, are. But decanted into plastic containers, it might have looked like a lifetime's supply.

"Milk?" he asked.

I pointed at the fridge.

He fixed his tea to his liking, and sat.

Twelve years ago, Jane Farlowe was found raped and murdered in a small untidy wood on the far side of the allotments bordering our local park. The year before, Jane, Dennis, Michelle and I had holidayed together in Corfu. There are photographs: the four of us around a café table or on a clifftop bench. It doesn't matter where you are, there's always someone will work your camera for you. Jane and Michelle wear dark glasses in the photos. Dennis and I don't. I've no idea why.

After Jane's death, I was interviewed by the police, of course. Along with around eighty-four other people, in that first wave. I've no idea whether this is a lot, in the context. Jane had, I'd guess, the usual number of friends, and she certainly had the usual number of strangers. I would have been interviewed even if Dennis hadn't made his feelings known.

Long time ago. Now he said: "Has she been in touch?"

"No," I said.

"It's just a matter of time, David."

"So I've been told."

"Everyone wishes you well, David. Nobody's . . . gloating."

"Why on earth would anyone do that?"

"No reason. Stupid word. I just meant—you know how it is. There's always a thrill when bad things happen to people you like. But there's none of that going on."

I was about as convinced of this as I was that Dennis Farlowe was the community's spokesperson.

But I was no doubt doing him a disservice. We had a complicated past. We've probably grown used to shielding our motives from each other. And more than once in the past year, I've come home to find him seated where he is now; Michelle where I am. And I've had the impression, on those occasions, that there was nothing unusual about them. That there'd been other times when I didn't come home to find them there, but still: that's where they'd been. In my absence.

That's what I meant by *newer history*.

He said, "David. Do you mind if I make an observation?"

"Have you ever noticed," I said, "that when people say that, it would take a crowbar and a gag to prevent them?"

"You're a mess."

"Thank you. Fashion advice. It's what I need right now."

"I'm talking hygiene. You want to grow a beard, it's your funeral. But you should change your clothes, and you should—you really should—take a shower."

"Right."

"Or possibly two."

"Am I offending you?" I asked him. "Should I leave?"

"I'm trying to help. That's all."

"Did you know this was going to happen?"

"Michelle leaving?"

"Well, yes, I—Christ, what did you think I meant? That we'd have *tea* this morning?"

He said, "I didn't know, no."

"Would you have told me if you did?"

"No," he said. "Probably not."

"Great. Thanks for the vote of confidence."

"I'm her friend too, David."

"Don't think I'm not aware of that."

He let that hang unanswered.

We drank tea. There were questions I wanted to ask him, but answers I didn't want to hear.

At length he said, "Did she leave a note?"

"Did the grapevine not supply that detail?"

"David—"

"Yes. Yes, she left a note."

Which was in a padded envelope, on the counter next to the kettle.

And I couldn't wait a moment longer. It didn't matter that Dennis was here; nor that I already knew in my bones what the experts would have decreed. I stood, collected the envelope, and tore its mouth open. Dennis watched without apparent surprise as I poured onto the table the postcard, still in its transparent wrapper; the letter I'd supplied as a sample of Michelle's hand, and another letter, this one typed, formal, beyond contradiction.

Confirm that this is . . . no room for doubt . . . invoice under separate cover.

I crumpled it, and dropped it on the floor.

"Bad news?" Dennis asked after a while.

"No more than expected."

He waited, but I was in no mood to enlighten him. I could see him looking at the postcard—which had fallen picture-side up—but he made no move for it. I wondered what I'd have done if he had. What I'd have said if he asked to read it.

At length, he told me:

"I'm going away for a while."

I nodded, as if it mattered.

"I've a new mobile. I'll leave you the number." He reached for the writing tablet on the sill and scrawled something on it. "If she calls, if you hear anything—you'll let me know, David?"

He tore the uppermost leaf from the pad and pushed it towards me.

"David?"

"Sure," I said. "I'll let you know."

He let himself out. I remained where I was. Something had shifted, and I knew precisely what. It was like the turning of the tide. With an almanac and a watch, I've always assumed, you can time the event to the second. But you can't see it happen. You can only wait until it becomes beyond dispute; until that whole vast sprawl of water, covering most of the globe, has flexed its will, and you know that what you've been looking at has indisputably changed direction.

With a notepad available on the windowsill, Michelle had chosen to unclip a postcard from the door of the fridge, and leave her message on its yellowing back.

Flipping it over, I looked at its long-familiar picture for what felt like the first time.

viii

The doorway into the second room is precisely that: a doorway. There is no door. Nor even the hint of a door, in fact; no hinges on the jamb; no screwholes where hinges might have swung. It's just an oblong space in the wall. The ghost of stone. She steps through it.

This is a smaller room. As wide, but half as long as the other. In a previous life of this building—before it succumbed to the fate all buildings secretly ache for, and became a ruin, scribbled on by weeds and tangled brambles—this would have been a secondary storeroom; only accessible via its larger twin, which itself can only be entered by use of a ladder dropped through the trap in its roof. Hard to say what might have been stored here. Wine? Grain? Maybe cheese and butter. There's no knowing. The room's history has been wiped clean.

And in its place, new boundaries:

To her left, a wall of tin. To her right, a screen of plastic.

The Yard of Ale was one of those theme pubs whose theme is itself: a two-hundred-year-old wooden-beamed structure on a crossroads outside Church Stretton, it was plaqued and horse-brassed within an inch of Disneyland. There wasn't a corner that didn't boast an elderly piece of blacksmith's equipment with the sharp bits removed, or something somebody found in a derelict dairy, and thought would look nice scrubbed up and put next to a window. The whole place reeked of an ersatz authenticity; of a past replicated only in its most appealing particulars, and these then polished until you could see the present's reflection in it, looking much the same as it always did, but wearing a Jane Austen bonnet.

Michelle and I had stayed there four years ago. It was spring, and we'd wanted a break involving long fresh days on high empty ground, and slow quiet evenings eating twice as much as necessary. An internet search produced The Yard of Ale, and for all my dismissive comments, it fit the bill. Post-breakfast, we hiked for miles on the Long Mynd; counted off the Stiperstones and scaled the Devil's Chair. In hidden valleys we found the remnants of abandoned mines, and sheep turned up everywhere, constantly surprised. And in the evenings we ate three-course meals, and drank supermarket wine at restaurant prices. The bed was the right degree of firm, and the shower's water-pressure splendid. Everyone was polite. As we checked out Michelle picked up one of the hotel's self-promoting postcards, and when we got home she clipped it to the fridge door, where it had remained ever since.

I set off about thirty minutes after Dennis had left.

THE RAIN BEGAN BEFORE I'd been on the road an hour. It had been raining for days in the southwest; there'd been weather warnings on the news, and a number of rivers had broken banks. I had not paid attention: weather was a background babble. But when I was stopped by a policeman on a minor road on the Shropshire border, and advised to take a detour which would cost a couple of hours—and offered no guarantee of a passable road at the end of it—it became clear that my plan, if you could call it that, wanted rethinking.

"You're sure I can't get through this way?"

"If your vehicle's maybe amphibious. I wouldn't try it myself. Sir."

Sir was an afterthought. He'd drawn back as I'd wound down the window to answer him, as if rain were preferable to the fug of unwashed body in my car.

I said, "I need somewhere to stay."

He gave me directions to a couple of places, a few miles down the road.

The first, a B&B, had a room. There'd been cancellations, the man who checked me in said. Rain was sheeting down, and the phone had been ringing all morning. He'd gone from fully booked to empty without lifting a finger. But there'd be more in my situation; folk who couldn't get where they were headed, and needed a bed for the night. It was still early, but he seemed confident there'd be little travelling on the local roads today.

"I was headed for Church Stretton," I said.

"You'll maybe have better luck tomorrow."

He seemed less worried than the policeman by my unshowered state. On the other hand, the smell of dog possibly masked my odour. The room was clean, though. I could look down from its window onto a rain-washed street, and on light puddling the pavements outside the off-licence opposite. When I turned on the TV, I found footage of people sitting on rooftops while water swirled round their houses. I switched it off again. I had my own troubles.

I lay on the bed, fully clothed. If it weren't for the rain, where would I be now? Arriving at The Yard of Ale, armed with enquiries. I had a photograph—that was about it, as far as packing had gone—and I'd be waving it at somebody. It wasn't the best picture of Michelle ever taken (she'd be the first to point out that it made her nose look big), but it was accurate. In some lights, her nose does look big. If Michelle had been there, the photo would be recognised. Unless she'd gone out of her way to change her appearance—but what sense would that make? She'd left me a clue. If she hadn't wanted me to follow, why would she have done that?

Always supposing it really was a clue.

Perhaps the rain was a blessing. It held off the moment of truth; the last ounce of meaning I could dredge from the note she'd left. The note there was *no room for doubt* that she'd written.

But had signed *Shell*. An abbreviation she'd detested. And what was that if not a coded message? It was a cry for help.

And no one was listening but me.

AT LENGTH, I TURNED the TV on again. I got lucky with a showing of *Bringing Up Baby*, and when that was finished I swam across the road to the shiny off-licence, and collected a bottle of scotch. Back indoors, before broaching it, I belatedly took Dennis Farlowe's advice and stood under the shower twenty minutes, using up both small bottles of complimentary gel. There were no razors. But the mirror suggested I'd crossed the line between being unshaven and having a beard.

And then I lay back on the bed, and drank the scotch.

Alcohol never helps. Well, alcohol always helps, but when there are things you need to keep at bay, alcohol never helps. Dennis Farlowe's appearance had disturbed me. Dennis's appearances inevitably did, though on most occasions I could mask the visible symptoms: could smile, give a cheery hello; ask him how things were going while I manoeuvred my way into my own kitchen; stood behind my own wife; put my hand on her shoulder, still smiling. All that newer history I mentioned. The history in which Michelle and Dennis had re-established the relationship we'd once all enjoyed, before the older history had smashed it all to pieces.

That history didn't end with Dennis's wife's murder. Ten days after Jane Farlowe's body was found a second victim came to light, in a town some distance from ours. I was at a conference at the time—that phase of business life was already in full swing—so didn't see the local press reports until they were old news. Wounds on the body indicated that the same man was

responsible for both murders. You could sense our local tab-
loid's frustration at the vagueness of this detail, as if it had hot
gossip up its sleeve it was bound not to share. Gossip relating
to the nature of those wounds.

"Have you spoken to Dennis?" were my first words to
Michelle on reading this.

"I tried calling him."

"But he wouldn't talk?"

"He wouldn't answer."

He would have been in shock, of course. Just a week and a
half since his own wife's body had been found: Did this make
it worse for him? To understand that his wife's end was sealed
by random encounter, not precise obsession? Because there was
surely—can I say this?—something of a compliment buried in
the murder of one's wife, if it was intended. If it didn't turn out
that the murder was just *one of those things*; a passing accident
that might have happened to anyone's wife, had they been in
the wrong place at the right time.

The random nature of the murders was confirmed with the
discovery of a third body: a little later, a little further away.

I poured more scotch. Switched the TV on. Switched it off.
It was suppertime, but I didn't want to eat. Nothing was happening outside. The rain had eased off, and I could see the
puddles dancing under the streetlights' glare.

In the gap between the discovery of the first two bodies—Jane
and the second woman, whose name I've forgotten—Dennis
Farlowe had suggested that I was the man responsible. That I
was a rapist and murderer. We had been friends for years, but in his
grief he found it possible to say this: *You wanted her. You always*

wanted her. The police would have interviewed me anyway—as they did all Jane's male friends—but Dennis's words no doubt interested them. Though they subsequently had to spread their net wider, with the second death; and wider still with the third . . . A local murder became a two-county hunt, but the man responsible was never caught, though he stopped after the third death. Not long after that, Dennis moved abroad.

He returned to England years later, a quieter, more intense man. Our friendship could never be what it was, but Michelle had done all she could. Jane was gone, she told me (I didn't need reminding). Dennis's life had been shattered; his attempt to rebuild it with a second marriage had failed too. With Michelle, he seemed to rediscover something of his old self, but between the two of us were barriers which could never fall, for all our apparent resolve to leave the past behind.

And it occurred to me that Dennis's old accusation—*You always wanted her*—could as justly be levelled at him. Wasn't his relationship with Michelle a little *too* close? How often had he dropped round in my absence; little visits I never heard about? Some evenings I'd find small evidences: too many coffee cups draining on the board; a dab of aftershave in the air. But it's easy to paint pictures like that when the canvas has been destroyed. And doesn't this sort of tension often arise, when couples are close friends?

Not that Dennis was part of a pair anymore, of course. And who could tell what effect a violent uncoupling like his might have had?

These thoughts chased me into sleep.

Where dreams were whisky-coloured, and stale as prison air.

X

She puts her hand to the wall of plastic. It gives, slightly; she has touched it at a gap between two of the objects it shields. An image startles her, of an alien egg-sac pulsing beneath her palm, about to spawn. But this is not an egg-sac; nor a wall; it is, rather, dozens upon dozens of two-litre bottles of mineral water, plastic-wrapped in batches of six, the wrapper stretched tight across the gaps between the bottles. That's what her palm lit on: a plastic-shrouded gap between bottles.

And opposite, the wall of tin; hundreds upon hundreds of cans of food. If they reach seven feet deep—which they might, if this room's as wide as the one adjoining—and reach ten feet in height, which they seem to, then . . .

But the number outreaches her ability to compute. Thousands, for sure. Possibly tens of thousands.

Put another way, a lifetime's supply.

xi

Next morning the rain had ceased, and though roads remained down all over Shropshire—and in neighbouring counties, marooned villagers waved at helicopters from the roofs of submerged cottages—it was possible to be on the move. But there were no shortcuts. Nor even reliable long cuts: twice I had to turn back at dips in B-roads, where the run-off from waterlogged fields had conjured lagoons. In one sat an abandoned van, rust-red water as high as its doorhandle. I reversed to the nearest junction and consulted my map. I should have brought a thick fat marker pen. Instead of marking possible routes, I could have deleted impossible ones.

But if progress was slow, it was at least progress. At last I reached the car park of The Yard of Ale, not much more than some poorly tarmacked waste ground opposite the pub. Three other cars were there. I'm not good on cars. I've been known to walk past my own while trying to remember where it was. But for some reason, one of those vehicles struck a chord, and instead of heading over the road, I sat for a while, trying to work out why.

There was nobody around. A stiff breeze ruffled the nearby hedge. The more I looked at the car, the more it troubled me. It was the configuration of the windscreen, I decided. But how? One windscreen was much the same as another . . . At last I got out and approached the offending vehicle, and halfway there, the penny dropped. A parking permit on the driver's side was almost identical to one on my own windscreen. Same town, different area. This was Dennis Farlowe's car.

The breeze continued to ruffle the hedge. After another moment or two, I got back into my car and drove away.

xii

It was dark when I returned. The intervening hours I'd spent in Church Stretton; partly sitting in a coffee bar, trying to make sense of events; the rest in one of the town's several camping shops. I'd intended to buy binoculars, but ended up with a small fortune's worth of equipment: the 'nocs, but also a torch, a waterproof jacket, a baseball cap, a new rucksack—with no real idea of what I was doing, I had a clear sense of needing to be prepared. I bought a knife, too. The instructions (knives come with instructions: can you believe it?) indicated the efficient angle for sawing through rope.

I believe in coincidence—if they didn't happen, we wouldn't need a word for them. But there's a limit to everything, and coincidence's limit fell far short of Dennis Farlowe's presence. He'd looked at Michelle's postcard, hadn't he? At the picture side, with the pub's name on. How long would it take to Google it?

Another possibility was that he already knew where it was; had already intended to come here. Which opened up various avenues, all reaching into the dark.

Whatever the truth of it, if not for the weather, I'd have been here first.

This time I drove straight past the pub and parked in a layby half a mile down the road, then walked back to the Yard, weaving a path with my new finger-sized torch. There was little traffic. When I reached the car park, my watch read 6:15. Dennis's car was still there

For four and a half hours I waited in the cold. *Lurked* is probably the word. Behind its thick velvety curtains the Yard was lit like a spacecraft, yellow spears of light piercing the darkness at odd angles. I could picture Dennis in the restaurant, enjoying a bowl of thick soup, or pork medallions with caramelised vegetables. Memories of my own last meal were too distant to summon. When I could stand it no longer—and was certain he was holed up for the night—I trudged back to my car and drove to a petrol station, where I ate a microwaved pasty. Then I returned to my layby, crawled into the back seat, and tried to get some sleep.

It was a long time coming.

IT WAS LIGHT BY seven, but looked set to be a grey day. I drove back to the pub and a little beyond, hoping to find a vantage point from which I could keep an eye on Dennis's car. But nowhere answered, the best I could manage being another layby. If Dennis passed, I'd see him. But if he headed another way, he'd be history before I knew it.

I sat. I watched. I'd have listened to the radio, but didn't want to drain the battery. All I had to occupy me was the road, and the cars that used it. My biggest worry was the possibility that he'd drive past without my recognising the car, and my next biggest that he'd see me first. There was a third, a godless mixture of the two, in which Dennis saw me without my seeing him: this further confusing a situation which already threatened to leave me at a waterlogged junction, rust-red water lapping at my throat. Is it any wonder I fell asleep? Or at least into that half-waking state where nightmares march in without bothering to knock, and set up their stalls in your hallway. There were more prison visions. Stone walls and tiny barred windows. I came back with a start, the taste of corned beef in my mouth, and a car heading past, Dennis at its wheel. In the same alarmed movement that had brought me out of sleep I turned the ignition, and drove after him.

I'D NEVER TAILED ANYONE before. When you get down to it, hardly anyone's ever tailed anyone before, and few of us have been tailed. It sounds more difficult than it is. If you're not expecting it, you're not likely to notice. I followed Dennis from as far behind as I could manage without losing track, once or twice allowing another car to come between us. This led to anxious minutes—he might turn off; I could end up following a stranger—but at the same time had a relieving effect, as if the intermission wiped the slate clean, leaving my own car fresh and new in his rearview mirror when I took up position again.

But it turned out I couldn't follow and pay attention to road signs at the same time. I've no idea where we were when he pulled in at one of those gravelled parking spots below the Long Mynd, leaving me to drive past then stop on the verge a hundred yards on. I grabbed my equipment—the new rucksack holding the waterproof, the torch, the binoculars, the knife—and hurried back.

It was midweek, and there was little evidence of other hikers. Besides Dennis's, two other cars sat sulking; the rest was empty space, evenly distributed round a large puddle. The surrounding hills looked heavy with rain, and the clouds promised more.

On the far side was a footpath, which would wind up onto the Mynd. That was clearly where he'd gone.

Stopping by the puddle, I pulled the black waterproof from the rucksack; tugged the cap over my eyes. From the puddle's wavery surface, a bearded stranger peered back. Far behind him, grey skies rolled over themselves.

The footpath dipped through a patch of woodland before setting its sights on the skyline. Just rounding a bend way ahead was Dennis. He wore a waterproof too: a bright red thumbprint on the hillside. If he'd wanted me to be following, he couldn't have made it easier.

xiii

Twenty minutes later, I'd revised that. He could have made it easier. He could have slowed down a little.

To any other watcher, it might have seemed odd. Here was a man on a hike, on a midweek morning—what was his hurry? Dennis moved like a man trying to set a record. But I wasn't any other watcher, and his speed only confirmed what I already knew: that this was no hike. Dennis wasn't interested in exercise or views. He had a specific destination in mind. He'd always known where he was going.

I couldn't tell whether his thighs ached, or his lungs burnt like mine, but I hoped so.

The red jacket bobbed in and out of view. I knew every disappearance was temporary; no way could a red jacket weave itself out of sight forever. But it also seemed that Dennis wasn't heading for the top. Every time the footpath threatened to broach the summit, he found another that dipped again, and some of them couldn't entirely be called footpaths. We broached hollows where newly formed ponds had to be jumped, and gaps where I couldn't trust my feet. I needed both hands on the nearest surface: rock, tree limb, clump of weed. More than once, a fallen tree blocked the way. At the second I was forced to crawl under its trunk, and an absent-minded branch scratched me as I passed, leaving blood on my cheek.

FROM THE HEAVY GREY clouds, which seemed closer with every minute, I felt the first fat splatter of rain at three o'clock.

I'm not sure why I'd chosen that moment to check my watch. Nor whether I was surprised or not. It can't have been later than ten when we started, though even that was a guess— what I really felt was that I'd never been anywhere else, doing anything else; that all the existence I could remember had been spent in just this manner: following a man in a bright red jacket through an alien landscape. But I do know that two things followed immediately upon my establishing what time it was.

The first was that I realised I was overpoweringly, ravenously hungry.

The second was that I looked up, and Dennis was nowhere in sight.

FOR SOME MOMENTS I stood still. I was possessed by the same understanding that can fall on a sudden awakening: that if I remain acutely still, refusing to accept the abrupt banishment from sleep, I can slip back, and be welcomed open-armed by the same waiting dream. It never works. It never works. It didn't work then. When I allowed myself to breathe again, I was exactly where I'd been. The only living thing in sight, nature apart, was a worm at my foot.

I took two steps forward, emerging from a canopy of trees. The ground sucked at my feet, and the rain picked up a steadier rhythm.

In the past hundred yards, the terrain had changed. Not four steps ahead, the path widened: I was near the bottom of one of the many troughs Dennis had led me through. Against the hillside rising steeply up to meet the falling rain was sketched the brick outline of what I assumed was a worked-out mine—Michelle and I had seen others like it on our holiday. On the opposite side, the incline was less steep, though you'd have needed hands and feet to scale it. Had Dennis gone that way, he'd have been pinned like a butterfly on a board. And as for directly ahead—

Directly ahead, the valley came to a dead end. The incline to my right became steeper on its passage round this horseshoe shape, and the cliffside in front of me was obscured by a rustic tangle of misshapen trees and unruly bushes. With no sign of Dennis, unless—and there it was: a ribbon of red flapped behind a bush, then merged again with the brown grey and green. A strap from a jacket, nipped by a gust of wind. The rain was coming down harder, as loud as it was wet, and Dennis must have thought this the right place to take shelter . . . Had Dennis really thought that, though? Or had Dennis just had enough of playing cat-and-mouse?

Hard to say when the game began. When I set off after him on the footpath? When his car passed mine in the layby near The Yard of Ale? Or further back, even; back in my kitchen, with Michelle's postcard in front of him, and an unused notepad next to the phone? He might have picked up on that clue. Dennis wasn't a fool. No one could call him a fool.

In fact, now I thought about it, you could almost say he'd brought it to my attention.

Which might have been the moment to pause. I could have stood in the rain a little longer, my cap soaking to a cardboard mess as memory made itself heard: *He reached behind him for the writing tablet on the sill, and scrawled something on it . . . tore the uppermost leaf from the pad, and pushed it towards me.* Was there more to it than that? If Dennis wanted me here, that was a point in favour of being anywhere else. I could have turned and retraced that long long ramble. Reached my car, eventually, and got in it, and driven away.

But I didn't. Momentum carried me forward. Only my cap stayed behind; plucked from my head by a delinquent branch just as I reached the bush I was after: surprise! Dennis's jacket hung like a scarecrow, flapping in the wind. What a foolish thing. The man must be getting wet.

Something stung my neck, and if it had been a mosquito, it would have been the biggest bastard this side of the equator. But it wasn't a mosquito.

Brown grey and green. Green grey and brown. Grey brown and—

I'd forgotten what the third colour was even as it rushed up to meet me.

xiv

"Do you remember?" he asks.

Well, of course I do. Of course I do.

"Do you remember we used to be friends?"

It was long ago. But I remember that too.

I'll never know what Dennis Farlowe injected me with. Something they use to pacify cows with, probably: it acted instantly, despite not being scientifically applied. He must have stepped from behind and just shoved the damn thing into my neck. I lie now on a three-inch mattress on a concrete floor. The only light spills from a barred window nine feet or so above Dennis's head. There is a strange object behind him. It reaches into the dark. My rucksack, with all it contains—the knife, especially—is nowhere.

Vision swims in and out of focus. I feel heavy all over, and everything aches.

I say, "Where is she?"

"She's dead."

And with that, something falls away, as if a circle I never wanted completed has just swum into existence, conjured from the ripples of a long-ago splash.

"But then, you already know that. You killed her."

I try to speak. It doesn't come out right. I swallow. Try again. "That's your plan?"

He cocks his head to one side.

"To make out I did it? To kill her, and make out—"

But that same head shakes in denial.

"I think," he says, "we need to clarify some issues."

It is only now that I realise what that strange object behind Dennis is. It is a ladder. There is no door into this room; there is only a ladder out of it. This reaches up to a trap in the ceiling.

And at almost the same time I realise that the room is part of a pair; that the shadow against one wall is actually a space leading somewhere else. And that somebody is hovering on that threshold.

"I don't mean your wife," Dennis goes on. "I mean mine."

The somebody walks forward.

Michelle says, "I found the locket."

XV

At last she nods. All this is fine. Barring one small detail.

"We need to unwrap these bottles," she says to Dennis Farlowe.

"Because?"

"So he can't stack them. Build himself a staircase."

She looks up at the barred window, about the size of eight bricks laid side by side, containing no glass.

"You think he can squeeze through that?"

"We're leaving him a tin-opener. He might hack a bigger hole."

"He wants to treat that thing with care. If he doesn't want to starve to death." But he concedes that she has a point. "You're right, though. We'll unwrap them."

In fact, she does this after he leaves. Leaves to return home; to find out what David's up to. To give him a nudge in the direction of the postcard.

Some things are best not left to chance.

xvi

"I believed you," she says. "For so long, I believed you. I mean, I always knew you had a thing for Jane—I'd have had to be blind not to—but I honestly, truly didn't think you'd killed her. Raped and killed her."

I so much want to reply to this, to deliver a devastating refutation, but what can I say? What can I say? That I never wanted it to happen? That would sound lame, in the circumstances. Of course I never wanted it to happen. Look where it's left me.

"But then I found her locket, where you'd kept it all these years. Behind that tile in the bathroom. Dear God, I thought. What's this? What's this?"

Jane and I had grown close, and that's the truth of it. But there are missteps in any relationship, and it's possible that I misread certain signs. But I never wanted any of it to happen. Or have I already said that?

"But Dennis recognised it."

And there you go. What precisely is going on with you and Dennis, I want to ask. Am I supposed to lie here while she reveals how close *they've* become? But lie here is all I can do. My limbs are like tree trunks. There is an itch at my neck, where Dennis stuck me with his needle.

"And those other women," she continues. "The way you made it look random—the way you killed them to make it look random. How can you live with yourself, David? How could I have lived with you? You know what everyone thinks when this happens. They always think the same thing—that *she must have known*. They'll think I must have known."

So it's all about you, *I* want to tell her. But don't.

"You told me you were at a conference."

Well, I could hardly tell you where I really was, I want to explain. I was doing it for *us*, can't you see that? To take Jane's story and put it at a remove, so we could continue with our lives. Besides, I *was* at a conference. Or registered at one, anyway; was there enough to make my presence felt. It passed muster, didn't it? Or it did until Dennis came back, and poured poison in your ear.

Did you really just find the locket, Michelle? Or did you go looking for it? It was the one keepsake I allowed myself. Every-thing else, all those events of twelve years ago—my seven-year itch—they happened to somebody else. Or might as well have done.

And I thought things were okay again. That's why I came looking for you. I didn't think your disappearance had any-thing to do with all *that*. All that was over long ago. And you said you loved me—in your note, you said *I love you*. Or was that just part of your trap?

And now Dennis says, "She's right, you know. All this will reflect on her. It always does. And that's not right. You destroyed my life, you ended Jane's. You killed those other poor women. You can't destroy Michelle's, too. We won't let you."

At last I find my voice again. "You're going to kill me."

"No," Dennis says. "We're going to leave you alone."

And very soon afterwards, that's exactly what they do.

I SOMETIMES WONDER WHETHER anyone is looking for me, but not for very long. They'll have parked my car far away, near an unpredictable body of water; the kind which rarely returns its victims. Besides, everyone I spoke to thought Michelle had disappeared of her own accord—only I believed otherwise; only I attached weight to the clue so carefully left me. I remember the conversation with her sister, and it occurs to me that of course Michelle had spoken to her—of course Elizabeth knew Michelle was fine. She had promised not to breathe a word to me, that was all. Just one more thing to be produced in evidence when Michelle returns, and I do not.

She hadn't known I'd take it so hard, she'll say.

I never imagined he'd take his own life—

Meanwhile, I have drunk one hundred and three two-litre bottles of water; eaten eighty-nine tins of tuna fish, forty-seven of baked beans, ninety-four of corned beef. There are many hundreds left. Possibly thousands. I do not have the will to count them.

I already know there's a lifetime's supply.

AN AMERICAN FRIDGE

Finally, she showed him the kitchen.

It was spacious, clean and modern, with gleaming taps and a brightly tiled floor. A fresh loaf of bread sat on the table, and though its aroma had reached into each of the apartment's seven rooms, it was here that it filled the air, soothing the senses and teasing the appetite. This was an obvious ploy, but some stratagems work almost despite themselves; no matter how transparent, they cloud the judgement. Before long, he would taste the bread. With that first meal, the apartment would start to become his home.

Not that the kitchen needed help. The kitchen was a paradise. If the apartment was a new life waiting for this man to step into, the kitchen was its heartbeat. Here was the modern world, reduced to the shape of a room. It was the space race; it was rock and roll. It was everything you hadn't known you needed; some of the devices so up-to-the-minute she didn't herself recognise their function. And in pride of place—taller than a man, and twice as reliable, with six shelves, an ice-making device and a freezer compartment—was a brand-new, belled-and-whistled, this-year's-model fridge.

NATHAN FLUSFELDER (1892–1964) WENT to his grave calling himself a merchant adventurer, but in his heart knew himself for a pirate, his wake littered with the wreckage of other people's dreams. He couldn't help himself. He had a genius for knowing what the Great American Public wanted, an ethical blind spot regarding the means of acquiring the patents thereto, and a talent for packaging it in such a way that it seemed the fruit of his own labours. On a small enough scale, this is termed theft. When done on an industrial level it is business, and accorded the respect it deserves.

So Flusfelder tempted electrical engineers away from their employers with gifts, lies and promises; bribed disgruntled nightwatchmen to ransack filing cabinets; and drove smaller businesses to the wall before scarfing up their assets at fire-sale prices, and re-labelling their products with his own beaming logo. A FAIR DEAL WITH FLUSFELDER was the banner under which he flew, it being a sound principle of commerce, as of politics, to trumpet your obvious weaknesses as your greatest strengths. If you cannot silence your critics, driving them to apoplexy is a suitable alternative.

Flusfelder's particular sphere of genius was the domestic, and during the 1950s, when his star was at its brightest, you'd have been hard-pressed to enter an American home without encountering at least one of "his" products. An electric juicer or waste disposal grinder; a food-processing device which sliced and minced and shredded; a toaster with eight separate slots of varying thickness; and especially, especially, especially, his pièce de résistance, his Rolls-Royce, his Koh-i-Noor diamond—the Flusfelder Isotron, which stood the size of a presidential coffin, and positively hummed with confidence. It was the American Dream in refrigerator form, available in any colour you wanted, provided it was white.

"HAVE YOU EVER SEEN one like it?"

He shook his head.

This did not surprise her. She had heard tales of what life was like over there. There was a great deal of deprivation.

"Let me show you."

She opened the door, indicating the brightness of the light that came on when she did so. He did not nod appreciatively, as she might have preferred, but did at least purse his lips and adopt a small frown, as if he were mentally picturing the connections required to produce this effect; the automatic illumination that came with the opening of the door, as if a metaphor were triggered by the action. He was an engineer, of course. He knew how such things worked. And knew much more than that, in fact, and had carried the information with him across borders, which was why he was here now, moving into this dream apartment, with its splendidly appointed kitchen.

"I didn't actually have a fridge back—" he began, but stopped himself before using the discontinued word. "We—I used to keep milk on the windowledge," he said. "That kept it cold enough."

"What about in the summer?"

"It didn't last long." He smiled suddenly. "But then, neither did the summers."

"Well. You don't have to worry about that now. No more windowledges. No more relying on cold weather."

She closed the fridge and, hidden from their view, its light went out.

AND NATHAN FLUSFELDER SOLD a lot of fridges. Not every home could afford one, of course, but he saw it as a sacred duty to make sure that those in that unfortunate position knew damn well how far short they'd fallen of the mark. Those without an Isotron in their kitchen might as well have gone the whole hog and admitted they weren't feeding their children properly. That they were dosing them with warm milk and perished groceries. It was a wonder the little tykes were shod, and had shirts on their backs. You wouldn't bet against malnutrition carrying them off.

Students of the retail game would later pinpoint as the key to his technique the subliminal suggestion that not to own a Flusfelder Isotron was downright unpatriotic. Other, lesser fridges would suffice for those down whose spines ran a streak of yellow, or whose tastes tended to the red. But those who saluted the flag before breakfast fetched that breakfast from the Flusfelder Isotron, and walked tall the rest of the God-given day.

Flusfelder's sales always saw a surge at times of great national pride.

THERE WAS NOTHING LEFT to see in the apartment, nothing he had not already been shown, and they stood for a while in an awkward silence. This irked her. He did not seem persuaded, she thought, of the privilege of his position. One moment of betrayal—to be fair, a series of such moments; nevertheless, a single course of action; hardly a lifetime's effort—and this was what it had earned him. A new existence in the kind of apartment few could afford through honest toil. It seemed unfair, as if his having been in a position to commit betrayal had been a loading of the dice.

But she knew that such thoughts were themselves a kind of betrayal. The comforts that were on offer here went with the territory, and that was all. The deal was this: You give up secrets, you give up information—you give up your homeland—and in exchange we make you comfortable. First, you have to stand in front of the cameras and proclaim your newfound allegiance. Then we shelter you; keep your body warm and your groceries cold. Ensure that the ties that once bound you are replaced by different but equally secure knots, and that any dreams you might have of the remembered hills of childhood remain night-time visitations, and never harden into longing. We accept that you are a hero, all the while knowing in our hearts that it is a strange kind of heroism, and one we hope we would not be capable of ourselves.

Perhaps—and this was a thought she would never utter, least of all to one in his situation—in the end, it did not matter whose side you were on. It was about crossing the line, that was all. Whatever your motives, whether rooted in honour or greed, the important thing was that you made the choice to move, rather than stay where you were put. Who knew? Perhaps, if such choices were not made, those same lines would harden until the opposing forces became ever more intransigent, ever more warlike. Perhaps these apparently unimportant defections were the small moments of doubt that kept the finger from the trigger.

These, though, were matters best left to history to decide. For the time being, her role was to make him comfortable in his new quarters; to show him where the rest of his never-unmonitored life was to be spent. As soon as he had finished staring round the kitchen, she would take him through the further details: where to do his shopping, where to do his laundry, and so on. His newfound freedom did not come without instructions.

BUT AFTER FLUSFELDER'S DEATH—AN untimely event involving a burlesque dancer, a chandelier, and a riding crop; the details were hushed up for the sake of the shareholders—it turned out that his enduring success had been matched only by his ability to spend his profits; and indeed, somewhat out-matched, technically. What had seemed a solid enterprise built on deep foundations was in fact teetering on the edge of an economic chasm: the bigger and shinier Flusfelder's products had become, the deeper and darker the hole they were intended to fill.

For a few short months Flusfelder Enterprises continued on an even keel, and then the rumours grew too ugly to ignore. Creditors began to circle, suppliers to chafe, and so the long process of liquidation was set in motion: factories were shut down, lines discontinued, workers laid off. To some, this was a life-crushing event, no doubt, but in the greater scheme of things, it was a minor blip in the annals of commerce: a business folds, and other businesses seep in to fill the gaps created. The Flusfelder toaster disappeared from the shelves, but twenty-seven other brands remained available. The Flusfelder

EasiSqueeze—"fruit to juice in two minutes flat"—was no more, but the ability to create juice at breakfast time remained within the grasp of all those with the income to afford it. Before long, Nathan Flusfelder's logo was only a dim cultural memory in the nation's shopping malls, though it would cling on for a while in kitchen cupboards and corners before newer, brighter, more convenient products arrived to displace those it adorned.

And as for the Flusfelder Isotron . . .

IT WAS NOT PRECISELY true that he had not had a fridge back home. There had been one in the kitchen of his lodgings, but it had been small, its use scrupulously regimented by an overbearing landlady, and had emitted an unpleasant smell ever since the power cut which had switched it off for an entire weekend. Like the other lodgers—most of them fellow technicians at the nuclear research laboratory—he had indeed kept his perishables on his windowledge.

Home, he thought. He had not had a fridge back *home*.

That was a word he was going to have to relearn. Home was your motherland, your fatherland, but what happened when you betrayed your parents and chose a new allegiance? This, of course, was life's natural pattern—leave the family home; start a new one—but betrayal cast it in a different light. Life is a series of bargains, and we are measured by what we bring to the table: what we offer, what we steal. Knowledge, secrets, power. He had given away such secrets as his job had allowed him to acquire, and this woman here—he could tell—believed that he had done so for the sake of a pleasanter life, one more luxurious, he suspected, than most in this city enjoyed.

But he hadn't wanted luxury. What he had sought was balance. Because while the balance held, everyone was safe, so safety depended on people like him repositioning themselves, to ensure that neither side held all the knowledge, all the secrets, all the power. It did not matter where knowledge came from. Science was for the world. What mattered was that the world did not tip one way or the other. As long as that balance held, it was possible to occupy oneself with smaller concerns.

And besides, didn't all systems have their own ways of committing theft? You couldn't nail information down any more than you could an idea. Everything made its own path round the world, eventually.

AND AS FOR THE Flusfelder Isotron, the remaining stock was sold off at bargain-basement prices, and the fridge's technical specifications auctioned at a trade fair in Nuremberg in 1965.

The successful bidder was a small electronics firm notionally domiciled in West Germany.

THE ENGLISHMAN REACHED OUT and opened the door of the fridge once more, and admired its cavernous recesses.

"Good Soviet technology," said Olga Ivanovna.

"Yes," he agreed. And closed the door.

THE OTHER HALF

When she'd finished with the computer she returned to the bathroom, set the boiler's timer to constant, and collected the shirt: a black silk affair evidently saved for special occasions. She carried this downstairs, turning the thermostat up as high as it would go as she passed, then hung it on the kitchen door while she sorted out her remaining tasks. The clock on the wall read Nearly Time To Go, but she didn't need telling; her body already sending out signals—pinpricks at the back of the neck, a fizziness in the blood; the on-the-edge messages the primal self transmits at useful moments. She'd promised herself ten minutes, max, and they were almost up. Kitchen jobs done, she retrieved the shirt and let herself out the back door, locking it behind her with the key from the hook next to the cooker. For a moment she stood fixed to the spot, gauging the quality of the neighbourhood noise. Nothing seemed out of the ordinary. She released the breath she'd been holding, then placed the key on the windowledge, before looking down at the shirt in her hand. "Now, what are we going to do with you?" she asked; though if the truth were told, she already knew.

"REFORMATTED," JOE REPEATED.

"The hard drive, yes."

"Which is bad," he ventured.

"You don't get computers, do you, Joe?"

Joe Silvermann shook his head regretfully. While he didn't mind that he didn't get computers, he hated disappointing people.

Tom Parker said, "Basically, Tessa wiped it. Erased all the work stored in the machine plus all the software loaded on it, which, trust me, comes to an expensive piece of damage on its own. Even without her other party pieces."

"Such as the heating."

"I was only away two days. Imagine if I'd been gone all week? Or a fortnight?"

"Or a long cruise," Joe suggested. "Four weeks, sometimes six. Two months, even. I've seen adverts."

"It doesn't bear thinking about," Tom said. "House was like a heatwave as it was. The bill'll be ruinous. Then there were the kitchen japes. Fridge and freezer doors swinging open, oven on full blast. And the phone, she'd left the phone off the hook. After dialling one of those premium rate chatlines. Jesus!"

"It's not good," Joe agreed, shaking his head. "Not good at all."

"And what she did with my shirt . . ."

He'd been steadily growing redder through this recital, and Joe was worried Tom Parker might have a seizure or something; perhaps a mild apoplectic episode requiring medical intervention. He was a youngish man, so this wasn't desperately likely, but as Joe's first-aid expertise stopped at dialling

999, he thought it best to steer conversation away from the shirt. "You'll forgive my saying so, I know," he said. "Not only because we are friends, but because you're a fair man. But you keep saying Tessa did this. Did she perhaps leave a note? Or some other declaration of some description?"

"Of course she didn't, Joe. We're talking criminal damage here."

"She seemed a nice young woman," he mourned.

"Well," Tom Parker said, "don't they all? To start with."

HE'D FIRST MET TOM Parker three months previously, at a French market in Gloucester Green, where they'd fallen into conversation over the relative merits of the olives on offer. Tom had been with Tessa—Tessa Greenlaw—and Joe, in the way of such meetings, had assumed them an established couple. He himself had been with Zoë at the time, and for all he knew, Tom and Tessa made the same assumption about them. Not that Zoë had been on the spot when the conversation started, of course—she had a way of bringing such encounters to an early close—but by the time she returned from a nearby wine stall, Joe was already ushering his new friends in the direction of a coffee bar.

"You'll never stop collecting strays, will you?" she'd said later.

"Hardly strays. He runs a language school? She is an NHS, what are they calling them now? Managers? Hardly strays, Zoë."

"It's the kind of thing old people do."

Joe would never get to be old, but neither of them knew that yet. Besides, as he said, the pair weren't strays: Tom Parker was mid-thirties, with a relaxed, confident way which expressed itself in his clothing, his smile, and the direct expression he wore when he shook Joe's hand. "Joe," he'd said. "Good to meet you. This is Tessa." Tessa was a few years younger: a sweet-faced blonde woman whose small, squarish, black-framed spectacles gave the impression that she was trying to look less attractive than she was, though to Joe's mind they made her look rather sexy. While waiting for coffee, the group swapped life details.

"I've never met a private detective," Tom had said.

Joe shrugged modestly.

"Well, now you've met two," Zoë told him.

"Do you solve many crimes?"

"That depends on what you mean by 'solve,'" Joe said carefully. "And also 'crimes.'"

"It sounds fascinating," Tessa said. She had a rather breathy voice, to Joe's ear.

"It sounds fascinating," Zoë echoed sarcastically as they made their way home later.

"She was trying to show an interest. I thought they were a nice couple."

Though as it turned out, they were no longer a couple by the time Joe next encountered Tom.

THIS HAD BEEN IN a bar in the city centre, where Joe had been watering a police contact of his, one Bob Poland, who had no useful information on a young runaway case Joe was working on, but managed to drag it out to five large scotches anyway. Joe himself had been nursing a beer, because there was no point getting competitive with a thirsty cop. He was only halfway through it when Bob had to leave—his shift was up—so was unfolding his newspaper when Tom Parker walked through the door. His language school, Joe remembered as he raised a hand in greeting, was just round the corner.

"You remember me?"

"Of course—Joe, isn't it?"

"Silvermann."

"From the olive stall."

"Well—"

"The private eye, don't worry. I remember."

He often dropped in here for a drink once the working day was done, he told Joe. The pair settled at a table by the window.

"And Tessa, how is she?"

"Oh, I'm not seeing her anymore."

"Tom! No! What happened?"

"Well, nothing. Christ, Joe, it's not the death of romance or anything. We dated for a while and now we're not. Simple as that." Something in his expression, though, suggested it wasn't that simple.

"But . . ."

"But what?"

But nothing, Joe had to admit. Nothing he wanted to say out loud. That they had seemed a nice couple, and that nice couples ought to stick together, if only to set an example to everyone else. "Should I—would you like another drink?" When all else failed, offer hospitality. "Should I go to the bar?"

"Joe, they have table service." Tom raised a hand for the waitress. "Why do it yourself when you can pay someone else to do it? How about you, you want the other half?"

"Perhaps I will."

Tom ordered their drinks, then went on, "Besides, she's unstable. Was right from the start."

"Unstable?"

"I used to get phone calls from her in the middle of the night. Checking up. That I was alone, and where I ought to be."

Joe clucked his tongue, shook his head. "Late-night phone calls. Zoë and I, we had a spate a while back. They get tired, they give up. You're sure this was Tessa?"

"Sometimes she'd arrive on my doorstep unexpectedly, or be waiting when I left work. You ever been stalked, Joe?"

"Is it stalking, this? Not just . . ."

"Just what?"

Joe shrugged. "Perhaps she just wants to be with you."

"Feels like stalking to me, mate." He shook his head. "It's a hell of a world, Joe, I'm telling you. And most of its problems caused by women."

Well, maybe half, Joe conceded. If you ignored war and famine and stuff.

They fell to talking about other things. The next Joe heard about Tessa, Tom was in his office, outlining the damage.

HE HAD TAKEN A cigarette from a pocket but didn't light it; just held it between finger and thumb as he spoke. "Those phone calls? They never stopped. Oh, she wouldn't speak, but it was her. Middle of the night, and I'm getting woken up to be given the silent treatment. Or not woken up, if you know what I mean."

"Sometimes you're already awake," Joe guessed.

"Not alone, either. You can imagine the damper that puts on proceedings."

"She sounds unhappy."

"And I care? She's fucking nuts, Joe. And driving me crazy while she's at it."

"Have you been to the police?"

"What good would that do? Look. I know it was Tessa, you know it was Tessa. Bloody Tessa knows it was Tessa. But knowing isn't proving. We get into an I-said-she-said situation, the best that'll happen's she'll get told to watch her step by the boys in blue. Meanwhile, I'm still paying the bills on her domestic terrorism, thanks a bunch."

"How did she get in?"

"In?"

"To your house," Joe explained. "She didn't look, pardon my saying, like a housebreaker."

"Oh, right. No, she didn't need to be. We'd swapped keys, but she never gave it back. Claimed she did, but she didn't."

"And your locks? Have you changed your locks?"

"Well, I have now, Joe. But that's a little late to help."

Joe nodded, as a change from shaking his head. There'd been a crime, and Tom seemed certain he'd identified the culprit. But it wasn't clear what Joe was expected to do about it.

Tom said, "That was my favourite shirt, too."

"It's not . . . salvageable? No, sorry, forget I spoke. Of course it's not."

Tom leaned forward. His unlit cigarette jammed meaning into every syllable. "She blocked the sewer pipe with it, Joe.

First I knew about it, the toilet's backing up. 'Course it's not bloody salvageable."

"Would you like coffee? Tea?"

"Neither. Not right now."

"You're upset, yes. Your shirt and all the rest, plus the sense of being invaded. I can see you'd want to talk to somebody about it."

"But why you."

"That's what I was wondering, Tom, yes. Why me?"

So Tom told him.

A HOMELESS MAN HAD made his pitch by an entrance to the Covered Market: teatowel in front of him for contributions to his wellbeing, he sat crosslegged, back to the wall, face obscured by a hood. A young Alsatian lay next to him, its head on his knee. Lots of homeless people—and there were lots; they seemed to multiply faster than any housing shortage could account for—lots of them had dogs, Joe had noticed, which was a detail which, if not a silver lining, at least provided a little insulation, he liked to think. There was comfort in knowing that no matter how hard you'd fallen, love was still available. He'd said as much to Zoë once, and she'd looked at him as if he were mad, which wasn't an unusual expression for Zoë.

"They don't keep dogs for something to love, Joe. They keep dogs so they've something to shout at. Something they can get angry with, which just has to sit and take it."

Which might or might not have been true, but one thing was certain: having heard it said, Joe would never look at a homeless man and his dog in quite the same way again.

"The glass is always half empty, isn't it, Zoë?" he'd said sadly.

"No, the glass is cracked," she'd told him. "And there's no way I'm drinking from a cracked glass."

Anyway, the dog he was looking at was the same he'd seen yesterday, because this was the homeless guy's regular hangout, and this particular entrance to Oxford's Covered Market was right by the doorway to Tessa Greenlaw's gym. Or the gym Tessa Greenlaw was a member of. Joe had spent long enough watching it to make such pointless clarifications to himself, as if somewhere inside his own head was a not entirely bright third party, in constant need of updating. Tessa Greenlaw came here once her workday was done, or had done so both days Joe had been following her. *Surveilling*, he amended. "Following" had a stalkerish air. And yesterday, after leaving, she'd done nothing more complicated than head straight home, giving Joe a tricky moment when he'd found himself boarding the same bus—but it had been crowded, and he'd sat where she couldn't see his face, and besides, they'd only encountered each other once, months ago. Chances were, all she'd have would be one of those vague city moments at the sight of a face from a forgotten context. And if that happened, she hadn't let on.

Tonight, though, there was no rush for the bus. Instead, on leaving the gym Tessa Greenlaw headed south, down St. Aldate's. Giving her a moment to get ahead, Joe peeled himself from his hiding place, thought for a moment about popping over the road to slip a quid to the man with the dog, decided he didn't have time, and set off in Tessa's wake.

IT WAS HARDLY A surprise. How many places could she have been headed? Well, okay, she could have been going anywhere—but a short distance down St. Aldate's, then a right turn, and what you reached was the building that housed Tom Parker's language school.

This wasn't a busy thoroughfare. Joe couldn't have followed Tessa along it without being spotted. But opposite the lane's entrance, on St. Aldate's itself, was a bench for the weary, from which Joe had a clear view of Tessa Greenlaw coming to a halt by the language school; of Tessa checking her watch, then leaning against the wall of the building opposite, looking up at the second-floor window where Tom had his office.

Joe spread his newspaper over his knees, in case Tessa noticed him.

He timed it at eleven minutes. Eleven minutes before Tom Parker came out. During this time, Tessa grew restless; checked her watch a number of times; fiddled through her bag for something she didn't find. She was wearing the same glasses Joe had admired the first time he'd met her—only time, he amended; you couldn't call this "meeting"—and her hair was shorter, but what he mostly noticed was that she seemed, what might the word be—frazzled? Yes: she seemed frazzled. As if things were not going her way lately, and the direction they had chosen instead were stretching her thin . . . Zoë would probably point out that Tessa had just been to the gym, which might account for it. But still: she looked frazzled.

Joe was staring straight at her when she looked his way. He dropped his eyes to the newspaper; made a bit of a thing about turning a page. When he risked another glance, Tom was in the lane too.

"YOU SAW?"

"I saw, yes."

"That's the fourth time. No, *fifth*. She's mad, Joe. Complete mentalist."

"Mentalist." Joe wasn't sure he'd encountered the term. "Certainly, she does not give the impression of being, ah, stable."

He hadn't been able to hear everything, but that she'd been shouting was clear enough. *Bastard* had floated Joe's way. And all the while Tom had been making soothing gestures in the air; smiling softly but never quite touching her, as if Tessa were a cornered animal in spitting mood, unclear of its own best choices. When he'd reached at last for her sleeve she'd pulled her arm away angrily and stormed down the lane, away from Joe. Slowly, he'd folded his newspaper and stood. When Tom reached him, he led the way to the bar without a word.

Now he said, "And has there been any *pattern*, any particular sequence to the way in which she comes and, ah, lurks outside your workplace?"

"I'm not sure. Would it make a difference?"

"Probably not," Joe admitted.

"You're thinking some kind of PMT thing?"

Uncomfortable with this direction, Joe shook his head. "Not really." Truth was, he had no idea what questions to ask, or what answers would help. Insights into the female psyche weren't his specialty. And if he'd ever claimed them to be, it wasn't like the

notion would withstand five minutes of Zoë's scrutiny. "Did you
confront her about her invasion of your property?"

"Did she give the impression of being up for a discussion?"

"I couldn't hear," Joe explained. "Traffic. Distance. Plus,
she was shouting and you were speaking softly. Neither was an
ideal volume."

"Well, trust me, she was in no mood for answering questions. More than likely, she'd find a way of blaming it on me,
anyway. You had much to do with madwomen, Joe?"

Loyally, Joe denied it.

"Lucky you."

She'd looked frazzled, he remembered. It wasn't such a
stretch to colour her mad. "What was she saying?"

Tom Parker ran a hand through his hair: a boyish gesture,
not without charm. "That we belong together. That I was just
being stupid, and should come to my senses. That *I* should
come to *my* senses." He shook his head in wonderment. "A
bloody baby. We're not even in a relationship, for God's sake."

"Does she have parents? Someone who could perhaps talk
to her—"

"Well, I don't know, do I? We weren't playing happy fami-
lies, Joe. We were only together for a couple of weeks."

"An official complaint, perhaps? Now that I've paid witness
to this stalking, this harassment, perhaps you want me to . . .
accompany you to the police station?"

Tom barked a sudden laugh. "You've never actually been a
copper, have you, Joe?"

"Never. Not ever."

"But you talk the talk. No, I don't want you to accompany

me to the station, thanks anyway. I want something more direct than that. I want you to put a stop to it. To all her crap."

Joe had been afraid that was where this was leading. "You think she'll listen to me?" He was older than Tessa, true—could easily be her father—and perhaps a little elder wisdom was what she needed: but still, he was afraid. Not of confronting a madwoman; more of being mortally embarrassed. "There is a law," he suggested. "The Protection from Harassment Act?"

"I know," Tom said. "You think that's going to carry weight? Quote section thirteen, paragraph six at her, and watch enlightenment dawn?" He leaned forward. "She's barking, Joe. You've seen what she's like, waiting round my office to harangue me when I leave. Not to mention she seriously messed me about, wiped my computer. I like things ordered, Joe. This was out of order. So. Are you going to help or not? I mean, that's what you do, right? You're a private eye. You take on clients."

"Yes." Joe sighed. "It's what I do. I take on clients."

"Good." Tom passed a key across the table. "I want you to mess her place up, Joe. Same way she messed mine. Fair's fair, right?"

"I suppose it is," Joe agreed. "Fair's fair. Yes."

TESSA LEFT HOME FOR work at nine-fifteen. It was all right for some, Joe noted, a judgement tempered by the knowledge that if he himself didn't reach the office before eleven, it wasn't like anyone would notice. As it was, this morning he'd been up at seven; by half-past, had been slumped twenty yards down the road from Tessa's front door, his trusty newspaper on the car seat next to him, in case a disguise was called for. Was it really necessary for him to observe, first-hand, Tessa's departure? Yes, it was. If he was going to let himself into her place with the key Tom had given him, he wanted proof positive she was off the premises. He figured that was the way Philip Marlowe would have played it, "What would Marlowe do?" being Joe's regular mantra. Marlowe wouldn't take unnecessary risks. Well, that wasn't true. But it was the answer Joe wanted, which was substantially more important.

"You still have this?" he had asked Tom on being given Tessa's doorkey. "Won't she have changed the lock?"

"Trust me, that'll get you through the door."

"But—"

"Trust me."

So Joe's hand had clamped round the key as if his fist were taking an impression.

Now he straightened in the driving seat as Tessa reached the corner, crossed the road, and headed for her bus stop.

Give her another ten minutes, he thought. It was likely she'd be waiting at least that long; time enough to remember she'd left her purse behind, or her paperback, or any one of a hundred items she never left home without. But his body was in unwilled motion, eager to get this part finished whatever excuses his mind could conjur; his body was excavating itself from its car, brushing the creases from its coat; was pulling its collar up in a completely unsuspicious attempt to obscure its face for the benefit of anyone curtain-twitching, wondering what the guy in the car was up to. Housebreaking in broad daylight was not a game for the nervous. So if he was engaged in it, he couldn't be nervous: QED. Unnervously, then, Joe made his way to Tessa's house; unnervously fished her key from his pocket as he did so; unnervously dropped it as he tripped on the kerb, then had to frantically scrabble before it disappeared down a drain.

Now *that*, Joseph—he chided himself—could so easily have ended in farce.

He looked around. Weirdly, there was nobody in sight; or maybe it was normal; what did Joe know about this particular street at this particular time of the morning? Key safely in his fist, he released a breath just as a bus passed the end of the road, on its way to collect Tessa Greenlaw and transport her out of the area. There was no more room for hesitation. He had the key in hand; the door in his sights. What he was about to do was illegal, but would only look unusual if he farted about while doing it. Farting about was not something Marlowe would do.

Nobody shouted as he walked directly to Tessa's door; no sirens blared as he slid the key into its lock. It turned. The door opened.

He was in.

THIS WAS ONLY THE second time he'd let himself into another person's house without their knowledge—not without help, either time. But this was different. He was here to do damage: well-deserved damage, he reminded himself, as his conscience threatened to kick in—this wasn't random vandalism; it was a message. That's what it was. A message.

Nothing immediately suggested itself as Joe scouted round the ground floor, but once he'd climbed the stairs and discovered what was evidently an office, his next move became clear.

He set to with a will.

"SO WHY DID YOU break into Tessa's place?"

"I wanted to see if the key worked," Joe explained. He took it from his pocket: a recent copy, shiny and unscratched. "They exchanged keys. He told me that. But when they broke up, he made an extra copy of hers before giving it back. That's why he was so sure she wouldn't have changed the locks. She didn't know he had it."

"It was Tom stalking Tessa, wasn't it?" Zoë said flatly. "Not the other way round."

"It's a creepy thing to do, isn't it? Keep a copy of your ex-girlfriend's key. Except he had me doing the actual stalking," Joe said. "There's the crux, you might call it. The nub." He recalled his self-clarification, following Tessa: that this wasn't *stalking* but *surveillance*. "Prior to persuading me to I think the word would be *trash* her place. Yes, trash." He recalled for her Tom's words in the bar: "Why do things yourself when you can pay someone else to do them? He was talking about fetching drinks. But . . ."

"You discerned a principle," said Zoë.

"You don't seem surprised."

"I didn't much like him."

"Yes, but . . ."

"But what?"

"You don't much like anyone, Zoë," Joe explained. "It's not like you were making an exception."

They were in the office, which was the mostly neutral ground of their marriage.

"Point," Zoë said. "But I thought you were his friend."

"I was, but was he mine? What sort of friend sends you off on a job like that?"

"The kind who's taking revenge."

"On poor Tessa, yes. She dumped him, I'm assuming."

"Guess so," Zoë said. "And he called her, didn't he? Asked her to meet him after work, once he'd arranged for you to be following her. Then blew her off when he eventually came out. So what you saw was her quite reasonably losing her rag, and you never did hear what he was saying."

"I think so, yes. There are ways someone clever could find out, probably, with phone records and technological trickery, but for myself, yes, I'm sure he faked it."

"Can't think why she went."

"Sometimes women are gentle like that," Joe suggested. "She would have been feeling guilty, perhaps, about dumping him. He maybe made an overture of friendship, or offered to apologise for something."

"And you're not worried she trashed his place first?"

Joe smiled kindly. "Don't you get it? He made that up so I'd be on his side. It didn't happen, Zoë. Not before today. And even if she had—well. I don't like stalkers."

"Me neither," Zoë said. And meant it. Tom had made a pass at her shortly after that meeting in the market, and evidently didn't take rejection well, hence the spate of late-night calls she and Joe had suffered a while back. But Joe had been right about one thing; there were ways, with technological trickery, that someone clever could find out who'd been making phone calls, no matter that they thought they'd shielded their number. Trashing Tom Parker's place had been her reasonable response. It hadn't occurred to her he'd think Tessa had done it, but the more she listened to Joe, the more she was sure he'd thought no such thing. He'd known it was Zoë. Using Joe—steering him to where he'd do to Tessa what Zoë had done to Tom— was the typical stalker's revenge: manipulative, distant, pleased with itself. His hard luck Joe had seen through him. Not that she was about to share any of this. "How'd you get into his place anyway?"

His second break-in. Harder when you don't have a key.

"Bob Poland helped," he said. For a fee. "Policemen know the strangest things. Like getting through locks."

Zoë nodded. Getting through locks was a skill she'd been tutored in by a local tearaway. "And what did you do?" she asked, curious. "Once you were in?"

There'd been a moment when he'd almost turned and left, overcome by the enormity of it: of breaking in, of wreaking havoc. But then he'd seen Tom's office. *I like things ordered, Joe,* he'd said. And there, to prove it, stood his filing cabinet, with its reams of carefully alphabetised records that Joe had carefully, randomly, reordered. Tom would be hours straightening that lot out. Hours. Maybe days.

"It's better you don't know," he told her.

He was sure that's what Marlowe would have said.

ALL THE LIVELONG DAY

Corvids flock in the winter months. They congregate in multi-species hordes—crows and rooks, jackdaws and magpies—where food is plentiful: open farmland, newly-ploughed fields, that sort of place. The flocks form in the early afternoons, and number thousands of birds, sometimes tens of thousands. Crows rarely travel far from their breeding grounds, but the rooks and jackdaws include visitors from overseas. In flight, they turn the sky black. At rest, they line rooftops and overhead cables. And when dusk comes they gather more tightly, and their raucous brawling gives way to a widespread silence until they rise as one, a boiling mass of life governed by a single impulse, and depart for their roost. It's a ritual that's existed for as long as there've been birds, and is one of those events that marry an unimaginably distant past to the ever-present now. It's about community, and information-sharing; about safety in numbers, and the celebration of flight.

But mostly, it's about food.

i

That morning they'd sat on a bench in a Derbyshire market square, in shade cast by a squat hexagonal building which might once have been a corn exchange but now housed a coffee bar and a unisex hairdressers, and while they checked their mobiles for incoming a man in a tri-cornered hat and red felt jacket arrived, ringing a bell which reminded Helen of schooldays; a bell the size of a bathroom plunger, with the same wooden handle. Before he'd opened his mouth, she'd known what he'd cry. *Oh yay, oh yay.* She watched, and the elderly couple chatting outside the woolshop paused to listen too. "Oh yay, oh yay," the town cryer boomed. Then he placed the handbell on the ground, and unrolled the scroll he'd had tucked under his arm.

Jon nudged her. "He's going to tell us someone's been rustling sheep hereabouts."

"Sshh."

"Or pilfering mangel wurzels."

"Shush. He'll hear."

But it was unlikely he'd have heard anything over the sound of his own voice. Out it thundered, with the local news: that the switchover to digital would happen in three weeks, and that leaflets explaining how to reset TVs to ensure uninterrupted service were available at the town hall.

"Well, I don't think either of us were expecting that," Jon said, returning to his mobile.

Helen had given him a sideways look, but he hadn't noticed. Too engrossed in whatever message had buzzed in since they'd last been somewhere with a signal. Too busy, now, replying to it; his fingers dancing on the little keypad as if he were playing a tune, not writing a message.

"Looks important," she said at last.

"Hmm?"

"Whatever it is you're saying." To whoever you're saying it to.

"Work." He wound it up, and pressed send. The town cryer finished his despatch, rerolled his scroll, collected his hand-bell, and left the square. His departure rang another change, it seemed to Helen. While he'd been there, she and Jon had been an audience, in a state of temporary suspension; their concerns an inaudible buzz. Now they were the cast again. Jon continued: "Nice to be indispensable, obviously, but you'd think they could survive a week without me." He put his phone away.

Helen looked down at her own. It had died while she'd been sitting there, its last bar of power blinking out without so much as a sigh. She didn't have a charger with her. But it didn't matter. Her own place of work puttered along fine without her, and the day's only text had been junk from a gym near her office; a plea for money disguised as an opportunity to enjoy a discount. She put the phone away. Their car was over the road. They would drive a few miles west, park in the spot Jon had identified yesterday evening on the map, and embark on a twelve-mile hike through countryside both dramatic and beautiful, before returning to the hotel for a beer and a bath and then supper. The third day of a five-day break, and this was the routine they'd found. There was comfort in routine. The more firmly it was established over these five days, the more entrenched it would become in their shared history; she would carry it back home with them, and embed it in their workaday lives. She thought of those little tubes of chemical adhesive which pump two liquids from separate chambers, causing them to bond fast on contact, routinely.

Jon was eyeing her. "You okay?"

". . . Fine. Yes. Let's go."

THAT HAD BEEN HOURS ago, and judging by the ache in her calves, they'd walked upwards of seven miles since. A directionless sense of competition had her mentally listing friends and acquaintances, colleagues and neighbours, who would no more dream of slogging across seven miles of countryside than they would of scaling the Matterhorn, but as a means of boosting self-esteem this was too vague to be effective. The sloth of others was best enjoyed in their presence. Here and now there was only Jon, who was less impressed by her fitness than he was by his own, and who mostly walked in front, stopping to confer only when geography let him down.

Because their route, though clear on the map, was less so on the actual landscape. The previous day's walk had followed the course of a disused railway track, with no confusing junctions; today, there'd been difficulties. Twice they'd found themselves on the wrong side of a field boundary, resulting on the first occasion in an undignified scramble through a gap in a hedge, and on the second, in having to retrace their steps half a mile. And while the scenery remained dramatic—the peaks stark against the skyline, and the trees fat and proud—the weather had turned overnight, and in place of yesterday's big blues and deep greens was a series of overlapping greys with a chilly edge. The only other walkers they'd seen had been far distant, their red and yellow jackets the day's sole smudge of brightness, if you didn't count the little blue bags that swung at head height from branches. These contained dogshit, and whether the dog-owners responsible were sociopathic or pathologically stupid, Helen couldn't begin to guess.

Meanwhile, clouds roiled overhead. Those to the west were dark and thick, and heading their way.

"I thought we'd be back before the rain set in," she said.

"Oh, I am *sorry*. Obviously that's my fault."

"I didn't mean it like that. I was just saying."

"It's a walking holiday, remember? Getting wet's part of the *fun*. Anyway, it's not raining yet."

Not yet, no. But she bit the words back, though they tasted of misery, and released herself from her backpack, and extracted a bottle of water. She passed this to Jon as a peace offering, but he didn't notice. He was sneaking a look at his mobile again, though there was no signal, of course.

He realised he'd been caught, and slipped the phone away without comment.

It's supposed to be a holiday, she wanted to plead. Can you not turn off for just a few days? But saying this aloud would be the verbal equivalent of lighting a firework, so she swallowed the words and looked back the way they'd come instead, blinking away the tears that had arrived without warning. Soon they were only watery eyes, not tears; the result of looking downhill into a stiffening wind.

There were sheep on that hillside, and sheepshit was scattered everywhere in a curiously raked fashion, as if someone had taken the trouble to ensure that it covered as wide an area as possible. Along the hill's crest was what appeared on the map as a boundary line, and manifested in the real world as a drystone wall, though an unsatisfactory one, barely three feet of it surviving at a stretch. Broken stones littered the gaps. It looked, thought Helen, much the way a drystone wall might if she herself had built one, and then leaned on it.

Jon was examining the map again. "We follow the wall, what there is of it, across the next three fields."

"Any more uppity bits?"

"No more uppity bits." His use of their private term gave her a sudden squirt of pleasure. "In fact, there's a steep—"

"Downty?"

"Downhill stretch in a mile or so. Then we're on-road for a while, which'll be a relief." Jon let the map, which was folded into a transparent plastic square on a cord round his neck, drop. "It's almost like they don't want people using this footpath. Well, not almost. It's exactly like they don't."

The path that followed the course of the wall continued in poor repair, potholed and brambly, and while Helen didn't suppose actual sabotage had been involved, she could sense there was little point trying to convince Jon. At the next stile, he paused to trace a finger round a pale circle in its wooden upright.

"Someone's unscrewed it," he said.

"Unscrewed . . . ?"

"The waymarker." He looked at the pale circle once more, where, presumably, a waymarker had indeed once been fixed. "Definitely."

"Why would anyone do that?"

"We don't be likin' no grockles, we don't," he said, in an accent strange to that county, or any county, but unmistakably intended to convey a sense of idiot localdom, of redneck threat.

"Or it just might have come off by itself," Helen said. "In the weather or . . ."

"Yes, because they weren't expecting weather when they started attaching waymarkers to stiles," Jon said.

"I only—"

"It's probably illegal," he said, vaulting over the stile. "Whoever took it down is pretending this is private land. And it's not."

She felt his critical eyes upon her as she manoeuvred over in his wake: one leg up, second leg up. Jon had made it one easy fluid motion, stiles being second nature to him by now, their third day's walking. One leg onto solid ground; second leg ditto. She was forty next year. The stilted movement made her feel fifty; probably made her look sixty.

He turned abruptly and strode on.

Helen became aware that for some moments she'd been

hearing a noise in the mid-distance; something like a high wind battering through a fairground. A disorganised, sprawling noise; lurid and awful, because it removed from the landscape one of its prize attractions, which was its sense of peace. Those peaks which lent the region its name: they'd been here longer than forever, and had remained the shape they were now. Whether this was geologically accurate or not, she didn't care; there seemed at that moment a truth in it anyhow, and there was peace to be found in the contemplation of such long-lasting changelessness, a peace unbalanced now by the squawling noise ahead.

It sounded modern, she decided. (She was wrong about this.) It sounded modern, and for that reason, she recalled the town cryer they'd seen earlier; of the ludicrous, though intentional, juxtaposition of his traditional appearance and the content of his message. This was a landscape steeped in ancient certainties, and they were ants crawling across it, that was all; just ants, with their carefully marked—or not—footpaths, and their little modern devices which needed perpetual upgrading, and often didn't work anyway. If these peaks ever decided to change shape, and shrug off the irritations modern people had become, well . . .

Jon had come to a halt. Here, the tumbledown wall ended and the land fell away to what Helen thought was the north, and was certainly the right. The sky had darkened further, and the probability that the rainclouds would catch them before they reached the hotel was another argument in waiting. But Jon wasn't looking towards the weather; he was pointing down the hillside, at the source of that mechanical-seeming clatter, which turned out not to be mechanical at all, but avian; another black cloud, a noisy twin of the one approaching, and made entirely of birds—black birds, crows; there must have been a hundred of them. Two hundred. They wheeled in low circles around the roofs of a farmhouse and barn which lay at the bottom of a steep descent, and their cries, now she understood what they were, were so obviously bird-made that she couldn't fathom why she hadn't recognised them as such immediately.

But there were so many of them. She'd never seen so many birds in one place, other than swallows gathering for exodus, or maybe gulls round a harbour.

"What are they doing?" she asked, but Jon didn't know.

ii

She said, "I'm not sure I want to go this way."

As soon as she'd opened her mouth, she knew she'd sealed his decision.

"It's that or go back the way we've come," he said. "And that'll take ages, and we'll get soaked."

"We're going to get soaked anyway."

"Maybe not. The road's down there. We might catch a bus if we're lucky."

The rules of the game had changed. Their first day, after ten miles, she'd raised the possibility of catching a bus for the last leg, and he'd accused her of malingering.

"Jon—"

"Hez, they're only birds. They'll flap off once they see us."

She hoped. But if there was strength in numbers, that flock was strong as, she didn't know what—an elephant? A tidal wave?

"There's probably a dead cat or something. That's all."

"That's supposed to make me feel better?"

"Five minutes' time, we'll be past them, on the road. But come on. Or the rain'll catch us."

He led the way down the footpath, which hugged a ditch from which stunted hawthorn trees haphazardly leaned. It was steep and jutted with rocks, and the strangly roots of those dwarfish trees, and was slick with mud in places. She supposed it rarely dried out, not in this shade. She wished she had a stick.

"Jon?"

"Come on."

"Can we go more slowly?"

"I'll wait at the bottom."

Which was hardly the point, she thought, reaching carefully for a low branch. One hand round it, she stepped over a gap in the path, where a root had caused a cave-in. That's where she was—one foot either side of a minor chasm—when Jon fell.

It was almost comical. Spurred on by his promise to wait once he'd negotiated the descent, Jon had attempted a canter over a rocky stretch, treating the outcroppings as stepping stones, and discovered they were less secure than they looked. One moment, he was trip-trapping downhill like a two-footed goat; the next, those feet were over his head, or that's how it seemed to Helen. Almost comical, then, but she screamed anyway, a noise swallowed by Jon's louder howl as his airborne adventure came to an abrupt end. Helen let go of her branch, and half skidded to where he lay.

"Are you all right?"

The cawing and crying of those birds had not diminished in the slightest.

"Jon!"

He lay on his back, his body arching over his backpack. His face was white, and as he struggled to sit up, his expression cracked in two; one half disgust at the stupidity of what had happened to him; the other half a growing awareness of pain. He reached for his right foot, but had to give up. It was too far away. He tried to lean back instead, but there was nothing to lean against.

"Jon oh God Jon, are you okay? Are you hurt? How bad is it?"

The questions seeming to answer themselves as she knelt and took his hand in hers.

He said, "I think it's broken," and his voice was wire-thin, stretched between two poles.

"Oh God!"

"It really really hurts."

He'd turned the colour of paper, through which his features shone like greasemarks.

"Oh God oh God."

A grumble rolled across the skies above, echoing the raucous choir below.

She could feel his fingernails in her palm. Take control, she told herself. You have to take control. And she stepped on the small voice beneath that one; the small voice perkily suggesting that Jon deserved this.

"How badly . . . ?" She couldn't finish the sentence. How badly did it hurt? It was broken, he'd told her. It hurt like hell. Obviously.

"Hurts," he said again, but his breathing was settling into normal, or more nearly normal. Deep breaths, but they were steadying him, as if he were taking on ballast.

"We should take your boot off," she said, with only the vaguest sense that they should in fact do this. What would they do afterwards? And it wasn't something they'd do together anyway; it was something she'd have to do, while he lay in pain. One of them might faint. Whichever it was, things would get worse.

"No," he said, but she was already saying it too:

"No, bad idea. We won't get it back on, and . . ." Again, she could find no ending for that sentence.

Wriggling her hand free, she fumbled at the zipped pouch of her sweatshirt.

"God!" he said. "Hell, that hurts—it hurts like, Jesus, did I ever break a bone before? I never broke a bone before." Something like a laugh bubbled underneath his words. "I broke a tooth and that was bad, but this, this is worse, except I think it's starting to fade, the pain, it's fading down. Still there, though. Hez? What you doing?"

"Maybe there's a signal here. Sometimes they come and go."

"Ah!" he said, or it might have been "Ha!" "Not going to happen, Hez, no signal, there's not been a signal since . . ."

"But—"

"Stupid stupid, don't be bloody—ach. God, it hurts, sorry, sorry."

The angry birds clattered below, with a noise like breaking crockery.

Fumbling the phone free, she stood. "I know. I know. But how stupid would it be not to check?"

She moved a step or two away, as if this would make all the difference. But even before her phone hummed into life—that slight hiccup it gave, as if reminding her it was high time she upgraded—she was remembering it had no charge. She thrust it back into her pouch angrily. "Stupid damn thing, there's no—here, give me yours."

"No signal. None at the top, not going to be one halfway down . . ."

She took it anyway, squeezing it out of his jeans pocket. It was something to do—was the next thing waiting to be done—but already she knew it would be useless; there'd be no bars of light, no bars of life. The signal was as absent here as it had been anywhere else these past few days.

"Helen?"

"Just give it another minute," she said, knowing that they could give it another week. Another fortnight. "Just wait, we're not that low down here."

But all she really meant was that there was further to fall, or at least, further to descend; because here they were, only half-way down a steep incline, the rest of which lay waiting.

"IT'S NOT FAR."

Half an hour had passed, either crawling or zipping by. It seemed to Helen that they'd spent all day halfway down this damn slope, but at the same time she felt that with only a slight adjustment to the way things were—one minor hesitation before Jon decided to dance downhill—and they'd be back where they should be; making their way to that farm-house, and the road beyond. The thought of how nearly things might have turned out all right caused a bitter taste to rise in her throat; she swallowed, and said again:

"Not far at all. And they're bound to have a phone."

She wasn't sure which of them she was trying to convince. The only alternative to her going for help was for the pair of them to stay where they were and hope help, by some miracle, would appear of its own accord. As if to underline how unlikely an outcome this was, another gust of wind shook through the stunted trees.

Jon's first plan had been that Helen help him down to the farmhouse. He could lean on her. She could hold him up. She'd had no words to counter this; she was too busy struggling with the image it evoked: that of her own inevitable collapse before they'd managed two steps. Instead of just him with a snapped bone, it would be both of them. Except, knowing her luck, she'd end up the worse damaged.

Perhaps something of this vision had escaped into the air around them, because his suggestion had faltered, then stuttered into silence before reaching completion.

If it weren't for the pain etched into his face, and the hissing noises he made, as if trying to release that pain through clenched teeth, Jon would have appeared uninjured. The offending foot, strapped in its heavy walking boot, looked unimpaired. But his so far only attempt to put weight on it had resulted in a cry loud enough to cause a ripple through the avian cacophony below; a momentary tremble in their screeching, as if in brief respect to a noise as ugly as their own.

With no other course open, Helen had told him she'd walk down to the farmhouse and call for an ambulance.

"How long will it take?"

In other circumstances, this might have provoked wry laughter; not only for its unanswerability—how could she know how long it would take? She had no idea where the nearest ambulance was—but for the very fact of Jon asking it; of his assuming, for a change, the role of anxious questioner. *What time will you be back?* How many times had Helen asked him that these past few months, in response to a text explaining he'd been held up at work. *As soon as I can*, was the standard answer.

But she said, "Not long. I promise."

At these words, the sky rumbled again.

He was sitting, back against a tree trunk, his backpack beside him. Opening it, she pulled out his rain jacket. "Let's get this on you." Obediently, he raised his hands, and she threaded it onto him. "There. Not raining yet. But this'll keep you dry in case."

It wouldn't, much. When it rained, he'd get soaked. They both knew that.

"Don't forget where I am."

"Have you seen yourself?" His jacket was bright red. "You'll stand out like a candle."

"Nice analogy. It's getting dark, Hez."

"So I'd better go. I'll be quick as I can." She kissed him briefly on the cheek, tasting salt. "See you soon."

iii

As quick as I can meant slowly; one step at a time, holding on to whatever came to reach. Mostly branches. Towards the bottom, Helen had to descend crablike on feet and palms, because it was too steep to manage any other way. Her hands were filthy and her elbows ached, and she was heading into a wall of sound.

And she had been wrong. The noise of hundreds of birds—easily hundreds; whirling round the farmyard like ashes round a bonfire—didn't resemble crashing crockery, but more a tray of steel knives, dropped on a marble floor. And if she'd thought they'd take to the skies at her approach, she was wrong about that too. Some flew up and settled in a row on the ridge of the barn; others flapped onto the farm roof, but they'd been doing this before Helen's arrival, as if taking part in some complicated queuing system. The rest continued wheeling round the front of the barn, out of Helen's line of vision. They took no notice of her. She could have emptied a shotgun, and she doubted it would have disturbed them for more than a moment.

A shudder ran through her. She wished she had a shotgun anyway.

She was approaching both farmhouse and barn from the rear. What seemed to be an empty livestock pen adjoined the latter, next to which was parked an ancient car. The ground beneath her feet levelled out, but remained stony and ill-prepared, and the ditch disappeared into a culvert. Barbed wire curled lazily round the topmost rail of the fence to her right. It was studded with chunks of wool, like countless others she'd seen these past few days. The sky rumbled. The birds screeched. A fat drop of rain hit her head.

So here it came, she thought. Here came the rain at last. She slipped her backpack off and pulled her rain jacket out. With the hood up, her world altered. When the next drip hit her it made a dull plastic *thock* that felt like it came from inside her head. And it drowned the sound of those birds a little. It drowned the sound of those birds.

Walking on, she saw that the ancient car was a car-shaped piece of junk, rather, with windshield and windows long gone, and its roof caved in, as if someone had dropped a fridge on it from a height. Its front seats were a rubbish bin, and it was so layered with dirt, there was no telling its colour. As for the farmhouse, this was a grey squarish box, as removed from traditional images of farmhouses—weathered stone and trellises; napping cats on windowsills—as a Rottweiler from a sheepdog. But still, Helen thought, leave that aside: it didn't matter what it looked like. All she had to do was walk up to a door, knock, and ask whoever answered if she could use their telephone.

But using the front door meant walking between house and barn, directly beneath that black mass of birds. Crows, she thought, now she was nearly among them; crows and probably rooks, she wasn't sure of the difference. And magpies too, and jays—weren't they all part of the same family? Ravens. There were legends about ravens, usually involving death. Helen shuddered. She didn't want to walk beneath that monstrous cloud. She'd try the back door. It seemed safer, and this was the country—back doors were what you used in the country.

No lights shone from any windows. By now it was dark enough that, if anyone was home, surely they'd have needed a light on?

But it was pointless speculating. All she had to do was knock on the door, ring the bell. Whatever.

First, though, she took a quick glance at Jon's phone. Still no signal. And this too was typical, she thought; typical of what the day was turning into.

Without looking back, she set off for the farmhouse door.

AND STILL THE BIRDS roiled and tumbled in the air.

There's probably a dead cat or something. That's all.

Thanks, Jon.

She'd seen that film, of course, *The Birds*, at so early an age it was indelibly part of her baggage. That scene where they poured from the fireplace like feathered smoke: she'd shrieked then, and might shriek now, remembering. But she had to swallow the thought, because she had no option. She couldn't go back up the hill and tell Jon she was too scared to find a telephone; that he'd have to lie in the rain with a broken foot until the birds departed. Though if she did, it would almost serve him right—might teach him a lesson, the precise nature of which eluded her right now.

The noise was unrelenting. Blocked out everything else, if there was anything else to block out. Her hands to her ears, squashing the plastic hood tight against them, Helen made straight for the door, not looking at where the birds swooped round the barn.

Which still left her a view of what lay the other side of the disappointing farmhouse. It was a mess; an abandoned junkyard, spoiled and oily in the lowering dark. She made out rusting buckets and springs, an upended mattress, a fridge with its door hanging off. Engine parts lined one side of a pot-holed concrete pathway, as if someone had been saving them for later, and in an untidy pile against the corner of the house itself slumped hubcaps and petrol cans; plastic flasks, some half full of dirty-looking liquid; lengths of wood arranged in a half-hearted wigwam; upended cans of paint and plastic milk crates. A broken bedstead obscurely reminded Helen of a fairytale; wasn't there one with a flying bed? But she didn't want to think about fairytales, almost all of which involved ogres or witches, and every kindness encountered masked a darker deed.

It was a house, come to that, where an ogre might live, if ogres came in human-sized packages. The windows were not only dark, they were dirty. From the upper storey, a tongue of curtain flapped.

She thought: I can't do this, either. Can't knock on that door, for fear someone might answer. You read about this sort of thing; about inbred hooligans who lived miles from anywhere because they hated people; hated them so much they'd sooner chop them into pieces and scatter them for the birds than offer them the use of their telephones . . .

For God's sake, Helen, belt up.

And that was her own true self talking, or the person she liked to believe was her own true self; the decent liberal who'd be the first to flare up when ignorant bigotry was aired. Although it was also true that the flaring up mostly happened on the inside—was mostly, indeed, a kind of seething—which rarely found external expression. She was good at raging after the event, at pinpointing exactly the moment when she should have made her voice heard.

Enough of this. Jon was hurt. Playing horror-film scenarios in her head wasn't going to help, and the next few minutes were out of her hands: she had to knock on that door, and ask if she could use the phone. No other option existed.

Meanwhile, off to her left, the birds boiled around a fixed point she could not see. Every second moment, several burst into the air like a black firework. They seemed unworried by her presence, but then, why would they worry? There were so many of them . . . When they'd been a distant noise, she'd imagined they'd formed some avian parliament, like the swallows that schooled in the autumn, practising for their African journey, or starlings murmurating in the dusk. But this was different. Crows—weren't they loners, essentially friendless? What would cause them to gather in a great noisy swoop like this? It could only be something to eat—a cow, perhaps, or a horse, or maybe a dog, though it would have to be quite a large dog to occupy so many birds for so long . . . She shivered, and another fat drop of rain landed, *bang*, on top of her head. And then another hit the ground in front of her, and another, and soon there were too many to count, because here it was at last, the hoarded rain, and she ran the last few steps to the door, and rapped on it loudly by its brass knocker.

Nobody answered. Instead, the door swung slowly open.

iv

Up on the hill sat Jon, his right leg rigid in front of him, and his head resting on his left knee. He was trying to ignore pain. This was possible for stretches of up to almost a second, and then it came back, insistent as a fire alarm, and throbbing with the same rhythm. He could smell himself, his rancid sweat, as if his whole body had curdled with the pain from his foot. It must be broken. He couldn't actually swear to it, for all he'd more or less done so to Helen—how could he know? He wasn't a doctor—but it felt broken, exactly what he imagined broken felt like.

This was the loop his mind had been spinning in since Helen left.

Which had been about twenty minutes ago. He couldn't be certain. Jon never wore a watch, and Helen had his mobile, but twenty minutes, something like that. Time enough, surely, to reach that farmhouse; to knock on the door and ask to use the phone. What earthly reason could anyone have to refuse such a request? And then—

Oh hell, it hurts. It hurts like hell. Oh hell oh hell oh hell.

Deep breath.

And then how long would it take? He didn't know how far the nearest hospital was, and the roads weren't brilliant, but even so, ambulances, they'd be used to navigating these byways at speed, so it couldn't be as long as an hour, could it? It couldn't possibly take that long, and as soon as they got here the nurses, the paramedics, whatever, they'd give him something for the pain, and this would fade into memory. After that, it was all just recovery. Meanwhile, he'd endure as well as he could, on his own, and he wouldn't even be on his own all that long, would he? Because Helen would return as soon as she'd made the phone call . . .

Once that thought had circled his brain the second time, it latched on and took hold.

He'd given Helen his phone.

Oh hell.

But it didn't matter, because there'd be no signal at the bottom of the hill—there'd been none at the top; how could there be one in the dip? She'd use the phone in the farmhouse and come straight back. She wouldn't even switch his mobile on. Nothing to worry about except he'd broken his damn foot—

Oh hell oh hell oh hell.

Except that it was something to worry about.

The patter on the leaves above him became more insistent, then more insistent still. Soon it was a constant battering, and rain was pouring through the tree's inadequate shelter as if someone had turned on a tap. It wasn't quite pouring directly onto Jon's head, but only because he was leaning sideways to avoid it in a stupid attempt to stay dry, as if dry might make a difference. As if anything could be measurably worse right now.

The noise of the birds was fading. Presumably they'd scattered now the rain had begun in earnest. He wished he knew what time it was—wished he hadn't given Helen his mobile.

Oh hell.

He raised his head and put his palms to the ground. Began the slow miserable process of trying to push himself up.

THE DOOR CREAKED OPEN an inch or two, releasing a dank odour, nothing Helen could immediately identify.

"Hello?"

Maybe the word echoed within the unlit reaches of the house. But nobody appeared.

Her finger to the door, she pushed it again. This time it opened fully, with that same painful screech, revealing a hallway, mostly brown, and the foot of a staircase ascending into darkness. On the left was a door, firmly closed, and at the far end of the passage alongside the stairs was another, this one ajar. Through the gap, Helen thought she could make out the shape of a kitchen chair.

"Hello? Is anyone in?"

Not even a dog answered. Didn't all farmhouses have dogs?

She became aware that the birds' noise had lessened as the rain increased. Though she was more or less sheltered here, under a small awning, a sinkful of water was flung at her back with each gust of wind. Waterproof as her jacket was, she didn't think this was what its makers had had in mind. Pretty soon, she might as well strip naked and dance about in the farmyard for all the protection her clothing would offer.

Leaning forward, she put a foot inside the house. Then the other. Now she stood on a worn coir mat, conscious of having done something she'd never done before—stepped into a house uninvited.

You were supposed to be able to tell whether a house was empty. It had to do with atmosphere; with the energy an occupied house holds. But all Helen knew was that she could hear nobody, and that the dank smell was deeper even just this little way inside. It was the kind of smell that infiltrates carpets and curtains and never leaves; the odour of neglect.

"I need to use a phone."

The house did not reply.

"My husband—he's had an accident. We think he's broken his ankle."

A clock was ticking. Now that she was aware of this, she couldn't understand why she'd not heard it immediately.

"We need an ambulance."

But she might as well be shouting down a well.

Behind her, a sudden squall threw rain through the open door. This was ridiculous. She could turn and go, but how would that help? Once again she fished out Jon's phone; watched it swim to life in a blaze of light and colour, but to no useful effect. What did they do round here when they needed to contact somebody? Send pigeons?

She opened her mouth to call again, then changed her mind. There was nobody here.

They might be in the barn, she supposed. Or in one of the other farm buildings; it wasn't likely they'd gone far in this weather. Didn't farm folk know when rain was coming? And did they always leave their doors open? Country ways were more relaxed, but wasn't that taking things a little far?

The light in her hand died, as Jon's phone lapsed into sleep mode.

She returned it to her pocket. She wasn't going back into the rain. This was an emergency, and required extreme behaviour; un-English it might be, but she was going to enter and use their telephone. Her husband was in pain on a soaking hillside. Good manners didn't come into it.

Still, she was trembling as she advanced down the hallway to that waiting door, behind which, probably, lay the kitchen.

"HELL," JON SAID AGAIN, this time out loud.

He was on his feet, or one foot, and leaning heavily against another tree, about two yards from his original post. Part of his mind was trying to calculate what his speed of descent was, and how much longer it would take to reach the bottom of the hill, but the rest kept flashing on a more distracting image: that of overbalancing while trying to hop on this slick path; of landing on his already fractured ankle, and broken edges of bone jarring against each other—the thought almost made him throw up. He sank down again, a tricky manoeuvre in itself. It was difficult to believe everything could go so pear-shaped so suddenly. Except it wasn't, really. Accidents were invariably sudden.

Helen would have reached the house and used the phone. Even now, an ambulance was heading this way; siren wailing, lights flashing. Very shortly, he'd hear Helen panting her way uphill.

His ankle was throbbing in time to his heartbeat. That was how pain worked, he decided; it coursed through the body in the blood . . . He was growing delirious. But it was true that his pain pulsed, and on the beat he could feel it everywhere: in his jaw, in his fingers, at the back of his neck. Hell.

Pushing away from the trunk he landed on his side, and rolled onto his front. It was undignified, and he'd soon be filthy. But he couldn't stay here, not with the dark upon him and the rain falling; not—and even the rhythm of the pain, thumping through him, couldn't keep this thought at bay—while Helen had his phone.

He began to crawl, to slither, down the hill.

THE OPENING DOOR SOUNDED like a cat on a black-board—Helen felt it in her spine and in her knees. Heart in mouth she waited as the door swung wider, revealing what lay behind.

A kitchen. An empty kitchen.

A *bam-bam-bam* replacing her heart's *lub-dub*, she stepped inside. It wasn't much less gloomy than the hallway. Through the window, what was left of daylight fell like a grey fog, illuminating dirty dishes in a chipped enamel sink; a table covered by a stained cloth; a french dresser, its shelves a hodge-podge of crockery and power tools, batteries and old newspapers, tinned food, battered pans. Small brown crumbs might be mouseshit. The air tasted as if milk had been spilt ages ago, and left to dry.

"Hello?" she called again, though it was obvious there was nobody here.

A doorway in one corner gave onto a small lobby, and what must be the front door. A coat hung on a hook, and a pair of

Wellingtons stood in the corner, one half folded over itself, as if exhausted by its wait.

On the wall, between the fridge and a chipped formica cupboard, hung a telephone.

Helen was so relieved that she stood simply savouring the feeling—this was the moment on which the day would turn, and the whole horrible event begin to be swallowed by the past. Later, she'd tell Jon about it; relate the incident in the company of friends—*And that's when I saw the phone. Just after I'd decided the place must be crawling with mice . . .*

None of this took more than an instant. It wasn't as if she was deliberately spinning out the time during which Jon lay in the rain with a broken ankle, and she committed trespass in a cold creepy house. She reached for the phone. Lifted the receiver. Held it to her ear as her finger poised to stab the emergency number.

Realised that what she was hearing was not the purr of the dial tone but an empty, windless silence, the kind you'd hear if you stood at the end of a tunnel in which nothing moved.

V

After a while she re-set the receiver on its hook, then lifted it
again. The same result. There was no life in the phone. It was
as useless as the pair of mobiles she carried.

Through the smeary window was a sideways view of the
barn. Its doors stood open. There were still birds there, looping
in and out of the barn, out of reach of the rain and screeching
viciously. It was like watching a tornado wrestle itself in a corner. She raised a hand and wiped a cleaner window in the glass.
Jon would be growing colder and wetter, and his broken foot
would be torturing his mind, snaking tendrils of pain into each
and every thought he had, even the thoughts he had about
whoever it was he was mostly thinking about these days. Helen
didn't know her name, though it hadn't escaped her attention
that it was within her grasp—the briefest examination of Jon's
mobile would render it up—but her name was an irrelevance;
would simply lend shape to what already existed as a shadowy
figure at Helen's shoulder. Even without a name, she made
Helen feel an unwelcome presence in her own life. Jon was
forever slipping away in front of her eyes; his attention visibly
shifting to what he'd claim, if she asked, was a crossword clue,

or a book he'd been reading, or a problem at work—all the lies he told every time he was thinking about his lover. Lately, she hated leaving him alone, knowing he'd use the freedom to wallow in the thought of her, or—God forbid—call her or text her . . . Well, he was alone now, and could think about her to his heart's content, except that pain would snatch him back to the here and now with every scrape of his broken bone. Which served him right. Maybe, out on that hillside, he'd catch a glimpse of the life she'd lived these past months; desperate for a tiny space, a single moment, where things didn't hurt, and the awful icy fingers that poked and prodded inside her, squeezing her heart with the regularity of a metronome, gave her a rest.

There were different kinds of pain. He wasn't suffering the worst.

She made another pass at the window with the palm of her hand, and saw the body.

IT LAY ON ITS side, facing away, and Helen could not tell whether it was male or female. What she could see of its grey hair was long, shoulder length, but that meant nothing in itself. But it was a body, that much was certain, by which she meant dead: wearing a red shirt and dark trousers. An extinguished life lay in the farmyard, in front of the barn, whose doors hung wide, and which now sheltered some of those big black birds, who'd been driven from their meal by the rain. The thought passed through Helen's mind, circled the room, then entered her mind again. They had been driven from their meal by the rain.

The birds, those huge black birds, they'd been feasting on the body.

That wasn't a red shirt. It wasn't the shirt that was red.

She was glad the body was turned away, because she had no desire to see what remained of its face. Already, the picture stamped on her imagination was bad enough—would remain there forever; would drop from the back of her mind at unexpected moments, causing her to gag or flinch or yelp. But for now she had to push it away, and do what had to be done in these circumstances. The next step was to call the police. Except that was no help, because the phone was as dead as the body.

Without being aware she'd done so, Helen had retrieved both mobiles from her pockets, and now held one in each hand, her thumbs already stroking their keypads, as if trying to coax them into life. But neither cooperated, and only Jon's offered the pretence of usefulness, beaming like a shiny matchbox. No signal, though. No signal.

Helen didn't know what to do.

Above her head, a floorboard creaked.

AT THE FOOT OF the hill, crawling through mud, Jon found a stick—most of a branch. It was forked at one end, and looked the right length for a crutch. He wouldn't have seen it at all if he'd been upright. This would pass as irony, he supposed. The pain from his foot thudded strongly as ever but the weird thing was he'd grown accustomed to it, as if it had always been part of him, like the shape of his ears.

He gingerly trusted a fence-post to take his weight. Hauled upright, balancing on one foot, he tested his newfound crutch. He wouldn't want to travel long distances on it, but it would do.

All around, rain pounded down. You'd think it would wash some of the mud off, but it satisfied itself with plastering his hair to his head, and streaming into his eyes.

. . . And where was Helen? He should have met her coming back by now: how long did it take to make a phone call? Did she have to do everything at half-speed? If she'd not been dragging behind all afternoon, he'd not have needed to hurry to make up lost time; wouldn't have taken that descent so quickly; wouldn't have fallen and broken his foot . . .

Damn. He wanted this pain to go away. He wanted to be warm, dry and mended, and wanted his phone back before Helen went trawling through its log, making unreasonable assumptions about a number he kept calling. His colleague, Effie. Well, more than a colleague. But whose fault was that, also?

Swearing under his breath, he limped towards the farmhouse. It was a big grey block in the darkness; a twin to the featureless shape that was the barn, around which those birds had been screaming. They'd taken off now, in the rain. He wondered where they'd gone.

And wondered, too, why there were no lights in the farmhouse.

ONCE, HELEN'S BRAKES HAD briefly failed—for a fraction of a second, her vehicle failed to respond to her instruction. And then it did, and everything returned to normal. Afterwards, mentally cataloguing the moment, she'd been aware that one part of her had risen above the imminent disaster, and had been planning damage limitation. That hadn't, then, been real fear. It had allowed space for alternatives.

Here and now, Helen turned to water.

When she was solid again, the world had changed. The phones in her hand were trinkets, and the collection of junk and household items on the dresser had acquired sinister shapes, as if arranged there with evil purpose. The rank odour had blossomed, and the air was grimy; streaked and smudged. Her knees did not want to hold her. Her mouth was full of salt.

After another moment, her thoughts ceased wheeling, and she was able to take stock.

The floorboard had creaked only once. It had been directly above her head, she thought; in a room that surely offered a view of the body in the yard. No one upstairs could have failed to hear her enter; she'd called and called—had made it clear she was coming in. Whoever was there had not wanted to make himself, herself, known. There were different ways you could add this up, but the total came out the same. Whoever was upstairs was responsible for the body in the yard.

Movement was like wading through wet sand. Like the worst sort of dream. Not making noise was now crucial, its importance far outweighing the stupid fact she was stupidly aware of: that she'd already made plenty of noise; that there was little point in pretending she wasn't here and never had been. The staircase, down which whoever was lurking upstairs might at any moment descend, was behind her now. She couldn't go back. Her only option lay ahead, through that door and into the yard. Once outside, she could slip back round the house, hugging the wall. She might not be seen. And she would be out of here . . . Criminally slowly she inched her way to the small lobby and its big wooden door, and as she reached for the handle, an overhead board creaked again. This was followed by another sound she couldn't identify; something organic, but not necessarily human.

She turned the doorknob, and felt its grinding complaint as if it issued from her own joints. But when she pulled, the door wouldn't give.

Bolts. It was bolted top and bottom.

The upper bolt was stiff, and it didn't help that she had to stand on tiptoe. Its handle bit into her thumb as she tugged, impressing its shape in the palm of her hand as she pulled with all her strength, and then a little more, as fresh adrenalin flushed through her. When the bolt gave it flayed the skin off her index finger, which she barely paused to lick before dropping to her knees to attack the lower.

The upper had been difficult. This one felt impossible, as if it had rusted into place. Which couldn't be true—couldn't— because there were Wellingtons here, a coat on this hook; why, if the door weren't in regular use? Something made her stop and she froze in place, there on her knees, head cocked like an anxious dog's for a sound that wouldn't come a second time, and maybe hadn't come a first. Perhaps she'd imagined it. Perhaps she'd imagined everything, but she hadn't. That body in the red shirt that wasn't a red shirt—that body in its bloody rags: she'd seen that. She knew she had. It had been left for birds to feast on. The bolt changed its mind without warning and hammered open. Helen lost her balance and fell forward, banging her nose against the door.

She sat back, head spinning. Touched her upper lip. It was numb but unbloodied. She wanted to cry, but didn't have time. Scrambling up, she grabbed the door handle again. Now she didn't care how loudly it squealed; she wanted the door open, wanted to be out. The handle turned. She tugged. It didn't budge.

An outside squall flung water against the kitchen window.

At the same moment a door slammed, and this time Helen screamed.

IN THE DARK, IT was easy to imagine things, to invent a different context for the darkness, and pretend he was inching towards a bright warm room, in which a fire chuckled, and a drink waited, and a hot bath, and soothing bandages. That was the story Jon conjured to make it possible to keep taking step after painful step. The warm room, the hot bath, and Effie, holding a huge fluffy towel: there, that made the picture perfect. Now all he had to do was limp across a puddled uneven path in the dark, leaning on a stick that might snap any moment, with driving rain pounding into him.

And there was no Effie waiting either, not in his immediate future. There were things to do first. Obstacles to overcome. Helen had to be told, for a start, and this was something that ought to be simple—was just a confirmation of what they both already knew; that their marriage was no longer working—but was proving anything but. He kept putting it off. He hoped to be able to do so indefinitely; failing that, he hoped to be able to find the right words, words that would allow everything to be over as swiftly and painlessly as possible. Which was why he needed to recover his phone before a quick study of his text-message history gave Helen all the hurtful information in one go. Because he didn't want to make things worse for her. He simply wanted things to be over. That much, at least, was clearer in this dark: he wanted things to—

Helen screamed.

Jon stopped dead. Had he heard that? Had it been Helen? He shouted her name, or tried to; it was washed apart in the pouring rain, which was louder than ever—it battered on the nearby barn roof; on the treetops behind him; on the metal surfaces of the scrapyard around the farmhouse. He hadn't appreciated how loud rain could be, so how could a scream have broached it? Maybe he'd imagined it, but—he should get to the farmhouse, make sure she was okay. He should do that. Do it now.

But there was another thing about the dark, he discovered; how easy it was to remain locked inside it, immobile. It was surprising what you could fail to do, when there was nobody there to see.

SURELY HER HEARTBEAT WAS audible? From where Helen now crouched, flattened against the wall beside the fridge, it sounded like a hammer pounding a mattress. She imagined the house trembling, as if she were the epicentre of a seismic disturbance which would spread ever outwards, shaking weathervanes for miles around; and, worse, much worse than that, bringing whoever was upstairs down to find her, flattened against this wall, and stop it stop it *stop it* she commanded herself. She held her breath while the message filtered through her limbs. She was shaking, yes, but nearly in charge of her thoughts.

A dragging sound. That was what she could hear; the sound of something pulling itself across a dusty floor, and here it came again: a dragging sound, followed by a thump, and brief silence. Then the dragging again.

The picture her mind drew was draped in bandages, stained with gore.

Shut up, she said. *Shut up.*

The door would not open. The bolts were drawn, but it remained locked, and no key was in sight—there were hooks along the dresser's shelves, the perfect place to hang keys, if only whoever had locked the door had thought of that, but they hadn't. So she was trapped in the kitchen, with a dragging noise overhead that was inching towards the top of the stairs. Soon it would start to descend, and there'd be nothing she could do about it.

Except leave this kitchen, head back down that passageway which ran alongside the staircase, and be out through the door into the outside world before it got there, she thought. She could do that. If she was fast enough.

It. She was thinking of it as an *it*, but it wasn't, of course; it wasn't an *it*. It would be a he. But men were worse than things, that was certain. Men were so much worse than things.

She didn't think she could make it down that passage. Didn't think her legs would carry her. She was frightened—so very frightened.

It was Jon's fault. If he hadn't been so keen on showing how fit he was, how agile; if he hadn't wanted to dance downhill instead of taking it carefully. If he hadn't been seeing someone behind her back, betraying nine years of marriage . . . If that hadn't happened, they wouldn't even be here. She wouldn't have been so anxious to get away, remove him from the scene of his adulterous crime. She'd be at home now, where all the doors opened at her will, and there was no body in the yard, no noises upstairs.

A thump, then another thump. And something whistled through the house, and more rain lashed the window.

This wouldn't do. She had to move. The kitchen was no haven, it was simply where she was right now, and she was allowing that fact to make it seem a place of safety. But in the absence of a key, there was no exit, unless she went through the window. In her terror at the thought of heading along that passage, in plain view of whatever lurked at the top of the stairs, she actually gave that some consideration, but it would have meant scrambling into the sink, and knocking the glass out, and crawling through . . . It couldn't be done.

Trembling, she hauled herself up. Her legs felt like an infant's; like limbs unused to movement.

Don't think about it, she thought. Don't pause, don't make plans. Just head for the door, then through it and into the dark. She didn't need to walk past the body. Just straight back the way she'd come . . . Though that, too, was no place of safety; it was a sodden hillside, on which her husband lay with a broken foot.

Damn this, she thought.

She headed down the hall. Moving quickly turned out not to be an option; she could only creep along, terrified that at any moment she'd be dropped on from above. Her life passed inch by inch. The stairs descended on her left; at their top, an unknowable darkness in which something was breathing. Every thought she had fed back into itself, endlessly. She could make it to the door unless the thing at the top of the stairs, the *man*, jumped on top of her, which wouldn't happen if she made it through the door first. But it might. It might happen.

And she was sure she'd left that door open, but now it was closed.

HE TRIPPED AND FELL. Oh, yes—perhaps he could break another bone, have a matching pair of useless feet. As it was, he dropped to his knees, and if it weren't for the makeshift crutch, would have sprawled in mud and gravel. Though it was the crutch at fault, having caught in something's prongs; a hoe, leaning against a fence Jon hadn't seen. He gripped it to regain his balance and found himself wrapping his fist round barbed wire, and swore as it tore his flesh, then swore louder—no one could hear; he was out in the dark and the rain, trying to get to that damn farmhouse, and he was frightened for Helen, of course he was, because it was dark and raining and they were miles from anywhere, but he was frightened for himself too because what was he supposed to do if she were actually in trouble—how could he help, half crippled, if she were actually in danger and not just frightened of her own shadow?

For a while back there he'd been tempted not to move, just remain where he was until everything sorted itself out, which was what usually happened. Things sorted themselves out. If you said nothing, did nothing, waited, everything eventually drifted towards resolution without intervening unpleasantness. He'd been hoping this would happen between himself and Helen; that if he simply allowed their marriage to continue on its unsatisfactory keel, she'd get fed up and let him go without his having to say anything. Damn it damn it damn it.

Damn it.

He held his palm level so the rain washed the blood away, then pushed himself upright. He couldn't leave her screaming in the dark, even if the only danger was in her head. And besides, this place, even now the birds had gone, gave him the creeps. It stank, and not just of shit and wet grass. It stank of neglect, underlaid with something he couldn't name, but seemed familiar. So it wasn't out of the question that whatever had made Helen scream—if it had been her, and a scream—wasn't some imaginary monster, but an actual person offering actual threat.

And again came the temptation to do nothing. How could he help, in his condition? He had nothing but a stick, barely enough to hold his own weight.

Then he thought: no, that's not right, actually. He had a hoe. And its end was sharp.

HOW LONG IS A minute? It was measurable, of course—its very name its own measurement—but how long did it last, exactly? Helen had no idea how many slipped past while she remained rooted, staring at the closed door, but however many there were, they came crashing to an end when something moved again at the top of the stairs—a dragging sound, hollow and awkward. She shrieked then, appalled at her own giveaway noise, retreated to the kitchen and its lobby where she tugged at the door again, as if it might have relented in her absence, and now allow her out. But it hadn't. Tugging gave way to pounding, which had as little effect. She slapped the door double-handed. She was sobbing, and there seemed little point trying to stop, though stop she did, sudden as if her throat had been cut, when she heard the dead weight of what must be a foot landing on the staircase.

I wasn't breaking in. I only needed a telephone. I haven't seen anything, I don't know anything, I won't say anything.

Let me leave, please, and I'll vanish into that darkness and never come near again.

Please.

But the words were hollow even in her head. Who claimed they'd seen nothing except those who knew there was something to see?

There was no further sound from the staircase.

Was it waiting up there—balanced, no, *poised,* poised to leap, as soon as it set eyes on her? The thing to do was stay where she was, make herself small as possible; tiny enough to slip through a keyhole; or failing that, small enough that she couldn't be seen in this dark lobby . . . But she couldn't stay. It was too enclosed here, too coffin-like—she froze at another sound, but it didn't come again; all she could hear was her own body trembling; that and her own breath slipping from her in short sharp bursts. She wondered if this was how it had been for the body by the barn; if she, he, whoever, had tried to flee, their heart pounding fit to burst their chest . . .

A creak now, and a shuffling sound.

She was pressed against the side of the fridge like a piece of kitchen furniture. If she couldn't be small she could be inconspicuous, and hadn't she had enough practice at that? This past year? Being invisible; being someone her own husband's glances slid off because he had better things to think about, someone else on his mind? And whose fault was it she was here now? A door opened, and a rush of air swept past her like a ghost. She whimpered and reached out, her hand brushing against objects made unfamiliar by the dark: a pepper pot a cheesegrater something leaking something sticky a knife—a knife? She grasped it, and its handle moulding into her fist was the first note of comfort she'd known since stepping into this damned house.

Something called her name in a hoarse whisper. Whatever it was, it was now dragging itself painfully down the dark hallway. She stiffened. Out in the hammering rain, just the other side of that window, lay a bird-chewed corpse, and she did not want to end down that road—end as food for birds.

Again, it called her name. But she wasn't fooled. This was how the creatures of the dark operated; they wheedled and crooned. They drew you in.

There was a scraping of steel on floorboards.

Something came nearer.

In her hand the knife grew warm.

vi

At morning light the birds returned, but were disturbed at their feeding by human commotion. Ambulances came, and cars with flashing lights, summoned by a postman making his first visit for weeks. Something was carried out of the house; something else, wrapped in a blanket, was escorted to a waiting car. The body by the barn was examined in situ before it too was wrapped and packed away. He had lived here for decades, the old man, sour and misanthropic; his days a downward spiral into a mess of unpaid bills and discontinued services; his only apparent pleasure prising waymarkers from public footpaths; his only companion his weak and failing heart. That this had decided to abandon him without warning was just the way life worked, until it stopped working.

One more corpse was found in the house, though this was disposed of with less delicacy. A crow had crashed through a bedroom window, lacerating itself in the process, and judging by the blood and feathers everywhere, had dragged itself about for hours before succumbing to the inevitable on the topmost stair. The draught that gushed through the broken glass made curtains flap and doors slam shut. Every hinge on every door could groan to wake the dead.

At length, the farmyard grew quiet. The birds returned in their dozens and perched on the barn roof, or strutted the junkyard that had grown up around the house, but found little to feed upon. Gradually, in ones and twos, they lifted up, and their wingbeats filled the air, then vanished. And in the abandoned farmyard, the puddles that were everywhere quivered when the wind blew, which the wind did all day long. Did all the livelong day.

THE LAST DEAD LETTER

Rules about access only took you so far. In St. Leonard's, a discreet brick establishment on a quiet close in Hampstead, they got you through the door courtesy of a concrete ramp, but after that you were on your own. The aisles were narrow, and the occasional memorial slab a hazard to cane- or Zimmer-users; the apparently random siting of a font might have been intended to force a congregation into a contraflow; and a set of railings sequestering an otherwise unremarkable example of twentieth-century stained glass jutted out a little far for those whose mobility was compromised, ensuring that, for a woman in a wheelchair, what might have been a quiet tour became a haymaker's outing. But St. Len's would not have been St. Len's if it offered itself for inspection without resistance. A notice in the porch suggested that mass was celebrated only irregularly, and locals knew that even these well-spaced events were invariably cancelled for illness or emergency. Funerals were the only reliable service, these more likely to be precipitated than postponed by such contingencies, and were strictly private affairs: family and friends; no hawkers, no tourists. Curtain twitching offered few clues. Those who arrived to pay their respects

might have been a caravan of civil servants, some of whom
had fallen on hard times. But Mrs. McConnell at Number 37
offered that she knew for a fact—had heard it from a friend
on the council, whose son, a Metropolitan officer, had been
assigned to take down numberplates of nearby cars during one
of these funerals—that St. Leonard's was where they buried
the spies. Those in the know, she claimed, called it the Spooks'
Chapel. And if her neighbours dismissed this on the grounds,
first, that surveillance techniques had long since outpaced a
bobby with a notebook, and, second, that Mrs. McConnell's
tales were famously taller than the hedge bordering St. Len's
itself, this suited everyone perfectly, since neighbours invariably enjoy seeing through each other, and Mrs. McConnell,
who in the long-ago had worked for the Intelligence Services,
was well aware that a truth from an unreliable source is twice
as effective as a rock-solid lie.

All of which Molly Doran knew, and none of which made
her passage easier, but she was accustomed to difficult journeys, and her wheelchair was robust enough to inflict more
damage than it suffered *en route*. Outside, behind the chapel,
the graveyard was a calm oasis in which visitors might forget
a city lay mere streets away, and in here, too, such noises as
filtered through were no more than light static on an old-time
receiver. Molly apart, the building was empty. It was a bright
cold day, and coloured light dropped in shafts onto benches
and an uncovered altar.

She had come to rest by the west wall, which was studded with nameplates instead of windows, plaques to those not
grand enough to occupy Hampstead's real estate, or whose

remains were beyond the reach of mortal transport. Messy ends, as Jackson Lamb had been known to remark, didn't lead to tidy burials, and there were bodies out in joe country that would never be found. So here their former owners were remembered, in a display informally known as The Last Dead Letter Drop, and if the names on the plaques weren't always accurate, the identities of those memorialised remained as true as they'd ever been. Few covers match those that shroud the dead. And if dates, too, were often fudged in the manner of a coy spinster, Molly Doran could read between lines like a harpist, and, for her, false facts often lit true pathways. There were stories here she'd followed through her archives, which lay below the pavements of Regent's Park, and she could tell a legend from a myth at a hundred paces—she always said "paces" when making this claim, staring hard at her interlocutor from the depths of her wheelchair, daring a furtive glance at her absent legs. Only Lamb had ever laughed, and she'd have been disappointed if he hadn't.

But not all stories laid themselves bare to her. Even for Molly Doran, some mysteries remained.

This section of wall contained seven plaques, ceiling to floor; the highest and lowest pair out of her reading range; the middle three dating back some years. In one of those curious jokes life plays, and death often chuckles along with, the upmost was for the name Huntley, and the one immediately below for a Palmer. The bottom-most, just below her eye level, read Gryff. One could easily mistake this for *Grief*, she supposed. For a while she remained there, the names dancing in front of her eyes. But maybe that was a trick of the light.

Behind her, a voice said, "No, don't get up."

She hadn't heard him enter, or approach across the clackety floor, but she had long grown used to this: that he could move stealthily when he wanted, though to all appearances had the grace and flexibility of a fatberg.

"You came," she said.

"I pay my debts."

Because that was what this was. He owed her a favour, and here she would collect, in the process illuminating one of the mysteries that haunted her archive.

Now that he'd revealed his presence, Lamb apparently felt no further need for stealth. As she manoeuvred round to face him, he lowered himself onto the nearest bench with a groan suggesting that movement cost him pain. The odour of smoked cigarettes wafted towards her. His raincoat was shiny here and there, not with recent moisture but with well-established stains.

"Limbs giving you trouble?" she asked, with a hint of sarcasm.

"You don't know the half of it." He paused. "I said—"

"I get it."

"Because you've only got half the—"

"I said I get it."

"Jesus, what's eating you? From the ground up, I might add." He pulled a sorrowful face. "Sense of humour failure's the worst disability of all. You don't even get free parking."

"Finished?"

"Wish I was." Lamb looked around. "God, churches give me the creeps. So why am I here? Just to watch you pondering the mysteries of the whatever-the-bugger-it-is?"

"Ineffable."

"I thought that meant can't be fucked."

"There are probably theologians who'd agree. But let's not waste time pretending you're duller than you look, Jackson. This is me you're talking to. Remember?"

"Hard to forget. It's like having a conversation with a demented armchair."

She came forward a few inches, effectively blocking any escape he might have attempted. "I've a story to tell."

"Oh, great. Jackabloodynory. Will it take long? Only I have plans."

"Plans? If you weren't here you'd be in Slough House, smoking and drinking."

"Like I said."

"Well, that'll have to wait." Her face was partly in shadow, so her messy cap of grey hair, her over-powdered skin, appeared two-tone. The effect should have been clownish, but somehow wasn't. "So make yourself comfortable."

Lamb took this as an invitation to fart, then stretched his legs under the bench in front of him. His collar was turned up, and he lowered his jaw to his chest. "And why exactly do I have to listen to this?"

"So you can tell me how it ends," Molly said, and began her story.

A LONG TIME AGO, when we all lived in the shadow, most of human life could be found in Berlin, for Berlin was the Spooks' Zoo, and every agency in the world had, if not an official presence, at least a tame weasel or two lurking there.

But it was a place where citizens and professionals alike could reinvent themselves, and not all those who checked their real names at the door were in the business. Some just liked the idea of being someone else, at least for a while. If it wasn't quite joe country, it was on the border, and more than a few passing souls never afterwards fitted back into their old lives. Travel's a way of finding yourself, it's said, but it's also a good way of getting lost.

("I saw this in a movie," grumbled Lamb. "Only they called it *Casablanca*."

"Hush now. I'm talking.")

There was a phrase at the time, describing Berlin's colours—*peacock shit*—because you had all these effervescent pinks and blues, these rainbow reds and greens, spraypainted onto cold grey concrete. There were party frocks for warehouse wear and glitterballs on bin lorries—the whole city was throwing a party; a rave-up in a wasteland, powered by whatever fuel was handy. Sex and drugs and rock and roll were all hard currency. But hardest of all was information.

So while young people danced and drugged themselves to oblivion in the shadow of the Wall, and made all kinds of music, most of which changed nothing, spies went about their business of soliciting betrayal: buying, stealing and seducing secrets from the innocent and the jaded alike. And some of these spies were young themselves, and some were old, and one was . . .

"Careful," said Lamb.

"Let's call him . . . Dominic Cross."

Cross wasn't young. He wasn't entirely old, either, but there's such a thing as joe years, which speed time up or slow it down, depending on your point of view. Minutes drag while glaciers form, and at the end of every hour you might have aged two, because that's how it was in the shadow of the Wall, especially on its wrong side. And Cross had spent time on the wrong side. Because Cross ran a network, a crew of informers, thieves and traitors—of heroes, idealists and freedom lovers, in other words—who required constant comforts, of cash or company, and Cross was a singular man, a man who could settle a bar tab, soothe a mad dog and calm a frightened asset in the same two breaths. Often his presence alone was enough, because that was no small thing. There were more ways round the Wall than people realise, but all were dangerous. There was barbed wire and concrete; there were forged greasy papers; there were cavities built into the underbellies of trucks. There were long drives up-country to apparently unregarded areas, where a stretch of land you could cover on foot in five minutes could be a twenty-four-hour journey. And even when you just handed the right guard the right amount of money, like skipping a queue in a nightclub, you might have been buying a ticket to the underworld, and wouldn't know until your last minute. So Cross lived on his nerves so that his assets might keep theirs, and if, by a peacetime clock, he should have been approaching his prime, his organs were run ragged by tension; with the effort of keeping others calm while they put their lives at risk. So he was a drinker, which barely needs saying, and a smoker too, because this was Berlin. Most things a man could do to ruin himself he did, but only on his own time. When it came to keeping his network safe, he was concentration itself.

But you can only live so long on such terms. Booze and fags and dangerous journeys, and too many nights in bars: these things take their toll. Dominic had been in Berlin for eight years, and eight was at the edge of the envelope: the sticky bit. Field agents were burn-out material, and reckoned to be past their use-by anytime after six. Only the complicated nature of handing over a network to a newcomer kept them in place longer. Jittery assets didn't like new faces. And most assets were jittery. But sooner or later, and most likely sooner, Dominic Cross would have been airlifted out and put behind a desk in a safer city, where no doubt he'd have finished the job Berlin started, and drunk himself into early old age. But before any of that could happen something else happened instead, one of those awful things a spook wouldn't wish on his best friend.

Dominic fell in love.

"HE WAS A GOOD man, I think," said Molly. "At the time. For that place."

Lamb grunted.

"I mean, he was a cheat and a liar, and probably sold his soul several times over. But he always got a good price for it, and always brought his assets home before the roof fell in."

"Not always," said Lamb.

". . . No. Maybe not always."

"Get on with it."

IT STARTED IN A bar, because when did anything start anywhere else? It was the winter of that particular year, one of the last spent in the shadow—though other shadows, God knows, would soon fall—and Dominic Cross was drinking near the station, not because he expected to catch a train but because you never knew. It was a workers' bar, with a low ceiling, tin-topped tables, and stools that warned you when you were nearing your limit, and Dominic had just lost at checkers against the blind pensioner who was a regular miracle there. Dominic had lost a small fortune trying to find out how he cheated, but was no nearer than ever as he shook hands with the old crook, and took his place at the counter. Gin was his tipple here, because everyone had habits and it was best to be everyone whenever possible, and while he was waiting he became aware of a small piece of theatre to his left: a blonde woman fishing in her bag, her expression a soliloquy. *I cannot find my purse. I cannot buy this drink.* It was a show he'd seen before, and had various endings, all of which left him out of pocket, but that didn't stop him buying a ticket. "I'll get that," he said to the bartender, which was the line written for him since before he'd got out of bed that morning, or any previous morning, come to that.

But as soon as he'd delivered it, it was capped.

"Ah—there you are!"

She produced a purse from the depths of the tote bag round her neck.

That had never happened before.

She smiled. "But you're kind. Let me get yours."

"No—really—"

"I insist."

Her purse snapped open, and a carousel of coins swarmed onto the counter. In the manner of barmen everywhere, the present example sorted those he required with an index finger, and swept them into his waiting palm.

"My name's Marta," she said. "What's yours?"

And the next part of that encounter was as inexplicable as the discovery of the purse, because one drink later Marta refused to allow him to repay the favour. Instead, she had looked at her watch, a chunky bootleg Timex with a Disney face, and told him it had been nice talking to him. And then kissed his cheek and slipped off her stool, made sure her purse was safe in her too-big bag, and walked out into the night. It was raining by then, and the windows were freckled with diamonds, which cast the street outside into a kaleidoscopic frenzy. She turned left, unless it was right, and vanished from view.

By the time the brief blast of cold air had swept its way around the room, the barman had already poured Dominic Cross a consolatory gin.

LAMB STIRRED. "JESUS. YOU'RE supposed to be an archivist, not Barbara bloody Cartland."

"And yet there you are, paying rapt attention."

"Only 'cause you're blocking my exit."

Perhaps in deliberate counterpoint to this observation, he farted again.

Molly didn't blink. "I've been wondering," she said, "what kind of woman might have proved so attractive to him. There's only one photo I ever saw. Dyed hair, dark roots. A little tacky."

"Said Coco the Clown."

"And her eyes looked hollow. Never a good sign." She glanced at Lamb, hoping for a reaction, but he had a hand down his trousers and was scratching his crotch while staring at the ceiling. "On the other hand, pictures don't reveal everything, do they?"

"Depends. I've seen a few could double up as X-rays."

"But she looked ordinary to me. I think mid-thirties, allowing her the benefit of the doubt."

"You don't have her birthdate? You're slipping."

"As you pointed out, I'm an archivist. Not an alchemist. I can't make something out of nothing. Everything I know about her is a detail invented by somebody else. Unless it wasn't, of course. Because that's the thing, Jackson. Maybe she really was who she claimed to be. And maybe she was shark bait. What do you think? All these years later?"

"I think you should hurry the fuck up," Lamb said. "Before the next funeral gets here."

SOMEONE ONCE CALLED THE spook trade a wilderness of mirrors, and that was never more true than in Berlin in those days, where, whichever direction you were facing, you always had to watch your back. So every working spook had a mirror-man, who wasn't quite a handler and wasn't quite a friend, and it was a mirror-man's job to take regular confession, which included any wayward encounters, professional or otherwise. Dominic Cross's mirror-man had been over the Wall himself, so knew how the big world turned. That should have given them common ground, but sometimes common ground becomes no-man's-land, and the pair had never clicked. Which might have been why Cross didn't mention that first pass, which was breaking the law in about five different ways. You always mentioned a pass, even if it didn't look like one at the time. You mentioned it when it was a woman, and you mentioned it when it was a man, and if it ever happened that it was a polar bear or a skunk you mentioned that too, because there was no end to the ways in which an approach might be made, and Berlin Rules were clear on the issue. You always mentioned a pass.

But Marta hadn't been making a pass. She was just a woman who thought she'd lost her purse, until she discovered she hadn't. If it had been a pass, she'd have let him do the talking, which was how these things went: first you opened your trap, then you walked into it. It was a ceaseless wonder how eager joes were to start talking. So she'd have let him buy a second drink, and then sat and let him talk, ears and eyes wide open. She wouldn't have left so soon, not on a rainy night. Not without taking a number or making a date. Not leaving them both with their virginities intact.

So plant or not, Dominic Cross kept her a secret. Didn't mention her to The Shit, which was his private name for his mirror-man, nor drop her name anywhere else. Instead, he told himself he'd forgotten all about her. It had been just another rainy night in a workers' bar, and anyway, he never saw her again.

Until, of course, he did.

IT WAS THE FOLLOWING year, about four months later. Far too long an interval for it to be anything other than accident—you didn't keep a man dangling that long. Not in Berlin, where four months might as well be a decade.

And this time it was in broad daylight, on a busy street. She was carrying a shopping bag over one arm, which gave her a domestic look, and they met in the middle of the road, crossing in different directions. Traffic waited, poised to pounce.

"It's you! Hello again."

There are better times, better places, to become reacquainted than the middle of a road, with traffic lights about to change.

"Hello again," he said, and then they were on opposite sides of the street, with traffic flowing between them; a metal river keeping them apart.

If it were a pass, it would have happened sooner. And wouldn't have happened here, with no chance of further conversation; unless one or other of them—unless both—waited until the lights changed again, and allowed passage across the road.

He rejoined her on the far pavement.

"Are you busy?"

He was. He wasn't. It didn't matter.

"We could have coffee."

They could. Anyway, he owed her a drink. And a good spy always pays his debts.

As they made their way to a café, Dominic found himself assessing how she looked in daylight: the eyes sadder than he remembered; the face more lined. The hair not naturally blonde. But a smile that showed she remembered him, and one which he now realised he had been carrying with him ever since that night. Any contact made is a memory filed. Even if that filing is a purely private matter.

And now might be a good time to remind you that we're in a church, and smoking is strictly forbidden.

Because Lamb was holding a cigarette, though Molly hadn't seen him reaching into a packet, or even a pocket. He hadn't lit it, but was making it dance between his fingers, as if hoping to mesmerise her, or possibly himself. The latter seemed likely at that moment, as his eyes were unlit too, reflecting whatever dark spaces filled him.

She sensed his objection without his having to voice it.

"We're all entitled to weave our own tapestries, Jackson. Don't you like a good backstory?"

"Depends whose it is." He looked down at his cigarette, then tucked it up his sleeve, or did something with it anyway: to all intents and purposes, it vanished. "Someone asked not long ago what happened to your legs. Should I have told him?"

Molly Doran wouldn't answer that. "Shall I continue?"

"Do we get a piss break?"

"It depends what you mean by 'we.' They don't have a disabled toilet."

"Well, I've disabled a few in my time," said Lamb. "I'll sort one out for you."

She wheeled back to allow him to exit the bench, and he got to his feet with none of the wheezing histrionics he'd occupied it with. The look he gave her as he passed would have caused a weaker soul to flinch, but even so it was mild, compared to what he was capable of. She watched as, instead of disappearing into the vestry to find a toilet, he went through the side door into the graveyard. To smoke, though he'd probably piss up against a tree while he was at it. The Lamb who'd been a spook in Berlin would have taken the opportunity to fade away: it wasn't dark yet, but Lamb had never needed much shadow to disappear in. But she knew he wouldn't, not now. Not because he'd want to know the end of the story—he knew how it ended—but because he'd want to match her ending against his own.

Though in the end it would all come down to peacock shit: different colours sprayed on the same grey facts.

THEIR AFFAIR BEGAN WITH that second meeting: the café might as well have been a hot-sheet motel, with the waiter bringing condoms along with coffee cups. And though it was weeks before they actually took each other to bed, at that same meeting they began to establish tradecraft, for affairs demand codebooks and secret practices. Dominic was that particular kind of bachelor, the kind you can't imagine being anything else, but Marta was married, even if her husband was such old news she might as well not have been. And this was Berlin, where it was axiomatic that, if you slept with someone, you were sleeping with the enemy; or, at the very least, with someone who had themselves slept with the enemy. So yes, tradecraft. They never met in the same place twice. Should they encounter someone familiar, Marta was from Dominic's old neighbourhood, bumped into by chance. Or Dominic was hoping for an apartment in Marta's building, and she was giving him the lowdown. Threadbare stuff, because it always is, and there's no amateur like a professional with his guard down. Dominic might as well have been walking round town bareheaded, which, for a spook, is as careless as it gets—a hat, in spook talk, is a whole identity. If Dominic Cross was wearing any hat that spring, it was one that identified him as a man in love.

He sublet a small apartment fifteen minutes from the office. There and back inside a lunch hour was doable. He plotted thirteen different routes between the two. He was more likely to be spotted as a spy when not being a spy than at any other time in his career, but what could he do? Her eyes were sadder than he remembered, the face more lined, the hair not naturally blonde. And the way she spoke, the way she called him *my Dominic*, all of it sunk a hook in his heart. He was haemorrhaging his savings, renting their lunchtime safe-house, but if they used his own apartment, it would all become official.

All encounters with civilians are to be logged and appended to the relevant personnel file.

They'd tear her life apart, looking for reasons why she was untouchable.

She had a child, of course. A five-year-old: Erich. This she told him on their third meeting, as if it had slipped her mind until that moment. He pictured a waddling cherub: Eros in lederhosen. Children did not come naturally to him. It was doomed from the start, obviously—he didn't have to be a spy to know that much—but still, he found himself imagining it wasn't.

Repeat encounters require follow-up.

The Shit asked him, "What's put a smile in your trousers?"

"Berlin in the spring," he said. "Always a joy."

"If you say so." Then, with a nod at the teleprinter, "They want you to resend the latest figures from Atticus. Seems they're not convinced."

They, in this instance, meant the Park—sometimes *they* were them, and sometimes *they* were us. And Atticus was an asset, an accounts officer at the second-largest machine-parts factory in the GDR, the output of which cast interesting light on agricultural requirements in the Eastern bloc. Or might do. One of the problems with information is that the useful and the useless can be snowflake-similar, and the ability to know the one from the other comes with hindsight, if at all. The intel Atticus provided, at risk to life and liberty, might be background chatter in the long run. But it all had to be processed, because it all had to be processed. That was written somewhere; maybe on the Wall, in pinks and blues.

Dominic had leave coming, after his quarterly debrief at Regent's Park, and it was an unwritten rule that it be spent well away from Berlin. He usually stopped in London; drinking too much, smoking too much, testing the patience of friends, and the wives of friends. "Something in the Foreign Office." It was a code that had brought him latitude in the past, but everything had its limit. Being thrown out of bars at two in the morning wasn't a good look after a certain age. More than that, he worried about Marta. Couldn't bear the thought of leaving her here, with all the temptations an unhappy homelife had to offer.

The husband was old news, but they still shared an apartment.

And she had a five-year-old, Erich . . .

She could easily fall back onto the straight and narrow, Dominic thought. He had lived all his adult life among people for whom lying was the simplest form of communication, and though she had told him she loved him, still, it was Berlin, and people told you what you wanted to hear. Usually in the full knowledge that all parties knew it was a temporary truth; built for the circumstances, and unlikely to survive the first wolf that came huffing and puffing. Was that what was happening here? He didn't want to think so.

Marta had told him—

"NO," SAID LAMB.

"Touching a nerve?"

"Yeah, my piles act up when a torrent of shit's on the way."

"That's so disappointing."

Lamb grunted. Or, if it was a word, it was buried under so much breath, he might have been huffing and puffing himself.

"Let's leave her be, then," said Molly. "But I picture him wondering what kind of life would have been awaiting him after Berlin. Whether he'd have ended up with an office job, maybe running one of the smaller desks. But he was a joe, not management material. He'd have been a disaster. Made everyone's life a misery. What do you think?"

"I think you're pushing your luck."

She laughed, a startlingly tinkly sound, something like angelic merriment.

SO DOMINIC WENT TO London, and had his debrief with David Cartwright at the Park. It was the usual slow-burn affair:

two days in a windowless office, with the same questions delivered in the same friendly but unyielding tone; the constant probing for information he might have but was unaware of; for weaknesses he was aware of, but didn't want to share. For signs that he was going native.

"You must be about ready to come home."

"I am home."

"For good, I mean."

For once an error had sailed past David Cartwright. He'd meant he was at home in Berlin.

"I've a year or two in me yet."

Cartwright had delivered one of those piercing gazes of which he seemed so proud: *I can read your small print*, it seemed to say. Dominic wondered how often it had resulted in impromptu confessions; in ghosts being given up before the haunting was confirmed. "If you say so," he said, contriving to make the phrase sound like its exact opposite. Then glanced at the papers in front of him. "I'd like to talk about Atticus. How do you think he is?"

"Well enough. In the circumstances."

These being that he was betraying his own country to a foreign power, and would face imprisonment, probably death, if this came to light. Balanced against which, he had been promised life everlasting, eventually: a new home, a new job, a lump sum, a different horizon. Though, as was ever the way with such new starts, this always seemed to be receding into the distance. Atticus had been asking for an escape route for more than a year. Dominic had been explaining the difficulties involved, their imminent solution, for precisely as long.

"Are you confident his product is still sound?"

"It's facts and figures, David. I can't answer for their useful-ness. I'm not an analyst."

"The last two reports, they've been wildly out of kilter with the previous few months."

"So things are changing. Isn't that what we're supposed to be on the alert for?"

"Some of our chaps, they're wondering whether we're being fed inaccurate data."

"You think he's been compromised?"

"I don't know, Dominic. What do you think?"

"I think he's been risking his life for little reward. I think he deserves our trust."

"It's important that we remain clear-eyed. Obviously, we want to do our best by Atticus. But if he's been blown, he's already beyond our help. And attempting to assist him fur-ther would be to put ourselves—to put you—at considerable risk."

David Cartwright had leaned across the table, as if to dem-onstrate their togetherness on this issue.

"And it's not as if he's high-value. I mean, all intel matters, I don't mean to suggest otherwise. But he's one small segment of a big jigsaw. We can work out what the landscape looks like with his part missing."

Dominic said, "Are you telling me to cut him adrift?"

"Of course not. But let's treat his product with caution. If they're using him to feed us sawdust, let's not put it in our loaves." He sat back. "Trust is our currency. Of course it is. But we have to know when to cash in."

There were other assets, other issues. Two days was a long time.

Dominic spent the tea breaks thinking about Marta, and counting minutes.

SOMEWHERE OUT IN HAMPSTEAD'S wilds, a bell was ringing. Perhaps a local school, releasing its charges for the day. There were always bells somewhere. This was London.

Lamb, well-practised at sleeping through alarms, paid it no attention. His eyes were closed; his mouth slightly not. But he wasn't still, or not as still as he was capable of. Every so often something rippled through his frame: a digestive rumble perhaps, though if so, an uncharacteristically silent one. It was as if his whole body were frowning.

"I'm not sending you to sleep, am I?" Molly asked.

"No," he replied at length. "You're keeping me awake."

"It's your fidgeting doing that. I never had you down for the fidgety type. Memories stirring?"

Lamb opened his eyes, and yawned. "Might be crabs. Christ knows who sat here before me." He stood, suddenly, and his head broached the shaft of light falling from a window. Jackson Lamb, enhaloed. An unexpected sight. "Am I supposed to believe you've read transcripts?"

"The debriefing's on record. And I'm an archivist, remember?"

"'He spent the tea breaks thinking about Marta, and counting minutes,'" Lamb quoted. "Funny fucking records someone's keeping."

"I fill in gaps. It's what I do."

"These aren't gaps. They're canyons."

"What are you worried about? That I'll get things wrong? Or get them right?"

"It was all years ago," said Lamb.

"That's not an answer."

It was the best she was getting. After turning for a moment to face the light, Lamb sunk onto the bench again. His gaze was fixed on the altar, but Molly was pretty sure he wasn't seeing it.

"I think," she said, "that it was immediately after he returned to Berlin that Dominic was approached by an agent of state security."

GDR STATE SECURITY, THAT is.

Marta was rarely available in the evenings, and Dominic, on those nights when he wasn't working, often found himself drifting through the city, joining its dots. Most of these were clubs and bars, but the streets held fascination too. Amidst the larger sectors carved out by politics and history, Dominic had his own areas determined by appetite and inclination. He was far from alone in this. Students, young people, often huddled near the Wall, sitting round fires, smoking, drinking, making music, while being studied overhead by watchful soldiers, their rifles unslung from their shoulders, as if the youth might be planning an assault. There were few things most students looked less capable of. On the other hand, Dominic thought, if anything were to shift that barrier, it would be the will and cooperation of the young, not the machinations of their elders. If politics was the art of banging your head against a wall, in Berlin it had found its apotheosis. As such, it seemed unlikely to provide solutions.

But that was no surprise. After years in a divided city, he had long ceased to expect it would ever be anything but. Even if the Wall were to disappear overnight, its stones picked apart by the youngsters who'd grown up in its shadow, where would that leave everyone? Berlin was a city twinned with itself: it had two zoos, two operas, two everything. Even if it healed, its divisions would remain; it would be a pair of mirrored images, neither side trusting the other. No wonder it was a habitat for spooks. Thoughts like this propelled him on his wanderings, and he found himself drawn, as so often before, to the water-tower, a halfway point between two of his usual bars, and a place to sit for a smoke, or have a piss in the bushes, which is what he was doing when he found he wasn't alone.

"I hear you've been keeping company with my dear friend Marta."

Dominic braced himself for a punch in the kidneys, which didn't come, so he finished what he was doing, zipped himself away, then turned.

"I think you must have me mistaken for someone else."

"In that case, I apologise. It must be a different Dominic Cross I took you for."

That the stranger was a thug was no surprise; that he was a civilised thug was less expected. He wore a soft brown raincoat to match his soft brown shoes, and Dominic knew he could peel layer after layer from this man, and everything he found would be soft and brown, right to the steel black core. For one brief moment he considered throwing a punch, just to short-circuit whatever was about to happen, but it wouldn't help in the long run. Not that violence couldn't be a solution, but it was best to have the problem laid out in full beforehand, in case he was asked to show his working.

"What do you want?"

"I think a beer would suit the purpose. Over there, perhaps?"

A lit corner of the nearby square.

"They serve a reasonable Guinness. That's your drink, am I right? In this part of town?"

There might have been a soft brown space in the air behind him as he walked away.

Dominic followed. He didn't see what else he could do. There were tables outside the bar, though the night was cool and curtained with damp, and it was here that his new friend chose to sit. He was lighting a cigarette when Dominic caught up, and a waiter was already asking if the gentlemen wouldn't prefer to be inside, and quickly understanding that the gentlemen wished only to be served their drinks, and then left well alone. Two beers arrived shortly afterwards. By then both men were smoking, and from a distance might have been taken for old acquaintances, comfortable in each other's company, and finding no need to talk.

An old woman walked past tugging a dog on a string, as if it were a reluctant kite.

The man spoke at last, continuing an interrupted conversation. "She is a citizen of the Democratic Republic."

Choosing to misunderstand would have been a waste of time and breath.

"She's a West German," Dominic said.

"Oh, is that what she told you?"

He sounded genuinely curious.

Dominic didn't reply. He had never asked, it occurred to him. Marta was here, in the West; of course she belonged. For her to be otherwise would have cast their reality in doubt.

The stranger was watching him through their joint veil of cigarette smoke. Like his overcoat, like his shoes, his eyes were soft and brown. The colour was probably his by birth, but the softness was a disguise he'd donned since. He said, "She was granted exit papers nearly twenty years ago, to visit an elderly grandmother who had the misfortune to be stranded on your side of the anti-fascist barrier. And she never returned after the grandmother's death."

He might have been remarking on the dampness in the air; how, for all its lack of bite, you could still catch your death if you lingered too long.

Dominic said, "She's lived here for years. Her papers are perfectly in order."

"I'm sure that's true."

"And it's not like they'll send her back."

His new friend was nodding: this also was true. They could hardly be more in agreement. "And yet, if she were to stray across the border by accident . . ."

"Nobody crosses the border by accident."

"But you know what they say. There is a first time for everything."

The old woman and her dog were long gone.

"What do you want?"

"I want you to know that we have your best interests at heart, Dominic. That there are many of us who wish to see a happy ending for you, and for your Marta. And we would be so unhappy were anything to come between you."

He flicked his cigarette in the direction of the Wall, and left Dominic with an unfinished beer.

THIS TIME, THERE WAS no doubt. It was a pass. But the moment for confession had gone: if Dominic bared his soul now, there was only one possible outcome. He'd be on the next flight home. What happened to Marta afterwards, he might never know. Perhaps nothing. If he was out of the picture, Soft Brown Raincoat might heave a soft brown sigh and move on, leave Marta untouched. But Dominic didn't think so. The morning after their encounter, he'd gone through their files on Stasi agents: Soft Brown Raincoat was one Helmut Stagge, whose paperwork was marked with a satanic squiggle, a line drawing of a horned devil whose meaning didn't require a footnote.

That lunchtime, Marta didn't turn up. He spent an hour pacing the bare floorboards of the flat, pulsing at every squeak; called her eventually, from a café four streets away.

"Erich isn't well. What could I do? I couldn't phone you. Not at work."

An unshakable rule, except in absolute emergency. Which this was, though she didn't know that.

"There's a man I met last night, he says he knows you."

"What's his name?"

"I can't remember. He has brown eyes? A brown coat?"

She laughed. "These are not distinguished features."

"Distinguishing."

She had to end the call; Erich, she said, was wailing again.

Blackmail was a favourite weapon—he'd used it himself, many times. You didn't always recruit an asset by showering them with kindness, or appealing to principle or greed. So by the time Stagge showed up again, two days later, Dominic had grown weary of expecting him. He knew that sometimes a joe was happy to be caught, or if not happy, at least aware that a weight had been lifted. Part of that was guilt, but mostly it was the relief of not having to wait any longer; of knowing that, whatever it was you feared, it had arrived, and now you would discover how well you might face it.

"It's simple enough," Stagge told him. They were on adjacent tables outside a café, and the recent glum weather had subsided at last: spring was here, and graffiti had bloomed fresh and new in the sunshine. Stagge had appeared as suddenly as birdsong a few minutes after Dominic had chosen this spot to nurse his hangover. Across the square a group of mime artists had set up shop, and were acting out agony or unspeakable happiness. It was hard to tell. As far as mimes went, Stagge was the better. He was enjoying a pastry with his coffee, and to the casual observer was ignoring Dominic and reading a newspaper.

"Whatever it is, I'm not doing it."

"Then I hope you've made your goodbyes. We'll be glad to see the prodigal return." The newspaper rustled in his hands. "Her son, though, his place is with his father. He'll be staying here."

This was delivered as fact, like a builder with an estimate. *This will be made to happen. I have all the tools at my disposal.*

Dominic's hand shook as he raised his cup to his lips. Experience with hangovers accustomed you to them, but didn't lessen their effect. He knew that Stagge could fulfil his threat. The very fact that he wandered at will through West Berlin would have indicated his status, even if Dominic hadn't been through his file. That satanic squiggle some Stasi-watcher had doodled: it might have been a comic flourish, but it wasn't a joke. So yes, Stagge could do as he threatened, and in the end it would just be another Berlin story: one that got away turned out not to have done so after all. Nobody strayed across the border by accident. But it was possible to end up in the boot of the wrong car, and wake up in your own past.

He wasn't aware of having spoken the words. Maybe he had picked up a trick from the mime group, and whatever expression was plastered across his face had done the work for him.

"A token of goodwill, that's all. You give me one of yours. I let you keep one of mine."

"She isn't yours."

"But she can be. You're not in a position to protect her, are you? A secret flat? Really?" Stagge bit into his pastry with care. A few, not many, crumbs fell free. "If your Service knew you were having an affair with a local, you wouldn't be going to such lengths. But then, that's the trouble with spying, isn't it?" His tone sounded almost kind. "It becomes an addiction. All this secrecy."

"I have nothing to offer you."

"I'm not looking for the crown jewels. A name. There must be many to choose from. One name, that's all. Anyone you like. You give me something I can take home to my masters, and your mistress can stay here with you." He smiled at his newsprint, proud of his wordplay.

"I see you again, I'll bring you in," Dominic said. The threat was for his own sake, they both knew that. Berlin Desk would have a stroke if he did any such thing, and besides, Stagge could cut him off at the knees without dropping what was left of his pastry.

"That watertower you're fond of," Stagge remarked to his paper. "There's a loose section of brick round the back."

"I'm not interested."

"One name," he said. "Is it really so much to ask? One name. Twenty-four hours."

Dominic watched as he strode off across the square, pausing only to drop a coin or two into the mimes' hat as he passed.

THE BELLS HAD CEASED, and nothing now disturbed the sanctified air, unless it was the aroma of stale cigarettes unleashed by Lamb's restless movements, or the whisky-tinted breath he expelled in a soft belch as it became apparent that Molly had come to an end, of sorts.

At last he said, "Mimes?"

"I told you. I fill in gaps."

"And that's what you brought me here for? To let me know you'd uncovered this little episode from the past?"

"Your past."

Molly reversed her wheelchair, and came to rest by the same stretch of wall she'd been looking at when he joined her. Lamb, for his part, stood again, and stretched loudly. A cigarette had appeared behind his ear. It was possible, she thought, that they grew there, like fungi. She was surprised, truth to tell, that he'd suffered in more or less silence this long: it would have been in character for him to leave as soon as her subject became clear. But he owed her, as he'd said. And spooks pay their debts, or the best of them do.

They both knew the ending of her story, of course, but she suspected the endings they knew were different.

She said, "So tell me what happened next."

"You know what happened next."

He sounded bored.

"I know what happened officially."

"Ought to be enough. That's your job, isn't it? Keeping the truth and the bullshit separate." He collected the cigarette from his ear and inserted it in his mouth. "But you seem to be treading a lot of bullshit around today."

"Atticus was for the chop," Molly said. "David Cartwright had made that clear. And maybe he'd already been compromised, but even so, he was still in play, and offering him to Stagge would have been a show of good faith. Enough to buy a little time."

Lamb said, "Stagge wouldn't have accepted a name he already had. And either way, he'd have wanted another one two days later. When a shark tastes your toe, he comes back for the rest." He moved the cigarette back to his ear. "But here's me, preaching to the legless."

"So he did nothing. He called Stagge's bluff. Remind me, how did that turn out?"

Lamb shrugged. "About how you'd expect."

"Marta disappeared."

He said nothing.

"Well, I say disappeared, but we both know where she went. They took her over the Wall. That must have been . . . difficult."

Lamb said, "No, they were pretty good at that. Ambulances were popular." He made a gentle swipe at the air, demonstrating a swift passage through all obstacles. "Unconscious patients don't fuss much at the border."

"Not what I meant. Do you think she was a plant?"

"I don't much care. It was a long time ago."

"There's a lot of stuff you don't care about, but the difference between a joe and a civilian was never one of them."

Lamb didn't answer for a while. At length he said, "I thought she might have been at the time. But it turned out there really was a kid, and he stayed behind when she left. So no, I don't think she was a plant. I think she was who she said she was. Just a woman called Marta."

"What about Atticus?"

"He was compromised, like Cartwright said. They fed us fake figures a little longer, but their heart wasn't in it. They knew we knew they had him. He went off air a month later. There was a report of a firing squad. We assumed that was him."

Molly patted the armrest of her chair. "So nobody got to live happily ever after."

"Imagine my surprise."

"Maybe a swap would have been a better outcome. Atticus for Marta."

Lamb said, "Sharks, toes. Remember?"

"So, then. No regrets?"

"What do you expect me to say? That I'd have done it differently now?"

She said, "That's what I thought."

He paused, then said, "Oh, Christ. That was a schooltwat's error, wasn't it?"

"I was already sure it was you," she said. "Not Dominic."

"No," he said. "It wasn't Dominic. Dominic gave up Atticus. I was the one took him back."

"No wonder he called you The Shit," Molly said.

"I SAVED HIM," LAMB said at last. "Even if he wouldn't have seen it that way."

"From what, exactly?"

"From leaving a name in a dead letter drop behind a loose brick in a watertower." He lit his cigarette in a brief, almost invisible gesture. Smoke pretended to be incense for a while, weaving in and out of coloured light. "From sacrificing an asset."

"So you waited till he used the drop, then removed the letter before it was collected. How long had you been following him?"

"Months, on and off. He was clearly hiding something. And I was his mirror-man, so I was the one he was hiding it from. That never lasts." He sat down. "So I knew about the apartment, I knew about Marta. I knew it was only a matter of time before someone put the screws to him. It didn't matter whether Marta was a plant or not. Bait doesn't have to know it's bait."

"But you didn't throw him to the wolves. *Our* wolves."

"He didn't like me. I didn't like him. But he was a joe. He'd earned the benefit. And Atticus was one of ours."

"Atticus was already lost."

"Doesn't matter. You never pull the plug. How did you know about Stagge, anyway?"

"His report turned up in a Stasi file we bagged in the nineties. He had it down as a failed attempt to turn a British agent." She smiled a sour sort of smile. "He thought Dominic had chosen duty over love."

"Like I said," said Lamb. "Barbara fucking Cartland."

Molly said, "Did Dominic discover what you'd done?"

Lamb shrugged.

"When Marta disappeared, he gave up, didn't he?" Molly said. "Came back to Blighty and drank himself to death inside a year."

"In a manner of speaking," Lamb said. "Hanging himself helped, mind."

"He was drunk at the time," said Molly. "And at least he got a plaque." She nodded towards the name at her eye level: Digby Palmer, which was who Dominic Cross was once he ran out of names. A pair of dates was his only epitaph. "I'm glad it wasn't him who sold Marta out."

"No. He sold Atticus instead."

"He wasn't in love with Atticus."

"What the fuck's that got to do with it?"

Molly silently allowed that this had no answer that Jackson Lamb might accept.

While he rammed his hands into his raincoat pockets and stood, all in the same huge motion, putting her in mind of a bin lorry performing one of those complicated hoisting operations which always threaten to leave spillage everywhere, she reached out and traced Digby Palmer's engraved name with her right index finger, feeling the shape of each letter unfold under her touch. She meant what she had said: she was glad that he had intended to sacrifice one of his agents for the woman he'd loved; but equally and inconsistently glad that this intention had been thwarted by Lamb. Mostly glad, though, that she could stop wondering where the truth lay. And it occurred to her to ask whether Lamb had ever met Marta, and if so whether he understood his poor mirror-man's fascination with her, but by the time her finger finished tracing the last dead letter of Digby Palmer's name, Lamb had gone.

THE USUAL SANTAS

Whiteoaks, the brochures explained, was more than a shopping center: it was a Day Out For The Whole Family; a Complete Retail Experience Under Just One Roof. It was an Ideally Situated Outlet-Village—an Ultra-Convenient Complex For The Ultra-Modern Consumer. It was where Quality met Design to form an Affordable Union. It might have been a Stately Pleasure Dome. It was possibly a Garden Of Earthly Delight. It was almost certainly where Capital Letters went to Die.

More precisely, it was on the outskirts of one of London's northwest satellite towns, and, viewed from above, resembled a glass and steel rendering of a giant octopus dropped headfirst onto the landscape. In the gaps between its outstretched tentacles are parks and play areas and public conveniences, and at each of its two main entrances were garages offering, in addition to the usual services, full valet coverage, 4-wheel alignment and diagnostic analysis, as well as free air and a Last-Minute One-Stop Shop. Cart stations—colored pennants hoisted above them for swift location—were positioned at those intervals market research had determined user-friendly, and were assiduously tended by liveried cart-jockeys. From ten minutes before dusk until ten after daybreak the area was bathed in gentle orange light, the quiet humming of CCTV cameras a constant reminder that your security was Whiteoaks' concern. And in a hedged-off corner between the center's electricity substation and one of four home-delivery loading bays—perhaps the only point in the complex to which the word "accessible" did not apply—lurked a furtive row of recycling bins, like a consumerist *memento mori*.

As for the interior, it was a contemporary cathedral, sacred to the pursuit of retail opportunity. There was a food mall, a clothing avenue, an entertainment hall; there were wings dedicated to white goods ("all your domestic requirements satisfied!"), pampering ("full-body tan in minutes!") and financial services ("consolidate your debts—ask us how!"). There was a boulevard of sporting goods, a bridleway of gardening supplies; a veritable Hatton Garden of jewelers. No franchise ever heard of went unrepresented, and several never before encountered had multiple outlets. Whiteoaks' delicatessens carried sweetmeats from as near as Abbotsbury and as far as Żywocice; its bookshops shelved volumes by every author its readers could imagine, from Bill Bryson to Jeremy Clarkson. The shopper who is tired of Whiteoaks, it might easily be asserted, is a shopper who is tired of credit. During the summer, light washed down from the recessed contours of its cantilevered ceilings, and during the winter it did exactly the same. Temperature, too, was regulated and constant, and in this it matched everything else. At Whiteoaks, you could buy raspberries in winter and tinsel in July. Seasonal variation was discouraged as an unnecessary brake on impulse purchasing.

Which was not to say that Whiteoaks ignored the passage of the year; rather, it measured the months in a manner appropriate to its customers' needs. As surely as Father's Day follows Mother's, as unalterably as Harry Potter gives way to the Great Pumpkin, time marches on; its inevitable progress registering as peaks and troughs in a never-ending flow chart.

For there are only seventeen Major Feasts in the calendar of the Complete Retail Experience.

And the greatest of these is Christmas.

AT WHITEOAKS CHRISTMAS SLIPPED in slowly, subliminally, with the faint rustle of a paperchain in early September, and the echo of a jingle bell as October turned. Showing almost saintly restraint, however, it did not unleash its reindeer until Halloween had been wholly remaindered. After that, it was open season. Taking full advantage of its layout, the complex boasted eight Santa's Grottos—one per tentacle—each employing a full complement of sleigh, sacks, elves, snowflakes, friendly squirrels, startled rabbits, and (counterintuitively, but fully validated by merchandise-profiling) talking zebras. And, of course, each had its own Santa. Or, more accurately, each had an equal share in a rotating pool of Santas, for the eight Santas hired annually by the Whiteoaks Festive Governance Committee had swiftly worked out that no single one of them wanted to spend an entire two-month hitch marooned in Haberdashery's backwater, or worse still, abandoned under fire in the high-pressure, noise-intensive combat zone of Toys and Games, while another took his ease in the Food Hall, pampered with cake and cappuccino by the surrounding franchisees. So a complicated but workable shift system had been established by the Santas themselves, whereby they chopped and changed each two-hour session, swapping grottos three times a day and generally sharing the burden along with the spoils. This worked so well, so much to everyone's satisfaction, that the first eight Santas hired by the Governance Committee remained the only Santas Whiteoaks needed, returning year after year to don their uniforms, attach their beards, and maintain an impressive 83-percent record of hardly ever swearing at children whose parents were in earshot.

Santa-ing was not an easy undertaking. It was not a task for sissies. And while the Usual Santas didn't always do things by the book, by God, they got the job done!

And each year, once they'd managed just that—after the shops had lowered shutters on Christmas Eve, and Whiteoaks slumbered, preparatory to the Boxing Day rush—the Santas met in a hospitality room adjoining the security suite, and relaxed over a buffet provided by the grateful merchants of the quarter, and exchanged war stories until the hour grew late, and generally luxuriated in the absence of children.

But however relaxed they grew, they kept their beards on. And remained zipped inside their red suits. And never addressed each other as anything other than "Santa"; and in fact, would have been unable to do so had they wanted, because while they might, for all they knew, be friends and neighbours in civvy street—might drink in the same pub, or regularly catch the same bus to the same football ground—on duty they remained in uniformed character, and always had done. This had started in jest but had quickly hardened into custom. Not long after that, it calcified into superstition. In their dealings with toddlers and hyperactive infants, the Usual Santas had suffered in undignified, frequently unhygienic ways that had bonded them in a manner few civilians could hope to understand, but on every other level they were strangers to each other. And with this, they were perfectly comfortable.

Until, one day . . .

THE BUFFET THAT YEAR was particularly handsome. There were sausage rolls and bowls of crisps; there were slices of ham and fingers of fish; there were rice salads, and things on cocktail sticks, and mince pies, and individual plum puddings. There was a huge plateful of turkey-and-stuffing sandwiches. There were Christmas pizzas: deep and crisp and even more cheesy. There were eight paper plates, and eight plastic knives and forks. There were eight red napkins, with jolly Rudolph patterns. And, most crucially of all, there were several large bottles of brandy, and eight glass snifters.

The Santas turned up one by one. Whiteoaks had emptied of punters, but still: it would never do for two Santas to be seen together in public.

The first to arrive poured himself a brandy, downed it in a single swallow, poured another, then helped himself to a turkey sandwich. "Ho, ho, ho!" he said as the door opened behind him.

"Ho, ho, ho! Indeed," the incoming Santa agreed. He too headed straight for the brandy. "What a day," he said. "What. A. Day."

"Christmas Eve."

They both nodded. The words carried a weight a non-Santa couldn't hope to understand.

"You know what happened to me? I was—"

"Ho, ho, ho!"

"Ho, ho, ho!" they both replied as another Santa entered.

Whatever had happened to Santa became lost in a general flurry of opening doors and greetings and fillings of glasses. Joe, the security guard, popped his head in too. He wouldn't stop for a drink.

"Let yourselves out through the emergency exit, yes? I'll leave you the master so the alarm doesn't go off. Just pop it through the box when you're done."

"Of course," said Santa. He put the key on the table. "Merry Christmas, Joe."

"Merry Christmas, Santas. Mind how you go with that brandy."

"Ho, ho, ho!"

Joe left.

And Santa arrived. "Ho, ho, ho!" he said.

"Ho, ho, ho!"

"Blimey. Christmas Eve, eh?"

Christmas Eve, they agreed.

Soon the room was full of Santas, bundled round the buffet table; each with glass or plate in hand, and most of them talking at once.

"Blinking cheek of him! Sitting on my knee, bold as brass, says if you're the real Santa, how come your reindeer's plastic?"

"So I said, you know like on *Doctor Who*? You know like his TARDIS? Bigger on the inside? So's my sleigh. And *that's* how come it fits all the presents in."

"I don't have a glass."

"I told her, 'course you don't need a chimney, darlin'. I carry a magic chimney with me. Pop it on your roof, Bob's your uncle. That dried her tears, I can tell you. You can borrow that line, if you like. No charge for a fellow Santa!"

"I don't have a glass."

"The next flamin' elf who tries to tell me Santa's suit should really be green, I'll—"

"Excuse me," said Santa in a loud voice. "But I don't have a glass!"

The Santas' chatter died away.

"Well, someone must have two," said Santa, jovially. "There were eight when we started."

"Nobody's got two," Santa said. "That's the point."

"What's the point?"

"There aren't eight of us here," Santa said. "There are nine."

There was a communal intake of yuletide breath.

"Ha!" said Santa. "I mean, ho! You must have added up wrong."

"I don't think so. You try."

The Santas fell to counting.

Then all started talking at once.

"But—?"

"What—?"

"I—?"

"Ho—!"

At length, Santa quietened the assembly by tapping his glass on the table. "Well," he said. "It seems I owe Santa an apology. One of us appears to be an imposter."

"Pretending to be Santa!" Santa said angrily. "I never heard of such a thing in my life!"

The Santas looked at him.

"Well, you know what I mean."

"Perhaps," Santa said, "we should have a quick roll call."

"What, where you call out 'Santa' and we say 'Present'?" Santa asked. "Did you see what I did there?" he added.

"That's not what I meant, no," Santa said. "I meant, we should all state clearly where we were today. The imposter Santa will have an impossible itinerary."

"Sounds like a plan," Santa admitted. "Who's going first?"

"Well, I was at the food hall this morning," Santa said. "Then electronics. No, then leisure. After that I was at—"

"You can't have been at electronics next," Santa objected. "I was electronics, second shift."

"No, that's what I said," said Santa. "Then leisure, then—"

"I finished up at leisure," Santa said. "Before that, I was at clothing, and before that books. Or was that yesterday?"

"Must have been today," Santa offered through a mouthful of sausage roll. "Because that's what *I* did yesterday."

"Oh, this is hopeless," said Santa. "Could we all just stop milling about?"

"If we all stop *milling about*," Santa said, "the Santas nearest the table will eat all the food."

There was general assent to this. Some of the more suspicious Santas immediately reloaded their plates.

"We need order," Santa said. "We need clarity. Everyone should write down their day's shifts."

"That's right," Santa said, reaching past him for a sandwich. "We should make a list."

"We should check it twice," Santa muttered.

"I heard that."

"Does anyone have a pen and paper?" Santa asked.

Nobody had a pen and paper.

"There's an elf behind this," said Santa. "Mark my words."

The elves were not popular with the Santas. They tended to be disruptive, and argumentative, and frequently indulged in non-traditional banter.

Santa said, "Why don't we take our suits off? See who we really are?"

"Which would help how?" Santa enquired testily.

"I was only saying," Santa mumbled into his beard.

"No, Santa has a point," Santa said. "We'd soon find out if we had an elf among us, if we took our suits off."

"Nobody is taking their suit off," Santa said sternly. "It would be—well, it wouldn't be right!"

"Hmm," Santa said. "That's *exactly* what an elf would say, if he was about to be unmasked."

"I hope you're not suggesting what I think you're suggesting," warned Santa.

"Everyone calm down," Santa said. "It's clear none of us is an elf. We're all far too shapely."

"Quite," Santa agreed. "Anyway, the elves are at their own party. They've gone clubbing."

The Santas shuddered.

"I don't suppose it would do any good to ask the imposter to put his hand up?" Santa suggested. "On an amnesty basis? He's welcome to stay and enjoy the buffet."

"Do you mean that?" Santa asked. "Or do you really think we should beat him up?"

Santa sighed. "Well, he's hardly likely to put his hand up now, is he?"

"Oh," said Santa. "Yes. Yes, I see what you mean. I shouldn't have said that, should I?"

Everyone helped themselves to more food and brandy. The Santa without a glass was making do with a hastily scraped-out trifle dish, though—as he pointed out several times—being last to arrive did not make him the imposter; on the contrary, the fact that he'd had farthest to come—all the way from Gardening—*proved* he was the genuine article, as well as indicating high career-commitment. Since his bowl held three times as much as a glass, and he was emptying it twice as quickly, the other Santas agreed with him, then sat him down in a chair.

"Well," Santa said at last. "Anyone got any ideas?"

Santas hummed and Santas hah-ed.

At length, a Santa spoke. "Suppose . . ."

A hush dropped over the assembly like a cloth on a budgie's cage.

"Yes?" Santa prompted.

"Suppose . . ." said Santa. "Well, suppose this imposter is the *real* Santa?"

A subtly different silence fell.

"Twit," said Santa, *sotto voce.*

"I heard that."

"There's no such thing as Santa," Santa pointed out.

"I can count nine of us."

"A real Santa, Santa meant."

"Who's to say—"

"Don't!" Santa interrupted. "*Don't* say, who's to say what's real and what isn't! Because I hate that sort of nonsense!"

"I was only going to say," Santa continued, "that in order to be the real Santa, our friend would simply need to *believe* that he's the real Santa."

The Santas considered this.

"That's pretty much what Santa told you not to say," Santa said at last.

"No, it's a different thing entirely."

"And anyway," Santa began.

"Anyway what?"

"If there *is* a real Santa—"

"Big if!"

"—or even just someone who *believes* he's the real Santa—"

"Which would make him a bloomin' loony," Santa muttered.

"—then why on earth would he come to Whiteoaks?"

The Santas considered this.

"Why wouldn't he?" Santa asked.

"Because it's a disgusting, crass, horrible place," Santa said. "That's why not!"

The Santas recoiled in horror.

"There!" said Santa. "I've said it!"

"Shh!"

"Quiet!"

"Don't!"

One by one, the Santas looked towards the door to the adjoining security room, where banks of closed-circuit monitors hummed; and where, just possibly, subversive and treasonous opinion was being recorded for later investigation.

"It's all right," Santa said. "We're the last ones here."

The Santas relaxed.

"And besides, it's true."

A delicious guilty knowledge susurrated through the Santas, like a winter's wind adjusting a snowdrift.

"We-ell . . ."

"Well, yes."

"Well, yes, it is."

The Santas nodded, one after the other. It was true. Whiteoaks *was* horrible, unless you liked autonomous commercialism writ huge, in which any suspicion of non-franchised individuality was stamped on before it made waves. The trouble was, the Santas had few alternatives as far as employment went. The local shops they'd once Santa-ed for had closed when Whiteoaks opened.

"But don't you see?" Santa said. "That's precisely why he'd come here!"

Santa said, "How do you mean?"

"Why would Santa bother visiting, I don't know, an orphanage or a children's hospital or a home for waifs and strays," Santa asked, "when the whole *point* of Santa is that he goes where he's needed?"

"Like Whiteoaks? Ha!"

"Ho!"

"I meant ho!"

"Exactly like Whiteoaks," Santa insisted obstinately. "Look at it. It's a soulless temple to rampant commercialism. It wouldn't know the meaning of Christmas if it came with a buy-one, get-one-free sticker. It's crying out for Santa, for criminy's sake!"

"But it has eight Santas," Santa said. "It has us. The Usual Santas."

A pleading note had crept into his voice.

"But it doesn't have the *real* Santa," Santa said quietly. "A Santa to teach it that profit isn't everything."

"That money doesn't matter."

"That it's better to give than to receive."

"That items can't be returned without a receipt."

The Santas stared.

"Sorry," Santa said. "I was thinking about something else."

The Santas fell silent.

Santa picked the last unempty bottle from the table, and passed it round the company. One after the other, the Santas solemnly filled their glasses; by a long-practiced choreography, each pouring an exact amount (except for Santa, who poured exactly three times that amount) which precisely drained the bottle to its last drop. Then each eyed the other morosely.

"If I have to wish one more kiddy a Merry Whiteoaks Christmas—" Santa began.

"—or remind one more parent where to go for all their yuletide needs—" Santa continued.

"—or explain one more time that Santa's gifts are for children with store-validated tokens only—" Santa embellished.

"—I don't know what I'll do," Santa admitted.

Though all agreed that it might involve punching an elf.

Santa by Santa, they raised their glasses; Santa by Santa, they drained them dry. Then, simultaneously, they plonked them down on the table, forming a neat row of eight brandy snifters and a small trifle dish.

"Well," Santa said. "Do I need to spell out our next move?"

"I think we're of one mind," said Santa.

"All for one?" asked Santa.

"And one for all," Santa replied.

"A Santa's gotta do—" said Santa.

"—what a Santa's gotta do," Santa agreed.

"It's a far far better thing—" Santag began.

". . . I can never remember the end of that quote," said Santa, after a slight pause.

"Gentlemen," said Santa. "To the grottos!"

WHAT BECAME KNOWN AS the Great Whiteoaks Christmas Looting was never solved—whoever coordinated the daredevil heist had somehow contrived to get hold of a master key, which not only gave access to every shop on every floor of every avenue of the complex, but also allowed every alarm and CCTV monitor to be switched off. Nor, given the tendency of store managers to estimate losses upwards for insurance purposes, was it clear exactly how much was stolen. Police investigations did suggest, however, that some very big sacks must have been used.

And nor was there any obvious connection between the daring robbery and the appearance, on Christmas morning, of some very big sacks on the doorsteps of the surprisingly large number of children's hospitals, orphanages and homes for waifs and strays to be found in the surrounding countryside. The sacks contained toys and games, and books and clothes, and food and drink, and sporting goods, and any number of DVDs and mobile phones and Wii consoles, and some little sewing kits, and various beauty products, and brochures containing useful information about how to consolidate debt, liquidate assets and set up a trust fund, and the odd item of gardening equipment, and some small brown muslin bags which proved to be full of not-quite-priceless but certainly very expensive jewelry. This, the governors, directors and head nurses of the various establishments concerned swiftly liquidated into cash which they then used to set up trust funds, to ensure that all their charges' future Christmases would be celebrated in an appropriately festive manner. And also to give themselves a small raise, because it was valuable and underappreciated work that they did.

Back at Whiteoaks, the only thing approaching a clue that was ever discovered came to light some weeks later, when a truck arrived to collect a recycling bin that was stuffed full of Valentine's Day cards. As it was moved, a large red and white bundle rolled into view. This turned out, on closer inspection, to be made up of nine Santa suits and nine Santa hats.

And eight false bushy white beards.

WHAT WE DO

She said, "Not sure why I'm here, really."

Venetian blinds adorned the windows, and afternoon daylight slotted through them, painting onto the opposite wall horizontal shadows that looked oddly solid. They seemed to take up space, like shelves. Given time, you might try placing other solid objects upon them: cups and saucers, books.

She said it again. "Not really sure why I'm here."

"That's not uncommon."

"Thanks."

There was no reply.

"For making me feel special."

"You do that a lot."

"Do what a lot?"

"Hide behind humour."

"Thanks again."

There was no reply.

"No, seriously. Not everybody finds me funny."

The only response to this was a note scribbled on a pad.

The session would last fifty minutes, and it made no difference if she sat and said nothing: the fee would be the same.

That was the first of the ground rules Neil Soltano had laid down, the second being that the session would finish fifty minutes after its scheduled start time even if she arrived late. And that the fee, in such circumstances, would remain the same.

"It's important you remember," he'd explained, "that in this room, you can say anything at all. I won't judge you, won't be shocked. And a big part of the reason for that is that I'm not your friend, I'm your therapist. It's a professional relationship, so it needs a clearly understood framework."

Spelling that phrase out so carefully, he might have been worried she'd never encountered the notion before.

Zoë looked around again. The room, she thought, was somehow self-possessed. Everything here had weight, Soltano included—if he wasn't exactly heavy, he was hovering on that borderline where the paunched become padded. He wore a goatee, as if in deference to an unwritten rule of his profession, and his hair, receding at the brow, was long enough to warrant a short ponytail. His clothes were casual: chinos, an open-necked shirt.

The last time she'd spoken to Sarah Tucker, Sarah—before hanging up—had told her: "You ought to see someone."

"I see people."

"A professional. Get help, Zoë. You need therapy."

Zoë wondered what Sarah would have made of this: Zoë Boehm, seeing someone. A professional. "Getting help."

She would probably assume Zoë had some hidden agenda.

The room, anyway. There were bookshelves against several walls, and an innocuous-looking landscape on one; snow-clad fields, presumably intended to promote a sense of peace. Because this was a room that served a function, and was entirely geared towards that end, in the same way a dentist's surgery was. And give me the drill, thought Zoë; give me the drill sooner than expect me to sit and talk about myself—reveal myself—to a stranger, however professional. A stranger with a goatee and a room full of books, here in his office on North Parade, only a few doors from where Zoë had shared an office once: Oxford Investigations.

These days she worked solo, and didn't use an office.

And the drill wasn't an option.

She said, "So I just sit here and open up, is that the idea?"

"The idea," Soltano said, "is that you sit there and tell me whatever you want. It's your stage."

"For fifty minutes."

"You're very focused on the time element."

"I run my own business," Zoë said. "Hard not to be aware that the clock's ticking."

"Mmm-hm."

It was, in fact, hard not to be aware that the clock was ticking. It sat on a bookshelf; a friendly, old-fashioned sort of clock, with a proper face rather than a digital display. Seven minutes past the hour now. Seven minutes and thirty-two seconds.

"I'm a detective," she said suddenly. "Did I mention that?"

"It's on the form you filled in."

"Of course. You meet many in this line of work?"

"I can't discuss my other patients."

"No. Stupid of me. I'm more used to asking the questions than I am to . . . well, filling in the awkward silences."

"You find silence awkward?"

"Not usually. Do you?"

He didn't reply.

Zoë laughed. "Got me again."

Seven minutes and fifty-one seconds. Whether that meant time was passing slowly or had speeded up, she couldn't tell.

To speed it up, she spoke again. "I've been busy lately. Don't know how it's been in your line of work, whether things have tailed off with the recession, but I've had plenty to do. And one of those things—well, it came out of the past a bit. My past, I mean. Is that the sort of thing you want to hear about?"

"I'm comfortable hearing whatever you want to tell me."

"Well, if you're already comfortable, I might as well begin."

IT HAD BEGUN, AS many things did, with a phone call. Zoë had been leaving the house of a new client, mulling over potential approaches to the task she'd taken on, when her mobile buzzed: unknown caller.

"Remember me?"

Lots of people imagine their voice is instantly recognisable, that it only takes the slightest nudge for their image to swim into view. Where this particular voice was concerned, though, its owner had a point.

Some years back Zoë had crossed paths with a minor hoodlum called Oswald Price. He was no great catch, Price—had resembled Mr. Toad—but his driver, Win, made an impression. The thing about Win, Zoë recalled, was that you always noticed her size first. She was not someone you'd want to get in a lift with, or become trapped under. But once you got close, it became apparent that size wasn't the end of Win's story; that, basically, she was a screen goddess trapped in a weightlifter's body; her skin pale and baby soft; her lips full roses; her eyes brown and damp. Her hair, worn buzz-cut short, was so blonde it was colourless, and this too gave her a doll-like aspect, but it was a doll whose head had been transposed onto an action figure, with broad shoulders, branchlike arms and thick columns of legs wrapped in black leather as form-fitting as sausage skin. All in all, what you had was a real-world approximation of that tutu-wearing hippo in *Fantasia*, which made it all the more cruel that her voice came out like Minnie Mouse's.

It was a case that had ended badly, though not for Win. And however life had treated her since, it hadn't altered her voice.

Zoë said, "What do you want?"

"That's kind of unfriendly."

"Great to hear from you, Win. Keeping well? What do you want?"

"Not much better."

"You still with Price?"

A question expecting the answer yes. Of all the oddities Win embodied, none was stranger than her obvious love for her boss. Where others saw Mr. Toad, she saw who knew what. Richard Gere? George Clooney? Anyone but Toad.

"Yes. And how are things with you, Zoë?"

"They're what they are," Zoë said. Confidential chats with girls held little appeal for her, especially when the girl in question carried bags for a crook. "What do you want, Win?"

"I've something might interest you."

"A new pair of boots? A tropical disease?"

"A job," Win said.

"I'll email you my rates."

"I was thinking we might come to an arrangement about that. This is something that could turn out very positively for both of us."

"I could swear I've heard this song before," Zoë said.

"Come on, Zoë. Would it hurt to hear the details?"

"I'm going to take a wild swing at that one, Win. Yes. It'll probably hurt to hear the details." Ending the call, she turned her phone off. The risk she might miss something important was one she was willing to take.

ZOË LIVED IN JERICHO, where mornings tended to be calm and unhurried. When she emerged onto the street the following day, there were few people about: a couple of young mothers pushing prams; older folk on their way to or from the shops. And a sixteen-stone woman in leathers, perched on a wall by the university press.

She sighed. Now Win had turned up, it was blindingly obvious there'd never been a chance she wasn't going to—when a woman like Win set her sights on something, everything either got out of the way or became collateral damage. Right now, she was eating a bag of cheesy snacks, and her fingers were coated with chemically-orange dust. At Zoë's approach, she tipped the remnants into the palm of her hand, and poured them into her mouth, then dropped the bag and slapped her hands free of crumbs. Then said, "Ever heard of a man called Nipper Ratcliffe?"

Their recent conversation did nothing to lessen the impact of that helium voice.

Zoë said, "They keep saying there's going to be a cold snap, but I don't know. Barely had the heating on yet."

"He was a wheelman. Best in the Midlands in his day."

"But it can't last forever. And even if it did, people would complain about the seasons blurring. No pleasing some folk."

"His day being the late eighties."

"There is absolutely no way I'm not going to hear this, is there?"

"Not much," said Win.

"Then buy me breakfast," Zoë told her. "If I'm going to have to listen to harebrained schemes, I'll need feeding."

"You can't call it harebrained when you haven't heard it yet."

But last time Zoë had listened to Win, a crossbow had been involved. She thought she was on safe ground pre-judging the issue.

"There's a place on Walton Street. It's pretty expensive. Let's go there."

"I MADE HER TAKE me to Le Petit Blanc," Zoë said. "I wish it had been lunchtime, not breakfast."

Neil Soltano said, "I can't get a handle on whether you like this woman or not."

"That sounds fair. I haven't got a handle on that myself." Zoë glanced at the clock on the wall.

"You're still worried about the time."

"We're on a meter, aren't we?"

"We've half an hour. Are you sure you want to spend it talking about someone else?"

"Wouldn't be right not to tell you what happened next, doc. I suppose smoking's not an option, is it?"

"Absolutely not."

"What I thought. Never mind. Here's what Win had to say."

THE CAREER OF NIPPER Ratcliffe, one-time best wheelman in the Midlands, came to an abrupt end shortly after a job in Birmingham: a jewellers' convention at the NEC. There were big takings, and in an understandable hurry to be somewhere else immediately afterwards, Nipper had clipped a teenage girl on departure. A hit-and-run would have been bad enough; a fatal hit-and-run worse still. But a fatal hit-and-run in the course of a getaway from an armed robbery was only ever going to have one outcome. After a two-day manhunt Nipper had been hauled out of a flat in Balsall Heath, slapped silly by the arresting officers, and, in due course, given a twenty-year-minimum sentence, which he'd been three quarters of the way through when he'd keeled over from a myocardial infarction: bang.

"Sad story," Zoë said. "Could you pass the butter?"

"There's more."

"I know. It's in that little dish in front of you."

Win thumped the butter down in a manner that a less charitable private detective might have interpreted as hostile. "I haven't got to the important bit yet."

"We've had crime, punishment and untimely death. You going to sing the final credits?"

"A crew of three pulled the jewellers' job. They separated long before Nipper was picked up, and they'd split the takings first."

Zoë said, "I so know what's coming next."

Win ploughed on regardless. "And they never recovered Nipper's share. The others gave it up for a reduction in sentence, but Nipper must have figured there was no percentage in that. He knew he was going down for serious time. Might as well have a nest-egg waiting when he got out."

"And you know where it is."

"Haven't a clue," Win said. "But I know a man who does."

IT WASN'T LIKE ZOË was short of work. She was halfway through a job for a local small employer, who was worried he'd end up smaller still if one of his employees didn't quit ripping him off; plus she'd recently come to an arrangement with a solicitor which mostly involved chasing up witnesses to traffic accidents, either to prove they'd happened the way the victim claimed, or prove they hadn't, depending on where the money lay. Then there was the missing husband ("I'm worried he's got amnesia," the woman had said; though if so, it was an intermittent condition that allowed him to remember her debit card PIN at regular intervals), not to mention the blackmail victim of the previous day, who was anxious to recover incriminating material. Plenty of work, and all low-key and minimal hassle; a necessary de-escalation after her last job, which had taken her to the northeast and nearly left her there. Among the things that hadn't survived was her friendship with Sarah Tucker, and only now that was gone had Zoë come to realise how much she'd relied on it. So one way or another, the last thing she needed was Win turning up with some idiot plan to find long-forgotten treasure.

On the other hand, she wasn't in the business of shutting her ears to freely-offered information, so she ordered another pot of coffee, and let Win have the floor.

"The other thing Nipper did—"

"The other thing?"

Win sighed, or it would have been a sigh if anyone else did it. Coming from her, it was more a squeak. "Apart from driving, Zoë."

"Right."

"The other thing was, he played chess."

"Nothing I like better than a thug with intellectual aspirations."

"Don't know about that," Win said. "Being good at chess is something you're born with. Doesn't make you intellectual any more than having sticky-out ears."

"But moving on," said Zoë.

"Yeah, anyway. I don't know how good he was, but he was keen. And being banged up for twenty years, well, he was only going to get keener, right? Not like he could have taken up hang-gliding instead."

"I get the picture, Win. I do know how prisons work."

"So he was always on the look-out for someone to play with. And found him in the shape of Reece Dobney."

REECE DOBNEY WAS JUST a kid, twenty-two, doing a year for burglary, which would be six months in real terms. His first stretch.

"Probably meaning his tenth offence," Win glossed. "Not one of your hard lads, mind. Not stupid, either."

"But a criminal," Zoë said.

Win shrugged. "Takes all sorts."

She drove for a second-echelon gangster; possibly did other stuff for him too. She was pretty well acquainted with the various sorts it took.

"Anyway, he's not the kind to hit the gym, so he ends up in the rec room, or whatever they call it, which is where Nipper asks if he plays chess. And while Reece's never played chess in his life, he figures now's as good a time as any to learn, and it turns out he's a natural. One of those who can see the board whole, know what I mean?"

"I'll take your word for it."

"Do that. And Nipper's not letting go of the first halfway decent opponent he's come across behind bars, so that's it. Veteran wheelman and new-fish. They get to be . . . friends."

"And then Nipper croaked," said Zoë. She'd finished the last croissant. There didn't seem much point stretching the story out, especially now she could see the direction it was headed.

"Then Nipper croaked," Win agreed.

Except, it turned out, he wasn't quite dead before he hit the ground. In fact, he'd lingered for about five minutes while the screws faffed around putting in an emergency call. Five minutes during which he'd lain flat on his back in the rec room—picturing the scene, it was hard not to imagine an overturned chess board; pawns and rooks and knights scattered everywhere—while his young mate Reece Dobney held his hand (why not?) and bent forward to let the older man breathe his final words into a waiting ear.

NEIL SOLTANO SAID, "REALLY?"

Zoë paused. "Wasn't sure you were supposed to interrupt, doc."

"You don't need to call me that . . . But you're right. I'm sorry. Please continue."

"You have to understand," Zoë told him, "that it might not have happened that way. The overturned chess board, the dying words . . . All this was what Win wanted to believe, get it? Because if that was how it happened, if Nipper Ratcliffe, in his dying moments, had really told Reece Dobney where he'd stashed the proceeds of that jewel robbery, well, that gave Win a chance to get her own hands on it. And if it wasn't, she had nothing."

Soltano nodded. "How did she know all this, anyway?"

"Good question. One I asked her myself, as it happens."

"HOW DO YOU KNOW all this, anyway?"

Win blinked. Sitting up close, Zoë was struck again by how Disney-like her face was. Big eyes, long lashes. The former grew damp now. "I just do."

"Somebody else was there," said Zoë. The croissants had left a buttery sheen on her fingers. She wiped them on her napkin. "You want me to take twenty guesses?"

"He wasn't in the room when it happened. But it was all over the prison within minutes."

"Sure." Prisons were villages when it came to gossip. "This is Price we're talking about, yeah? Your boss."

"He's doing two years."

Zoë didn't ask for what. Mostly because she didn't care. "And you're there every visiting day, right?"

"You wouldn't understand."

That was true too. Zoë really wouldn't.

"So he whispered all this across the visiting room table? That's sweet. You know it's all cobblers, don't you?"

"It happened."

"Nipper died, I'll grant you. There's probably a body to prove it. And played chess with young Reece, I'll give you that too. But the rest of it, the dying message, that's the kind of fairy story cons tell themselves after lights out. Because even a two-year stretch must feel pretty damn long once that cell door shuts at night."

"He'll be out in a few months."

"Price? I bet you're counting the days."

"Yes. But that's something else you'll never understand, isn't it?"

"AND HOW DID THAT make you feel?"

Zoë blinked.

"The notion that Win's, er, attachment to this Price fellow was something you'd be incapable of empathising with. Did you think it fair comment?"

"You'd have to meet Price, doc. Frankly I'd find it difficult to believe his mother had strong feelings for him."

"And how about attachments in general. Romantic attachments. Are they something you shy away from?"

"We're getting a little removed from the story. Because Win didn't really care what I thought about her boss. What she wanted was my help with Reece Dobney, who was also about to be released. Not in a couple of months. In a couple of days."

"AND HE LIVES WHERE?"

"Just up the road."

"Suddenly, my part in this becomes clear."

They'd left Le Petit Blanc, and were walking down Walton Street. It was another bright day, though the calendar was steadily working through November. By rights they should have been bundled up against the damp, watching their breath fog the air.

"His share would have come to half a million. Nipper's share."

"And he hid it somewhere it's never been found, but now little Reece knows where it is."

"Exactly. So all we have to do—"

"Win. Thanks for breakfast. Drive carefully."

"You don't mean that."

"Sure I do. There's some idiots on the roads."

"Zoë. Have you been listening? Half a million pounds."

"Win. Yes I have. It's a fairy tale."

"Okay, so maybe it is. But I want to float one small idea in front of you. You can handle that? One small idea?"

By way of answer, Zoë sighed.

"What if it isn't?"

"That's not really an idea, Win. More a pipe dream."

"So it's long odds. So what? Because what we're talking about is a couple of days at most. If Reece Dobney really knows where Nipper's share of the take is, he's not going to be able to sit on the info long, is he? Not a kid like that. So there's your investment. A couple of days max, and you'll know whether you've wasted less than half your week or made yourself a tidy little fortune."

"Because if it turns out to be true, you plan to take it away from him."

"It's not his."

"It's not ours either."

"Not yet."

Zoë said, "And that doesn't worry you at all?"

Win shrugged. "It's what we do," she said.

"AND WAS SHE RIGHT about that?"

"About Dobney knowing where the stash was? I'm not gunna spoil the ending, doc."

"I meant about what she said. That it's what you do. Is it?"

"Do I make a habit of ripping off minor crooks, you mean?"

"Well . . ."

"Or to put it another way, am I a crook?"

Neil Soltano said nothing, but pursed his lips, as if pursuing that train of thought to a station not so very far away.

Zoë too was silent for a while. The clock continued ticking, and the shadows shifted minutely. "I could just tell you if I was, couldn't I? I mean, like you said, I can say anything within these walls, can't I? You won't judge me and you won't be shocked."

"I've heard worse," Soltano said. "Believe me."

"Oh, I do. I'm sure you hear lots of things. But you can relax, because no, as it happens, it's not true. I'm not in the business of ripping off anyone, crooks or otherwise. Win was just trying to draw me inside her circle. Paint me as one of her crew."

"I see."

"And I'm not just saying that because your promise of confidentiality doesn't cover admissions of crime. Does it, doc?"

Soltano smiled briefly, but concealed it by wiping his mouth. "If Win has a, ah, crew, how come she needed you anyway?"

"Well, she's Price's driver, and I suppose he's got various legmen, one sort or another. But Price is out of the picture, don't forget, and it's not likely Win's held in huge esteem by his associates. You probably don't mix in such circles, but I've got to tell you, career criminals can be pretty conservative."

". . . Interesting."

"Shall I continue?"

"It's your session."

IT TOOK A WHILE, but Zoë got rid of Win—not so much by dint of outright rudeness (skins came no thicker than Win's) as by leading her into town, then losing her on the crowded High. She turned her phone off, settled into a day's work for her solicitor client, and once that was over tarried in the King's Arms, gently supping a large Pinot and watching undergraduates enact the age-old rituals they thought they'd invented themselves. It was mid-evening before she headed home, half expecting to find that bulky shape sulking nearby. But the coast was clear.

Inside, Zoë poured another glass of wine, threw a ready-meal in the microwave, and fired up her laptop. She wasn't getting involved, she told herself. But there was no harm in verifying Win's tale, if only as a prelude to congratulating herself for not falling for the bullshit. Win only looked like she'd escaped from an animated flick. She was more than capable of laying out a complicated play, luring Zoë into something that would leave her broke, clueless, and wondering what just happened, while Win disappeared in a cloud of pink smoke, her pockets stuffed with someone else's dosh.

But it turned out the basics were true. Edward "Nipper" Ratcliffe was much as described, including dead, and while Reece Dobney wasn't leaving many skidmarks on the surface of the web, he'd certainly been sent down for burglary, and prior to that had been living in Cutteslowe, or "just up the road" as Win had put it.

And yes, a hefty chunk of the takings from the Birmingham robbery had never turned up.

All smoke and whispers, as someone had once put it, but still; chances were, whatever the truth of the matter, Win believed every word she'd said.

Once she'd eaten, Zoë turned her phone on and checked her texts. *that was unkind but have it yr way. youll wish youd listend when im rolling innit.* She ought to be glad Win was gone, and that whatever slapstick scenario had been unfolding was going to play out without her. Still, it was some hours before she took herself off to bed, spending the intervening period gazing into the recesses of her coal-effect gas fire. The flames danced and flickered, as if reflections of her thoughts.

CUTTESLOWE WAS THE OTHER side of the ringroad that wrapped Oxford the way moats encircle castles. Reece Dobney lived there with his girlfriend, a young black woman called Deedee Timothy, a trainee hairdresser. Zoë had no illusions about young love, and guessed that whatever ties bound the pair together were knotted more to his advantage than hers. But either way, this was where Reece Dobney would be heading, after his holiday in the Big Stone Hotel came to an end.

Zoë drove round after work the following evening. Deedee Timothy's place was a grey-brick two-up two-down, with a patch of garden out front a little smaller than Zoë's car. It was a rental property, but displayed signs of pride of occupancy; a hanging basket dangled from a hook by the front door, and a stained-glass bird had been hung to catch the light in an upstairs window. Zoë parked opposite for five minutes, not entirely sure what her purpose here was. There was no sign of Win, but then Dobney wouldn't be released for a few days yet. This information, like the address, like Deedee Timothy's profession; it all came via the internet. Nothing took long to find, if you knew where to look.

That was presumably the principle Win was working on too.

THE NEXT COUPLE OF days—the last two Reece Dobney would be spending behind bars—were busy ones for Zoë. She confirmed that the local small employer's main worry wasn't so much that one of his employees was ripping him off as that all of them were, and discovered that the missing husband's "amnesia" extended to his having forgotten to tell his wife that he had another wife in a different city. She also enjoyed an interesting discussion with her solicitor client as to the propriety of questioning an accident victim's eight-year-old son about how severe his mother's whiplash was when there was nobody around, and then, having brought that income stream to an abrupt end, went cruising through various charity shops up and down Walton Street, and along Summertown's main drag. She'd forgotten how many of the damn things there were. And if she kept sawing off branches she was sitting on she'd end up outfitting herself from these places, she reminded herself. She couldn't afford to tell paying customers she didn't care for their so-called ethics. On the other hand, it had felt good to tell the solicitor he was a toerag out loud, instead of just in her head, and a small victory like that was worth a paycheque. The kind of thing Sarah would have enjoyed hearing about, if Sarah was still talking to her.

("This woman, Sarah—you miss her, don't you?" Soltano asked.

"Blimey, doc," said Zoë. "I can see why you went into this line of work. Not much gets past you."

"I'm simply wondering why you don't just call her."

"Yep, that's a professional talking all right. Maybe you'll convince me to do just that. Where'd you get your doctorate, anyway?"

"Manchester."

"That's refreshing. I get so bored with everyone having an Oxford degree, don't you?"

"It's an overrated institution."

"Lots of people say so," agreed Zoë. "Of course, they're mostly people who failed to get in. Shall I continue?")

A couple of busy days then, and when they were over Zoë was back where she'd started; sitting in her car near a grey-brick two-up two-down, with a hanging basket by the front door, and a stained-glass bird in an upstairs window. It had been dark by five, and Reece Dobney had been home since lunchtime. Deedee had taken the day off work, and Zoë had been there to see the moment of reunion, the young woman opening the door to her long-absent boyfriend, and had discovered there were limits to her ability to observe others without their being aware of it; she had turned away before the door closed. Looked back in time to see the curtains being drawn behind that stained-glass bird. That had been it for some hours.

And now it was after nine, and the front door was opening again.

Reece Dobney was small, thin-boned; it was plain to see burglary might have come easy to him—all those tight openings, and narrow-gauge windows—but less apparent was his appeal to Deedee Timothy. Zoë wondered if he was aware how much out of his league he was playing, and answered her own question immediately: No. Men never were. As the pair emerged, Dobney held a hand out and Deedee dropped her car keys into it. They climbed into a Mini, cream with a black roof, and drove away.

Zoë waited.

Down the road a pair of headlights came to life, and a moment later, a dark blue BMW sailed past, Win at the wheel.

Here we go, thought Zoë.

She waited two minutes before following.

IT WASN'T AN ESPECIALLY strange procession, that small convoy of cars which soon vanished inside a larger convoy. They were just three more elements in the daily onrush of hot metal, which even at this time of night, this time of year, showed few signs of relenting. And besides, they were divided by time and space; the first two cars a mile and some minutes ahead of Zoë's on the drive towards Birmingham.

Some way short of that destination, the car containing Reece Dobney and Deedee Timothy peeled off the motorway, abandoning its ribbon of red and white light for a less important road. This was lit as it trundled past houses and shops, then faded into darkness as countryside took over, lined either side by hedgerows and fields. A garage forecourt was bright as a flying saucer in the surrounding darkness. The Mini briefly entered its brightness, like a sparrow flying through a lit dining hall, then disappeared into the darkness beyond, coming to rest a mile up the road near a stile. This gave onto a footpath which wound uphill to where a lone tree waved on the skyline, like an illustration on a book jacket. From the boot of the car, Dobney retrieved a spade. Then the pair of them mounted the stile, and trekked up towards that tree.

When Win passed she kept going for a few hundred yards, before parking. From her own boot, she dug out a baseball bat.

By the time she reached the stile, the young pair were at the top of the hill, and it looked like Reece was digging.

ZOË PARKED WELL SHORT of the Mini and killed her engine. When the car's lights died, she felt herself at the centre of an enormous darkness: she was not big on the countryside, Zoë Boehm. More at home with streetlights and paving stones. But she liked to think she was adaptable; besides, growing attuned to the dark, she realised how much light in fact there was: a dim glow westward from the motorway, and a moon somewhere above. And noise, too; not only the hum of traffic, but a dull thumping noise accompanied by a glassy rattle, as if someone big were running down a slope, say, carrying a half-full tin . . .

Zoë shrank into the hedgerow, and watched as a large shape clambered over the stile, then trotted off in the opposite direction. A few moments later, Win's car lit up, and drove into the night. As the sound of its engine was swallowed by the winding road, Dobney and his girlfriend hopped over the stile. He held a spade in one hand, and Deedee's hand in the other.

Extricating herself from the hedge, Zoë went to join them.

"OKAY. HOLD UP."

"What's that, doc?"

"You've missed stuff out, haven't you?"

"Have I?" She checked the clock. They had eight minutes to go. "Why do you think that?"

"That stuff about doing the rounds of charity shops . . . You faked her out. Win. You bought a load of cheap jewellery and planted it like it was buried treasure."

He seemed to be quite enjoying that possibility. Was pleased with himself for having sussed it out.

"You'd spoken to her, hadn't you? Deedee Timothy. In those intervening days."

Zoë ran a hand through her hair. It was shorter than it had been in a while; a curly cap, neatly cropped. "I thought she did quite a good job of it."

"She cut your hair."

"Yeah, that's how I made contact. Mind you, when I mentioned Reece's name, I nearly lost an ear."

"WHAT DID YOU SAY?"

"I asked when Reece is due home. He's out tomorrow, isn't he?"

Deedee had looked both ways, to see whether anyone was listening—though Zoë was the only customer, and her two colleagues were chatting over magazines in a corner—then met Zoë's gaze in the mirror. "How do you know Reece?"

"Did I say I know him?"

"Then what you on about?"

She was generously shaped, Deedee Timothy, and if the thick red frames of the glasses she wore were a little large for her face, Zoë could spot a very real beauty waiting to flower: give it a year or two. Her long hair was beaded, as if to demonstrate her establishment's expertise, and behind her lenses, her eyes were currently flashing. "You trying to make out he's done something wrong?"

Mindful of the scissors Deedee held, Zoë's tone was mild as she said, "Well, he has been in prison."

"Keep it down. And what if he has? Paid for his mistakes, hasn't he? Not that it's any of your business."

If her eyes grew any angrier, they might shatter the mirror.

Zoë said, "I know. And I'm not here to cause trouble. Trying to save you some bother, if you want to know the truth."

"What sort of bother?"

"She's called Win," said Zoë.

"SO YEAH," ZOË SAID. "There were fake jewels in a tin box. We buried it together that evening. Once I'd convinced her I wasn't there to give her boyfriend grief, Deedee got quite into it. So after Reece's, ah, homecoming party, the pair of them set off to dig up the treasure, knowing Win wouldn't be far behind. And of course, once they did, there she was to take it away. The bat was just for show. She didn't hurt them."

"And what happens when she discovers she's got a load of junk?"

"Oh, that happened already. She's not stupid, Win. Soon as she checked them in the light, she knew she had a load of rubbish."

"And?"

"And she was on the phone a minute later."

"THAT WAS YOU, WASN'T it?"

"In your rearview? Might have been."

"No, I meant you're the reason I'm holding a biscuit tin full of crap."

Zoë said, "Win, the reason you're holding a tin full of crap is that you insisted on chasing after it. So yes, I planted it, and yes, Reece and Deedee led you to it, but only to make you realise what a waste of time the whole thing is. Buried diamonds? Seriously?"

"It could have happened."

"Not in the real world."

"You do realise," Win said—and for all her high-pitched weirdness, or maybe because of it, she was a woman who could put a weight of threat into her words—"that your little game tonight doesn't mean Reece doesn't know where they really are?"

"Earth to Win. You listening? The kid knows nothing. Trust me, he played chess with the old man, end of story."

"But—"

"But nothing. Look, if you've spent fifteen years in prison for stealing diamonds, the last thing you're gunna do with your dying breath is give them away. I expect Nipper spent his final moments trying to work out how to take them with him. I told you that the other day, but you wouldn't listen. Maybe now you've had a wasted evening and a big disappointment, you'll think harder. Seriously, Win. Think about it."

There was silence.

"Win?"

"Maybe."

"When's Price get out?"

". . . Next year."

"So maybe you won't have a bag of diamonds to give him. But you know, maybe that's not what he's looking forward to."

"Zoë?"

"What?"

"You can jerk me around to make a point. But don't think you can be my shrink."

And Win had hung up, and Zoë had thought: well, perhaps she'd stepped over the line there. Still, it sounded like Win was coming round to the idea that dreams of buried treasure were idle fancies. Perhaps she'd leave Deedee and Reece Dobney in peace.

SOLTANO SAID, "SO TELL me. What was in it for you?"

Zoë glanced at the clock. It showed forty-nine minutes past the hour. "I don't know, doc. You remember that thing Win said, about this being what we do? When she was talking about ripping off stolen property?"

"Mm-hm."

"Maybe I just wanted to make it clear she could count me out. That it's not what I do. Besides, that woman's trouble. Deedee Timothy hadn't done anything to deserve her."

"And that's it?"

"You sound suspicious, doc. I thought you were the non-judgmental type."

"I'm simply encouraging you to examine your motives."

Zoë fell silent, examining her motives, perhaps. There was a buzzing from her pocket, and she took out her mobile while Soltano frowned. "Sorry, doc. I thought it was off." She put it away, then said, "What do you want me to say? That I thought it might come in handy, having a burglar owe me a favour?"

"No. I just wondered if you thought those two really did know about Nipper's stash."

Zoë smiled. "That would make a better story, wouldn't it? That Nipper really did spill his soul, and the pair of them let me convince Win otherwise."

"Which would mean they were cleverer than you give them credit for."

"That could happen. I mean, he's not stupid, despite his career choice. And she's a smart woman. No ill will to young lovers or anything, doc, but I'm kind of hoping she upgrades from him sooner or later."

"You didn't like him?"

"I didn't say that. But she could do better."

"And do you think he'll give up his, ah, life of crime?"

"What, jack in the burglary trade? I doubt it, doc."

"Really?"

"Really. In fact, I'd put money on it."

"What makes you so sure?"

"Because that was him texting me. To let me know he'd finished turning over your place."

AND NOW THE CLOCK had completed its course, or the truncated course it was allowed in this room—the fifty-minute hour was up, and Zoë stood. All this while, she'd not taken her jacket off, and she removed a pack of cigarettes from an inside pocket now, and slotted one into her mouth.

Neil Soltano remained in his chair, transfixed—Zoë hoped—by what she'd just said.

She told him: "It's not that difficult, setting yourself up as a therapist, is it? I mean, you never actually claim you're professionally qualified, do you? And Manchester Uni doesn't count, by the way. They never heard of you."

"What is this, a shakedown?"

Zoë laughed. "Shakedown. Love it. To come up with words like that, you really have to know what you're talking about, don't you? But then, it's an area you've done your research in. Blackmail, I mean." She lit her cigarette. "I know, I know. Against the law to smoke in workplaces. But this isn't really a workplace anymore, doc, because the way I look at it, you're retired. Reece Dobney just collected a set of tapes from your

house, the ones you made during your sessions with Carol
Enderby. Remember Carol? Having serious guilt issues about
defrauding the charity she works for?"

"I don't know what—"

"—I'm talking about, yeah yeah yeah." Zoë blew out
smoke. "All stops here, doc. You repay the money you extorted
from Carol, she repays the charity, and everybody's happy. Oh,
except you. Because I ever hear you've hung your shingle out
again, here or anywhere else, and I will close you down." She
zipped her jacket up and headed out the room, but paused in
the doorway. "I have to ask, doc. How does that make you feel?"

DOBNEY REALLY HAD BURGLED Soltano's place as a
favour, which was handy: there was no way Zoë would have
been able to claim payment as a business expense. Still, she
owed him a thank-you, so drove by a couple of mornings later.
But the hanging basket had disappeared from its hook, and the
stained-glass bird in the upstairs window was nowhere to be
seen. Nobody answered when she rang the bell. So she returned
to her car, where she sat trying not to allow a small possibility to
grow any larger; trying so hard, she became unsure whether to
swear or laugh. Eventually, deciding she needed advice on the
matter, she fished out her mobile, and made a call.

"Sarah?" she said. "Don't hang up. It's me, Zoë."

ACKNOWLEDGMENTS

Novels, in my experience, tend to bully their way centre stage; short stories require encouragement if they're not to fade away into might-have-beens. My thanks, then, to the editors of the magazines where these stories first appeared, notably Janet Hutchings of *Ellery Queen's Mystery Magazine* and Mike Berry of the sadly departed *Bookdealer*, without whom this collection wouldn't exist.

And I'm grateful, too, to Juliet Grames of Soho Press, whose idea this publication was. In fact, without Soho Press, my whole career would be a might-have-been. So my ever-lasting gratitude to Bronwen Hruska, who steers that ship, and to Paul Oliver, Mark Doten, Rachel Kowal, Janine Agro, Rudy Martinez, and all other Soho Peeps past and present. I've never found myself knee-deep in Minnesota snow, en route to a reading in a deserted bookshop, without having deep warm thoughts about all of you.

Back here in the UK, huge thanks to everyone at John Murray, for their care, their support and their kindness. Yassine Belkacemi is a rock: ever-inventive and on the ball as editor and publicist; ever-dependable as friend. Becky Walsh, Caroline

Westmore and Emma Petfield deserve acknowledgments pages all of their own. Nick Davies and Jocasta Hamilton keep it all together. And thanks and *au revoir* to Jess Kim.

   Last but never least, my agents Juliet Burton and Micheline Steinberg probably know these stories better than I do by now, because they work hard while I mostly woolgather. I'm happy to have them on my side. The last story here, "What We Do," references a novel called *Smoke and Whispers*. That was dedicated to Juliet. This, long overdue, is for Miche.

MH
Oxford
April 2021